THICKER THAN BLOOD

JAMES P. SUMNER

THICKER THAN BLOOD

Second Edition published in 2021 by Both Barrels Publishing Ltd.

Copyright © James P. Sumner 2017

Editing and Cover Design by: bothbarrelsauthorservices.com

ISBNs:
978-1-914191-21-3 (Hardback)
978-1-914191-22-0 (Paperback)

Visit the author's website: jamespsumner.com

JOIN THE MAILING LIST

Why not sign up for James P. Sumner's spam-free newsletter, and stay up-to-date with the latest news, promotions, and new releases?

In exchange for your support, you will receive a **FREE** copy of the prequel novella, *A Hero of War*, which tells the story of a young Adrian, newly recruited to the U.S. Army at the beginning of the Gulf War.

Previously available on Amazon, this title is now exclusive to the author's website. But you have the opportunity to read it for free!

Interested? Details can be found at the end of this book.

This won two awards...

THICKER THAN BLOOD

ADRIAN HELL: BOOK 7

1

June 6, 2017 — 10:47 PDT

The sun feels within touching distance as I stand alone, taking in the stunning, panoramic view from the mountaintop. Dust dances around my feet, caught in the light breeze sweeping across the deserted plateau.

It was surprisingly easy to get up here. I'm not an expert climber, or even that good with heights, but there's a footpath on the opposite side that winds up on a gentle but steady incline. It wasn't too strenuous, despite the heat, and I actually enjoyed the walk. It gave me time to clear my head.

It's been a weird few weeks, to say the least. Yesterday marked the one-month anniversary of my official death— and if that statement doesn't highlight how messed up my life is, I don't know what does. I'm beat-up and tired. The bandage around my head is stopping a large gash from re-opening. My right hand is still effectively useless, due to nerve damage I sustained during an explosion. The cast I'm wearing is molded to provide as much comfort and protection as possible, and I'm popping painkillers every couple of hours to help take the edge off. My wounds are a constant reminder of the choices I made and the consequences I must live with.

I spent the last few weeks living someone else's life. I had a nice house, an expensive car, all the money in the world... and it didn't mean a damn thing. I realize now that I simply used it all to hide the fact that I'm angry with myself and slowly being driven insane by my own guilt. But that life is gone now. I'm sure a new one will be created for me by the people who enslaved me.

A bird screeches overhead, interrupting my quiet moment of reflection. I focus on it for a moment, watching it glide effortlessly in a circle. I wonder what it feels like to live so free. Ever since I was pronounced dead, I've been expecting to feel overwhelmed by not living within the confines of a normal life. I'm a phantom, able to roam the world without consequence. Ironically, having committed myself to serving The Order of Sabbah as payment for this new life, I've never felt more trapped.

I take in a slow, deep breath and briefly close my eyes. Now isn't the time for such musings. I need to focus. I have a job to do.

I crouch beside the black sports bag currently resting at my feet. It's fifty inches long and weighs around twenty-five pounds. Having this with me certainly made the walk up here harder, but it was a necessary burden. I unzip it and carefully lift out the sniper rifle contained within. I fold down the bipod legs, click them into place, and rest it gently on the ground.

I pause for a moment to admire it. It's a beautiful weapon, one of only three ever made—a rare collection referred to as the Holy Trinity by the people who live in my world. Each bolt-action rifle has a distinctive emblem engraved on the stock—a golden bullet standing on its end, with a crown on the tip and a number on the casing. The one I have with me is number three. Last I heard, number one was somewhere in Africa.

The story goes that they were manufactured by the son of a former Marine sniper, who was some kind of engineering prodigy. No one knows exactly how the weapons are capable of such extreme long-distance shooting. They're worth so much money that anyone fortunate enough to have owned one hasn't dared take it apart and reverse engineer it to find out.

I reach back inside the bag and take out the scope. It's military-grade, with 20x zoom and anti-glare technology. It has thermal, infrared, and night vision sighting options—perfect for targeting under any circumstances. I fasten it in place on the upper receiver, directly above the trigger, leaving the lens caps in place. A common mistake people make is taking the cap while they're setting up the rifle. It should always be the last thing you remove because once you expose the lens, you risk sunlight reflecting off it, giving away your position. You only remove it when you're ready to look at your target.

Finally, I take out the magazine, which contains five .338-caliber Lapua Scenar rounds. They're a very-low-drag round, or VLD for short. Each three-hundred-grain bullet is roughly three-point-six inches long and has a lead core designed specifically for long-range shooting. I cup the magazine in my left hand and slam it firmly into the breach.

I move the rifle nearer to the edge of the plateau and lie on my front, stretching my legs out behind me. Resting on my elbows, I tuck the stock into my left shoulder, adjusting it for comfort. I need to position myself on the opposite side from what I'm used to, since I can't use my right hand for the trigger.

I work the bolt and hear the mechanical clanking of a round being chambered. I flip the lens caps up and close one eye, focusing on the view through the sight. The building I'm looking at is twenty-three hundred yards away, give or take. That's a long shot. Not impossible but incredibly difficult, even for me. There are numerous calculations to run through before firing—bullet velocity, wind resistance, gravity, motion delay... even the rotation of the earth. It's a complex skill even military snipers struggle to master. The reality is that most people, even with intense training, can't hit a target more than thirteen hundred yards away with any degree of accuracy.

Fortunately, I'm one of the people who can.

The longest shot I ever made was just under twenty-two hundred yards, in conditions far worse than those I have right now. My spotter said it was an incredible shot but lucky. He said the wind was too strong to guarantee accuracy, and despite the first bullet finding the target, he argued that he knew a marker shot when he saw one. He might have had a point, but I never confirmed or denied it either way. The way I see it, if you try to do something and succeed, it's skill, not luck. It was a great shot, and I'm twice the shooter now than I was back then, so this distance doesn't concern me.

I look at the slightly blurred building in front of me, almost a mile-and-a-half away. I adjust the zoom on the scope until the image sharpens. It's only six stories high, yet it seems to tower over the surrounding structures.

I consciously slow my breathing, pushing my heart rate as low as I can. Beginning at the roof, I work my way down, one floor at a time. I move left to right, checking each window, searching for my target. At this distance, the slightest movement makes a large impact, so I keep the adjustments as gentle as I can while I scan the offices for—

Bingo.

Two floors down, in the window farthest right. It's huge inside—typical of a corner office—and has two walls that consist of glass running floor-to-ceiling. The anti-glare technology of the scope makes it easier to see inside, despite the reflection of the sun. I can make out two chairs facing the east side. Opposite them is a large desk, with a man sitting behind it. It looks as if he's writing something, but I can't be sure from here.

What I *am* sure of, however, is who he is. I smile to myself. He hasn't changed much since I last saw him. Not that I would expect him to, really. It may feel as if a lifetime has elapsed, but it's only been a couple of months.

I take another slow, deep breath, trying to push the rising pulse of emotion from my mind as I stare at my best friend through the scope of my sniper rifle.

"Hey, Josh."

2

Okay, now what? I don't want to shoot him, obviously, but what choice do I have? The Order knows I'm here. They can track me anywhere in the world, to within about three feet of my position. If they don't like where I am or what I'm doing, they press a button and... poof! Off with my head.

Talk about a rock and a hard place. Literally. I'm on top of a massive rock, facing yet another tough decision. Do I kill my best friend? Or do I refuse, which would result in my own swift, messy demise? I'm too young to die. Okay, that's not true. I'm forty-five and probably deserve to. But I don't *want* to die. I also don't want to shoot Josh.

I focus on my breathing, trying to calm my mind. It's racing in every direction at once, trying to find a solution, but ultimately gets me nowhere. I close my eyes for a second and flick the switch inside my head that turns off my emotions. I need to look at this objectively. I've been far too emotional lately, and I'm forgetting all the skills I spent my life honing.

...

...

...

Right, if I shoot Josh... then what? It's clear that whatever he's doing is getting in the way of whatever The Order wants to do. Otherwise, I wouldn't be here. So, what's he *actually* doing? Thanks to President Schultz, I know he now runs the largest privately-owned military in the world. In addition to manufacturing weapons and their research toward technological and pharmaceutical advances, GlobaTech has replaced the UN Peacekeeping Force. They're now active all over the world, trying to restore order to regions affected by 4/17.

He's also an advisor to the National Security Council, which is an unprecedented appointment. He's the first person from the private sector to play such a pivotal role in government. Consequently, he's a prominent figure nowadays. Maybe taking him out is nothing more than a show of strength by Horizon? Proof that The Order can manipulate government at any level? Or, more likely, it's precautionary. I imagine Josh is in a unique position to influence many things The Order wouldn't like. They might want him out of the picture to make sure he doesn't do any of them.

Now, remaining objective, what if I *don't* kill him? Well, I die. That's easy. But what impact would my death have? I smile regrettably. The sad, lonely answer to that is absolutely none. Everyone, including Josh, already thinks I'm dead, so it makes no difference to anyone if I die right here, right now.

So, what do I do?

I suppose I could—

No, I couldn't. That would be stupid.

There's always—

Wait, no, there isn't.

Shit. Come on, Adrian. *Think*!

...

...

...

Hold on a second.

I could call him. Is that insane? I mean, I'm not entirely sure what I would say, but let's face it—if there's one person who can get me out of this shit, it's Josh, right? Plus, The Order can only *see* where I am. They can't hear me, so if we can work something out between us, it might buy us some time.

I trap the stock between my chin and shoulder to keep it steady and reach down into my pocket for my cell. Not the one Horizon gave me, which will almost certainly be bugged. It's a burner phone I picked up out of habit, for emergencies.

I rest it on the ground in front of me, beside the rifle, and tap in his number. I pause, my finger hovering over the call button. Seriously, what do I say? He would've been devastated when he heard I was dead. I know I would be if the situation were reversed. How do you tell someone who has been grieving for the past month that the person they're mourning is still alive?

Ah, screw it. I'll figure it out.

I hit call and then put it on speaker. The sound of ringing fills the air. I watch through the scope and can see him clearly, staring at his computer screen. He's just glanced at his cell phone, which he's now holding in his hand. He looks all around the room, as if he's debating whether to answer. I guess he's used to receiving calls from numbers he doesn't recognize. Half the world must want to speak to him nowadays.

I feel really, *really* bad about this.

He stands and begins pacing around his office. He puts the phone to his ear. The ringing stops.

"Hello?"

I take a deep breath. "Hey, Josh."

"Who is this?"

I roll my eyes. "It's me, man. It's Adrian."

"Look, asshole... whoever this is, it isn't funny. How did you even get this number? I'm gonna trace the call, find you, and—"

"Josh, relax. Take a breath and listen. It's me, all right? It's me."

He stops pacing.

"A-Adrian?"

"Yeah."

"I don't... What... Is this... How?"

I smile. "In all the years I've known you, this is the first time you've been lost for words."

"But... I don't..."

"I know, and I'm sorry to do this to you. I can't imagine what must be going through your mind right now, but I wouldn't be calling if it weren't urgent."

I watch him walk back over to his desk and rest on the edge. "What do you mean?"

"I'm in trouble, Josh. We both are. I need—"

"Whoa, whoa, whoa—hang on a minute. Back up. Are you telling me you've been alive this whole time?"

I sigh heavily. "Yeah."

"And you're making contact now, after a month, purely out of necessity?"

I close my eyes. "Yeah..."

"So, you let me believe my best friend was dead for a fucking month? Are you being serious?"

"Josh, it's not like that, okay? I didn't—"

"Adrian, you're *alive*, and you didn't tell me! It's *exactly* like that!"

I fight to keep my temper, which is frustrating because I know I have no right to get angry with him.

"Look, I get that you're pissed with me, Josh, but it's not that simple. Can we just—"

"No! We can't *just...* anything! You let me think you were *dead*, Adrian. All this time. Do you know how hard I worked to save your ass after you killed Cunningham? How much I begged Schultz to spare you? And when he wouldn't do that —when he *couldn't*—how much I pleaded with him to let me see you? I've spent every waking moment hating myself for not being able to save you. Feeling guilty and angry and sad because the man I considered a brother, whom I spent over half my life standing beside, was gone. Except, guess what? He wasn't! He just let me think he was, so I could go through all that for nothing! And the worst part is, when he finally tells me he's alive, the first thing he says is that he's not doing it because he wants to."

I let out a long breath, which tremors with emotion I can't subdue. "Josh, I—"

"You sonofabitch."

He hangs up.

Well, that went well.

I watch him through the scope. He's still sitting on the edge of his desk, staring ahead. Oh... no, he's not. He's throwing his computer monitor across the room. And the keyboard. He's banging his fists on his desk. There's more movement. I adjust slightly and see his door has opened. There's a woman standing there. Josh turns to her and gestures with his hand. She steps out again hurriedly, closing the door behind her.

I feel terrible. He's right. Everything he said was right.

But now isn't the time. Both our lives are in danger, and we need to deal with that first. He can be pissed with me later.

I call him again.

It clicks on after one ring. "What?"

"I'm sorry, all right? I'm *sorry*, Josh. You're right about everything. It was a real dick move letting you think I was dead, and I feel terrible about it."

"Oh, well, now that you've apologized, that makes everything okay..."

"Look, be pissed with me all you want—"

"I will. Don't you worry!"

"—*but*... it'll have to wait. I'm calling because you're in danger. We both are. And if we don't work together, we'll both be dead by morning."

He doesn't say anything. My words hang ominously in the tense silence. I watch him as he starts pacing back and forth again. The guy's worse than me! Finally, he sits back down on the edge of his desk. "Fine. What's the threat?"

I take a deep breath. "Me."

"What?"

"I've been hired to kill you. And if I don't do it, I'm going to have my head blown off."

I watch him run a hand through his hair. He sighs. "I suppose you'd better start from the beginning."

"I don't have that kind of time, Josh. Details will have to wait."

"Okay, then at least bullet-point it for me. Give me something, Adrian, for Christ's sake. You can't just say something like that and expect me to jump to your aid without any explanation."

I close my eyes and mutter, "This is going to sound crazy..." before opening them again. "...but you've heard of The Order of Sabbah, right?"

"What, that stupid myth you people tell each other?" I see him shrug. "Yeah, of course. What's that have to do with anything?"

"Well, they're not a myth. It turns out they're real. They recruited me after I killed Cunningham, helped fake my death, and gave me a new life on the condition that I make no attempts to contact anybody from my old one. They stuck something in my neck that not only tells them where I am at all times but also contains a small explosive that can be detonated remotely from anywhere in the world. Basically, if I don't kill who they tell me to, I'm a dead man. It hasn't been too much of an issue up until now, but my latest contract is you."

He starts pacing again. "Well, that's... awful."

"Yeah. I bet you're glad I called first, eh?"

"But... The Order of Sabbah? Seriously? They're a thing?"

"Sadly, yes."

"Bloody hell." There's some silence, then he sighs heavily. "Okay, fine. Being pissed with you can wait, along with all the questions I have. The first thing we need to do is take that device out of your neck."

"No can do, man. It has some kind of sensory trigger on it, apparently. If it comes into contact with the air..."

"It detonates. Yeah, I know what a sensory trigger is, believe it or not. Although, I'm surprised *you* do."

I ignore the justifiable edge to his tone. "I had it

explained to me in simple language by the prick holding the detonator."

"Okay, let me..." I watch him walk over to his desk and then stop. "Shit. Never mind."

"What?"

"Nothing."

I smile. "I bet you're wishing you hadn't thrown your computer across your room just now, aren't you?"

"How did you—wait a second! Are you *Jason Bourne*ing me right now?"

I laugh. "Yeah, sorry."

I see him looking out both windows. "Unbelievable. Where are you?"

"About a mile and a half away, on top of the mountain facing you."

He turns. Unbeknownst to him, he's now staring right at me.

"A mile and a... Christ! What gun are you using?"

"You wouldn't believe me if I told you."

"Really? I just found out you're not dead and you're working for a secret society of assassins no one believes really exist, but it's the gun that I'll find hard to believe?"

"Well, when you put it like that... Fine, I have one of the Holy Trinity. Number three."

He pauses. "Holy shit. Are you serious? Where did you find that?"

"No idea. The Order got it for me."

"What's it like?"

"Beautiful, man."

"Wow. I mean, that's..." He shakes his head. "D'you know what? It doesn't matter. I'm too angry and confused to get excited about the gun I have pointing at me right now. I guess I should be grateful. At least you're not using one of ours."

I smile. "Yeah, that would just be in poor taste."

"So, you've been watching me this whole time through your scope?"

"Yeah."

"I don't believe it..."

"Hey, remember what you said—being pissed with me can wait."

He sighs. "I know, I know. Okay, sit tight. I need twenty minutes."

I frown. "For what?"

"To save your ass."

3

I squint in the glare of the midday sun as I watch the chopper approaching. I saw it rise from the GlobaTech compound in the distance, and I heard the rapid thudding of the blades a few moments later, faint at first but growing louder as it neared the mountaintop.

I'm nervous, which isn't a sensation I'm too familiar with.

It hovers overhead for a moment. It looks like an air ambulance. The back is long, with double doors on either side. There's plenty of room for it to land, and it touches down gently about thirty feet away. The door facing me slides open. Josh steps out before the blades begin to slow, stooping as he hurries toward me. He's wearing a fitted shirt, with the sleeves rolled halfway up his forearms, dark-blue jeans, and brown shoes. There's another guy behind him, wearing a suit and carrying a briefcase, and two armed soldiers dressed in full GlobaTech attire—black outfit with a red trim, thigh holster, and an automatic rifle slung over their shoulder, held casually.

The noise fades as the blades slow to a stop. He stops a few feet in front of me, eyeing me up and down. "You look like shit."

I shrug. "Yeah. Feel like it too."

He gestures to the guy with the briefcase. "My friend here is a surgeon of sorts. He's going to help us get that bomb out of your neck."

"Awesome." I nod toward the soldiers. "And the Rambo twins?"

He smiles humorlessly. "They're here in case I feel you need to be shot."

"Oh."

"Show me where it was inserted."

"Okay, but you should know... they know I'm here and probably have eyes on us all right now. This thing could go off any second."

He shrugs. "So, quit whining and show me where it is already."

I raise an eyebrow. "All right, man. Jeez..." I turn around and point to the small scab on my neck. "That's where they injected me with it. I tried masking the signal it sends, so they couldn't track it, but—"

"Yeah, that wouldn't work."

An image of Yaz falling lifelessly to the floor in front of me flashes through my mind.

"No shit."

Josh takes a deep breath. "Okay, here's what we're gonna do. We've been developing a small, localized EMP device, similar in design to those you used a few years ago, back in Pittsburgh."

"On Trent's men? Yeah, I remember those."

"Well, we've been refining the tech to give it a more surgical application."

I frown. "How would they ever be useful during surgery?"

"You need them now, don't you?"

"Well, yeah..."

"So, shut up."

Wow. He's *really* pissed with me. Can't say I blame him.

I feel something cold on the back of my neck. "What's that?"

The doctor steps in front of me. He's short, with a thick, gray mustache and bushy eyebrows. His mottled skin betrays his advancing years. "I just placed one of the devices over the point of injection. It will emit a low-frequency electromagnetic pulse, which should short-circuit the device you have implanted there."

I look at him, narrowing my eyes slightly. "Should?"

He nods. "There's a... small chance it could *detonate* the device instead of disabling it. Without examining the tech beforehand, there's no way of being completely sure."

I shake my head. "Wonderful. Won't the EMP knock out the chopper too?"

"No, the blast radius of the device is approximately six inches. It's designed for surgical precision, not maximum carnage." He holds up a button. "You ready?"

"Not really, no!" I turn around to face Josh. "Are you okay with this?"

He shrugs. "I'm not sure what you want me to say. There are risks, but we're confident it'll work, yeah. If we're wrong, you'll die. But if we don't try it, based on what little you've told me, it'll likely be detonated anyway by whichever asshole has the trigger. So, really, you don't have anything to lose, do you?"

"Huh. Fair point, I guess. Callously made, though."

"Oh, I'm sorry. Did I hurt your feelings, Adrian?"

The doctor steps between us. "Gentlemen, please. I believe time isn't a luxury here. Shall I proceed?"

Josh nods. "Yes."

He looks at me. "Adrian?"

I point to the device he's holding. "You just press that button?"

"That's right."

I hold my hand out. "All right, give it here. If anyone's gonna accidentally blow my brains out, it's gonna be me."

I look at the small device and then at Josh. "If this doesn't work, I just... I want to apologize. I want to tell you everything that's happened... everything I've been through. I hope you'll understand why I did what I did, but if I don't get the chance, I need you to know that I'm sorry. I love you, brother."

His expression softens and his jaw relaxes. He glances down at the ground, then turns and heads back over to the chopper. The other men move to join him.

I frown. "Is that it? You're just going to walk away?"

He looks back over his shoulder. "Yeah. I don't want to get blood on my shirt if this goes wrong."

I shake my head and smile. "Asshole."

I close my eyes and press the button. I feel a sharp pinch in my neck, and—

...

...

...

I drop the button and place my hand on my head. It feels as if it's in one piece. I move it down, feeling for my neck. Yep, still attached too. I take a deep breath and open one eye, followed a moment later by the other. Josh is walking toward me. The doctor and the soldiers are still by the chopper.

"Did it work?" I ask him. "Is the device disabled?"

He nods.

I roll my eyes and breathe a sigh of relief. "Thanks, man. You have no idea how good it is to know that. I feel as if I've just been released from prison. I—"

I land heavily on my back, my cheekbone and jaw stinging from the punch Josh just hit me with. I put my hand to my face as I look up at him. He's not smiling anymore. He's looming over me, his expression locked in a hard frown, his nostrils flaring repeatedly. I imagine it's how he looked when he was throwing his computer around his office.

With him always being behind a laptop or on the other end of the phone, it's easy to forget how tough he is. He was British Special Forces back when I met him. Those SAS boys are crazy, and some of the shit they do... man, it's insane. Yet Josh always made it look easy. He may have made the transition from aging rocker to clean-cut corporate director, but he will always be the guy who left the SAS, and eventually the CIA, by choice. Not because he couldn't cut it—he was among the best either organization has ever had—but because he decided to work a computer and help me.

I nod. "Do you feel better?"

His expression stays the same. He shrugs. "A little."

"Wanna throw me over the edge?"

"Thinking about it..."

"Good. You wouldn't be human if you weren't, after what I've done to you."

He hasn't blinked in a while. Always a sign the adrenaline is pumping. After a few moments, he relaxes and extends his hand. I take it, and he hauls me to my feet. I dust myself down, and we stand in front of one another.

"I know you're hurting, Josh, and I'm sorry. But so we're clear, you hit me again, I'm gonna put you down. Understand?"

Josh looks around and takes in a deep breath, then looks back at me. We lock stares, and the tension is immediate and palpable. After a moment, he nods once and turns away. He looks over at one of the soldiers and gestures with his thumb to the sniper rifle, still set up near the edge of the mountaintop. "Grab that rifle, would you? I want it catalogued and then locked away in our secure vault." He turns to the doctor. "Good work. Thank you. We'll take the device out later. Hopefully, it will help us to improve our own tech."

He moves around the front of the chopper and looks back over his shoulder at me. "Come on. We're walking."

I follow him, frowning, confused. "But there's a perfectly good ride back right here..."

"Yes, and there's a perfectly nice path leading down to the bottom, which should give you plenty of time to explain yourself."

He strides over to the far edge and begins the steady descent. I look back at the doctor. "Thanks for, y'know, zapping me and everything. Appreciate it."

He nods, looking slightly bewildered. I turn and follow Josh to the path that leads back down the mountain. How am I supposed to even start explaining all this to him?

Ah, I'll figure it out as I go along. That always works... sometimes.

4

I've told him almost everything. He didn't say much. Presumably, he's saving all his questions for when I'm finished. I told him how The Order saved me and how they forcibly recruited me. How they threw me out of a plane in Vietnam, how they gave me a new life, made me kill for them, et cetera. I told him about Lily and how she died. I told him about Kaitlyn and how she helped me. I told him what happened to Yaz. I told him how I sustained my injuries. I told him how I struggled with suicidal thoughts. I told him the thing that ruined it all for me, aside from my inability to blindly follow orders, was my inability to let go of my past. I was honest with him. I didn't mask any part of how I'm feeling with humor. I didn't dismiss anything as irrelevant. For probably the first time in my life, I talked to him openly, just like Kaitlyn taught me to do.

We're maybe ten minutes from the base of the mountain. The sun is high, and it's a struggle to bear the heat. The walk back down has been gentle, but I'm aching everywhere. I'm thirsty. I'm hungry. I'm tired. I just want to—

Josh slows his pace and eventually stops. I turn to look back at him. "You okay?"

"I hate you."

I shrug. "Fair enough."

"No, I hate you because I'm trying to be mad at you, and then you go and tell me all that, which makes me feel sorry for you. I don't *want* to feel sorry for you. I want to hate you."

"Then hate me. I wasn't looking for your sympathy, Josh. I just wanted you to understand what I've been through and why I did what I did. I didn't expect you to like it. You're entitled to feel angry."

He gazes around for a moment, as if searching for the right words. "I'm... ah... I'm sorry about the people you lost, man."

I nod. "Thanks."

"I have a lot of questions."

"Figured you might," I say with a small smile.

We continue walking in silence for a few minutes, until we see a bench at the side of the path. He points to it, and we both sit down wearily. I stretch my legs out and crack my neck. It feels good not to move. I lean back and stare ahead, taking in the breathtaking view of the river and the tree line beyond. I look right, at more greenery and the faint outline of San Fernando in the distance.

This place is amazing. I mean, the temperature's a bit high for me. I know it's nowhere near as hot as Abu Dhabi was, but I hated the climate there, and I'm not much happier here. I like things mild—not too warm, not freezing. T-shirt weather but with a breeze. Mid-seventies is perfect. I know Texas was hot, but I had a new life there—and Tori—which made it worthwhile. However, the temperature in

California during the summer is definitely *not* in the mid-seventies. It's like Satan's sauna out here today!

Josh sighs. "So, The Order of Sabbah... they actually exist?"

I nod. "They do."

"That's messed up. I mean, they're, like, a ghost story to people like us, aren't they? If a bunch of hitmen sat around a campfire, *that's* what they would talk about to scare each other. Well, that and stories about you."

I laugh. "Yeah, that's what I thought too. But it turns out they're very real and powerful."

"What do you actually know about them?"

"Not as much as I'd like, but if Horizon is to be believed, they have... I dunno, *chapters* all over the world, headed up by people like him. They all answer to a committee, which ultimately calls the shots and decides who lives, who dies, and why."

"And this Horizon guy... you said that was his title, not his name?"

I nod. "That's right. He's a big deal, and if the other people who do his job are anything like him, they'll all be ruthless, intelligent, and able to play the long game better than anybody."

"And he wants me dead?"

"He does."

"But we don't know why?"

"Nope. He told me The Order has existed for centuries, influencing key moments in history by killing the people they believe are taking us in the wrong direction."

Josh leans back and runs his hands through his hair. "That's some real Illuminati shit, isn't it?"

"I haven't really thought about the consequences of disabling that device, but I'm pretty sure it's gonna piss them off, not having control over me anymore. They value discretion and secrecy as if they're commandments from God."

He turns to me, frowning. "And they hired *you*?"

I chuckle. "Screw you. My point is, I have as much knowledge about them as anyone else in their organization, except they no longer have the option of silencing me. That means I'm the biggest kind of threat they can imagine. I think after today, we're both at the top of their shit list."

He sighs. "Well, misery loves company, right?"

"I'm being serious, Josh. This is bad. Think about everything we've been through together. We've had every acronym in the U.S. Government trying to kill us at some point."

"Trying to kill *you*..."

"Whatever. The Order makes all that look as if a shopkeeper's been chasing us down the street because we stole a candy bar. They're an adversary we can't see, whose size we can't comprehend, whose resources are truly limitless, and who can hit us from all sides without any notice. They're a whole new kind of threat, and we need to up our game if we're going to get through this."

Josh looks at me. His mouth is a thin line on his grave face. "If I didn't know any better, I'd say you were scared."

I shake my head. "No, I'm not scared. I'm just aware of how deep in the shit we are. They say a little knowledge is dangerous."

"And yet, from what you've told me, you've done nothing but ask questions for the last month, which is basically what got us both into this mess."

I don't say anything. I know he's joking, but he's right. It's my fault we're both in this situation. I need to figure out a way to—

"Stop it."

I turn to look at him. "Huh?"

"Stop it."

I frown. "Stop what?"

"Sitting there feeling sorry for yourself, blaming yourself for everything. We don't have time for crap like that."

I go to speak but catch my words, smiling silently. I've missed him.

He stands. "Okay, here's what we do. We get something to eat, get that device out of your head, and then we sit down and figure this whole thing out, from the beginning. We find 'em and then we find a way for you to kill 'em."

I get to my feet. "Sounds like a plan."

We continue walking along the path, side by side, at a steady pace. I look across at him. "Does this mean—"

"Still not forgiven you."

"Oh. Okay."

I look away but not before I see him smile to himself.

5

I push the empty plate away from me and wipe the edges of my mouth with my napkin. I swallow a mouthful of beer and lean back in my seat. "Oh, man... *that* was a damn good burger."

Across from me, Josh sips a glass of water. "Thought you might like it."

We haven't spoken much since we got here. We're in some bar about a half-mile from GlobaTech's compound. Josh said it was popular with the employees and is the only place anywhere near here worth drinking in. It's also quiet at this time of day, which is a good thing.

News of my execution traveled fast, and the world's media was quick to run with the story Schultz felt compelled to feed them, to hide the truth behind what really happened. And I get it—the country needs to believe in its own government. Telling them what Cunningham really did would only add to the problems, not help fix them. Consequently, Schultz told everyone I was a crazy, lone gunman who needlessly shot the president, which meant I died with everyone in the world knowing who I was and believing I was a traitor to the United States. Regardless of the reasons, my lifetime of ruthless anonymity is over. Now that I'm back, I need to keep a low profile.

This whole place feels like a saloon in the Old West. The tables and chairs are made of old wood but are sturdier than they look. Same with the floor. The bar is a stained, waist-high counter, with thin posts periodically inserted along it for aesthetics, rather than necessity.

We're sitting at one of the tables in the middle of the main area, close to the entrance, about halfway between the door and the bar. Over in the opposite corner is a pool table, with a jukebox mounted on the wall across from it. It's the kind of place I would choose to drink in. It bears an uncanny resemblance to the bar I owned until a couple of months ago.

The feeling of nostalgia is still strong, and I force myself to ignore it. I lean forward and rest my elbows on the table. "It's weird, man. Everything I did was supposed to give me freedom. But the reality was, I never felt more trapped in my life. Eating that cheeseburger just then, it felt as if today's my first day out of prison."

Josh goes to speak, but his cell phone starts ringing. I smile as *Crazy Train* by Ozzy Osbourne sounds out in the near-deserted bar. He leans sideways and reaches into his pocket to retrieve it. He looks at the screen and slides his finger across it to dismiss the call. "Sorry about that."

I wave my hand. "Don't worry if you need to answer your phone, Josh. You're an important guy now. I understand."

He smiles sheepishly. "Nah, it can wait."

I fix him with a hard stare. "Hey, just because I showed

27

up and ruined your day doesn't mean your life gets placed on hold, man. You're running a multi-billion-dollar company. You have more important things to worry about than me."

"Yeah, I know." He sighs. "I'm telling you, Adrian, it's stress like I can't describe. I have shareholders breathing down my neck. I have Washington on the phone what feels like every hour. I have hundreds of thousands of security personnel deployed all around the world and billions of dollars invested in more projects than I can fathom, which all require constant monitoring and assessment."

I frown. "So, quit ignoring your phone. Anyway, don't you have, like, several thousand subordinates to do all that shit for you? I thought the whole point of getting promoted was to do less work for more money?"

"If only," he says, laughing. "I guess I just don't trust the employees to do as good a job as I can."

I shake my head. "Okay, let's take a moment to think about what your reaction would be if I said something stupid like that."

"Yeah, yeah. I just... I don't know. I just—"

"You're just *you*, Josh. That's always been your greatest strength and your greatest weakness." I take another swig, empty the bottle, and push it to one side. "Why do you think I kept you around all those years?"

He sips his water and smiles. "Since when did you become Dr. Phil?"

"I had my eyes opened a little these last few weeks. Probably the only good thing that came from it all. A little perspective was long overdue, and I like to think I made a lot of progress in a short space of time."

"Was that because of... what was her name? Kaitlyn?"

I nod. "Yeah, my therapist."

"Well, I'm impressed you realized you needed help and took it upon yourself to get some. There's hope for you yet."

"That's what she said."

"She sounds smart and good for you. You should call her now that you're free from The Order's grip."

"But I'm not, am I? Not really. You're still their target, and I'm the one that got away. We're both gonna be running for a long time unless we find a way to take them down. Calling her now would only put her back in the firing line, and she's suffered enough because of me."

"Fair enough." He gets to his feet. "I'm gonna get the drinks in. Then we'll discuss what we're gonna do about this Horizon asshole."

He walks over to the bar, signals the barmaid, and starts talking to her. I watch him. It's encouraging that he said, *what* we're *gonna do*. If we can work together, there's a chance we might get through this. But he's got a life and a job—a pretty important one, by all accounts. He can't lose focus on that to help me. This is my mess, my problem, and it's my responsibility to fix it. And to protect him. I owe him that much.

He's heading back over now, holding another bottle and another glass of water. He places them on the table as he sits back down. I point to his drink as he sips it. "What's with the whole not drinking thing?"

He shrugs. "The official reason is I'm trying to stay healthy. I have a physical once a week, so I have to watch my diet."

"Really?"

He nods. "Yeah. I'm insured for millions. Look at everything I do. It's in a lot of people's interests to make sure I stay alive and well. Besides, it's not as if I'm getting any younger."

"Maybe we can ask some of those people for help?"

We share a brief laugh. He shakes his head. "It's not just that, though. Honestly, the last few weeks, believing you were dead... it was hard. Really hard. I figured if I started drinking beer for comfort, it would be an easy habit to get into. Then, before you know it, I'm sipping whiskey from a hipflask during meetings with the Joint Chiefs."

"That's sensible, man. I'm sorry I had to put you through all that."

"Did you?"

"Did I, what?"

"Have to put me through it. Did you really have no choice?"

I shrug. "I was sitting in a cell, probably in some CIA-sponsored, off-the-books detention center, waiting to be executed because I killed the president. It was a long-ass twenty-four hours, and I had a lot of time to think about things. I mean, I put this life behind me. After years of running from myself, of ignoring your subtle pleas for me to move on, I finally did. I had The Ferryman, I had Tori... I even had a dog. All that was missing was a white picket fence, y'know? I was—dare I say it?—happy. And then, like a goddamn boomerang, my old life came back around and ruined everything. I got dragged into this whole conspiracy, which resulted in me fighting a corrupt government and watching the end of the world from the front row."

Josh holds up a hand. "Hey, I didn't drag you, Adrian. I asked for your help and then tried to talk you out of it when I saw what you had. Don't turn this around on me."

I shake my head. "I'm not saying you dragged me into anything, Josh. Relax. I'm saying I did. My Inner Satan did. *Adrian Hell* did. And d'you know what? It was the right thing to do. How could anyone with the ability to help not want to, knowing what we knew? But what I've lived, loved, and lost in the last two months is enough to fill three lifetimes, and I'm tired. I sat in that cell, barely able to move under the weight of the guilt I put on my own shoulders, and I felt..."

He leans forward, frowning. "You gave up, didn't you?"

I nod slowly. "I didn't like it, but I'd accepted it, yeah. After the life I've led, the things I've done and been through... yeah, I was ready to die."

"Christ..."

"But then this Colonel Sanders lookalike appeared. He told me he represents The Order of Sabbah and that they've been watching me this whole time. He said my hit on the president impressed them, and he was there to offer me a way out, to join their ranks, and fight the good fight. The proposal shocked me, and he disappeared before I could answer. As it turned out, he switched the chemicals in the lethal injection and hired me anyway, but I would've taken the coward's way out, Josh. I would've said yes, despite knowing what it would do to you. So, to answer your question, yeah... right or wrong, I felt I had to do what I did. It was selfish and cowardly, but that's the choice I made."

He takes a sip of his water and stares at the surface of the table. He absently scratches at a stain with his fingernail, clenching his jaw muscles, frowning with deep thought. Finally, he looks up at me. "There's this guy. Married, two kids, nice house—the works. He had a well-paid job that gave his family a good life, but he lost it because of a mistake, leaving them with nothing. He spent a few weeks spiraling, drinking, taking it out on his loved ones. Then he finally decided to kill himself. He blamed himself. He felt terrible about making his family unhappy, and he figured the world was better off without him in it. He drove to a bridge, climbed out over the side, and stood on the edge, looking down at the water below, prepared to jump. Is he a coward?"

I nod. "Yes."

"Why?"

"Because he's choosing the easy way out and leaving his family to deal with the consequences of his mistakes, instead of facing them himself."

"Correct. But you see, just as he was about to step off, he had an epiphany. He realized how much he loved his family and decided right there and then to fix the problem, no matter how difficult it might be, because he owed it to his family."

I don't say anything. I can see where this is going, but I'll let him make his point. It was a good story, after all.

He leans back in his chair. "Adrian, by sitting in that cell, accepting the lethal injection, and giving up because you felt you deserved it... *that* was the coward's way out. The Order offered you a second chance, a way of continuing your own fight. You stepped away from the edge, despite knowing how difficult it would be. Despite knowing the consequences and how your choice would affect others. You decided to keep living, and that takes a strength few people are blessed with."

I imagine it took a lot for him to say that after everything that's happened today.

I smile. "Thank you, Josh. That means a lot to me."

"You have to understand, Adrian... it'll take time for me to... y'know... deal with all this and get past it. But please, don't think for one second I'm not glad you're alive."

I extend my hand across the table, curling it into a fist. He nods and bumps it with his. I finish my drink. "So, now what?"

Josh gets to his feet, his chair scraping on the floor.

"Now... we do what we always do. We learn what we can about our target and take 'em out."

I laugh. "I admire the enthusiasm, man, but we've... ah... we've got a *lot* of targets."

He shrugs. "We'd best get started then, eh?"

I laugh again, then get to my feet and stretch. Josh throws some money down for the food and then we walk out of the bar side by side.

Time to go to work.

6

18:10 PDT

I'm sitting across from Josh in his office. He's behind his desk, tapping feverishly away on a laptop he's borrowed, since his computer is still in pieces on the other side of the room. His secretary nearly fainted when she saw me, but he said she can be trusted to keep my presence here a secret.

I had the device removed from my neck a couple of hours ago. They gave me a local anesthetic, and the procedure took maybe twenty minutes. The doctor from the mountaintop earlier today performed the surgery, and he was keen to analyze the tech afterward.

Josh also had his medical personnel work on my cut. They re-stitched it and secured it with some kind of surgical glue. It had already begun to heal, but now the wound looks a lot healthier no longer needs a bandage around it.

They examined my hand too but conceded there was little more they could do. It's still next-to-useless, but they've given me another cast, which allows for some minimal movement without sacrificing any support.

After all that, I'm feeling slightly more human than I have in a few days. It's nice to take a moment to relax while Josh does his—

"Adrian, can I ask you something?"

He's looking at me over the edge of his laptop.

I shrug. "Sure."

He scratches the back of his neck. "It's a random question, I know, but have you... ah... have you ever heard of a guy named Sayed bin Mawal? He was a Saudi Prince."

Oh.

Well, *this* is awkward.

Play it cool, Adrian.

I raise an eyebrow. "Why d'you ask?"

"He was a client of ours, paying ridiculous money to receive the best personal protection we could offer. He was murdered in his hotel suite a few days ago, along with the men we sent to protect him. In Abu Dhabi..."

Ah, shit.

I let out a heavy breath. "Okay, yeah, about that..."

He holds up a hand. "Before you say anything..."

He spins the laptop around and presses a button, which starts playing a video file. It's clearly security footage from the hotel. It shows me, in glorious, grayscale hi-definition, taking out a bunch of GlobaTech employees in a hallway before disappearing inside bin Mawal's suite.

I smile regretfully. "That's not how it looks."

He turns the laptop back around, closes the lid, and leans back in his chair. "Funny, because it looks a lot like you killing my men and my client..."

"Okay, so it's *exactly* how it looks."

"Would you care to explain?"

I take a deep breath as I recall the events of three days ago. I think of Lily, which creates this... bubbling inside me, like an emotional volcano preparing to erupt, filling me with both anger and sadness at the same time.

"Adrian?"

I shake my head. "Huh? Sorry. So, yeah, Abu Dhabi... Remember I told you about Lily?"

He nods.

"Well, The Order originally gave her the job of taking out bin Mawal."

Josh frowns. "Do you know why?"

"No, but I'll get to that. Anyway, she failed to kill him but lied to The Order about it. She then showed up on my doorstep to ask for my help in eliminating him before Horizon realized he was still alive."

"Go on..."

I feel as if I'm being interrogated. All that's missing is a light shining in my face.

"So, I talked my way into his suite. Now, by that point, I was already doubting The Order's true motives, so I thought I'd quiz bin Mawal as to why someone might want him dead. Maybe it'd give me some clue about what Horizon's planning."

"And?"

"And when I got there, I noticed GlobaTech was protecting him. I knew The Order would be pissed with me for getting involved in the first place, but I also knew if I violated their rules by allowing someone from my old life to find out I was alive, they would kill me without hesitation."

"Right, so you figured my guys would report the incident back to me, and I'd review the footage and see you weren't dead?"

I nod. "Pretty much, yeah."

He massages the bridge of his nose between this finger and thumb. "I'm trying really hard not to lose my shit here, Adrian..."

"I know, and don't think I don't appreciate it. Look, I didn't like it, but I knew my only option was to leave no trace I was ever there and hope you wouldn't find out. I figured The Order would wipe the video footage from the hotel as part of their clean-up procedure."

"They did," he replies with a short tone. "The footage I have is from our own security feed, which we installed ourselves once we knew our client was staying there. It wasn't on the same network as the hotel's own feed, so The Order wouldn't have known to look for it."

"Oh."

"You do realize I'm the one who has to contact the families of those people? I'm the one who has to tell wives and children their husband or father is dead."

I look away, feeling ashamed—not for killing those men but because I never once considered the implications. I mean, I've never thought about the people my targets leave behind. They're usually all scumbags of some kind. But now that Josh is in the position he's in, it's showing me a different point of view.

"I'm... I'm sorry, man. I didn't think. I—"

He holds up a hand. "Forget it. I shouldn't have put that on you. You're a professional killer by nature, and you were in an impossible situation. It's not your problem to worry about. It's mine. Just..." He sighs. "Anyway, did bin Mawal give you anything?"

I shake my head. "Nope. Not a damn thing. Don't get me wrong—there was something off about him that I couldn't put my finger on, but from what I read about him and from what he said, he seemed like a rich guy just trying to help out."

Josh frowns. "Help out?"

"Yeah, y'know, by selling cheap oil to people who needed it. I figured The Order was involved with the people who were losing money because of bin Mawal's business, and they wanted him gone because of the financial implications."

He suddenly sits forward, jumping slightly in his chair. He opens the laptop and starts typing again.

"What is it?" I ask.

"Fuelex," he replies, without looking up.

"The company bin Mawal owned?"

"Correct. Maybe it wasn't about what they were doing. Maybe it's about what they *would* do if he were dead."

I scratch my forehead. "Josh, I appreciate you're probably out of practice, but you *do* remember I'm not as smart as you, right? You need to say things slowly, in Adrian language."

He rolls his eyes. "The guy was rich, right?"

I shrug. "Yeah."

"And his companies are worth billions because of him."

"I guess..."

"So, do you know what happens to public companies that suddenly lose their majority shareholder?"

I shake my head.

He theatrically taps a key and spins the laptop around for me to look at. There's a news article displayed on the screen.

Josh points to it. "Their stocks crash."

I lean forward and start reading, skimming over the page to pick out the key words I need to get the story.

...

...

...

Okay, it says here that when bin Mawal died, Fuelex's stock prices hit the floor, resulting in the company being dramatically devalued and costing its remaining shareholders millions of dollars.

I look at Josh. "So, by killing the prince, I essentially killed his company too?"

He nods. "That's right. Maybe that's why The Order wanted him dead. Not because of something he was doing but because of the consequences his death would trigger."

I get to my feet and begin pacing around the spacious office. I stop in front of the window to look out. In the distance, I see the outline of the mountain I was sitting on this morning. Below me, GlobaTech's massive compound is alive with activity. It's an impressive sight. Hard to believe my best friend is in charge of it all.

I turn around to face him. "So, we look at who benefitted from Fuelex crashing, and maybe we find a link to someone in The Order?"

His head is buried in the laptop again. "That's what I'm hoping."

I walk back over to him, move around to his side, and lean on the desk. "Maybe that's why they want you dead too —to send GlobaTech down the same way. Can you cross-reference that to see if there's anyone who would benefit from both companies going belly-up?"

He glances up at me with a raised eyebrow. "Your research skills are improving. I'm impressed."

I smile. "Not through choice. I've had to do it all myself lately. I have a newfound respect for you, man. All this fact-finding is boring as shit."

He chuckles as his fingers dance over the keyboard, then

claps his hands after a few minutes of silence. "I think we have a winner."

I look at the screen. "Grant Sterling?"

"Uh-huh. Chairman and CEO of The Sterling Group."

"And they are..."

"An international conglomerate with headquarters up in Seattle. They have rather large fingers in a great number of pies. They proposed a takeover to Fuelex two days ago, for only a fraction of what the company was worth when bin Mawal was still alive. That's fast, man. Like, impossibly fast. Corporate mergers aren't put together overnight, and given you only took out bin Mawal three days ago..."

I nod. "This has Horizon and The Order written all over it."

"Looks that way. The shareholders will likely agree to sell. It's the only way they'll recoup anything close to the losses they will have suffered, which leaves Sterling with a huge piece of the global oil business. Not a bad industry to dominate nowadays."

"Jesus. So, what does this have to do with us? Or you?"

"I don't know. The conglomerate is big, but they're not in GlobaTech's league. I doubt the hit on me is for the same reason they took out bin Mawal. But one thing at a time. From what you've told me about this Horizon guy, he likes to play the long game, right? So, we need to look at why Fuelex is so important to them."

I stand straight. "What say we pay this Sterling prick a visit?"

Josh gets to his feet. "Not so fast, Adrian. We need to keep a low profile, remember? For a start, that means we're driving, not flying. Seattle's almost a day away on the road, and I can't just up and leave. I've got things I need to take care of here first."

I nod. "That's fine. Do what you gotta do."

He closes the laptop and presses a button on his desk phone. It buzzes and clicks. "Yes, Mr. Winters?"

"Kim, can you arrange a management meeting, please?"

"When for?"

He checks his watch. "Now."

"And which department heads need to attend?"

He sighs. "All of 'em."

The phone buzzes again, ending the call.

I smile. "Mr. Winters, eh? Fancy."

He smiles back weakly. "Yeah, you get used to it. Listen, everyone who's coming to this meeting, Schultz and I vetted personally when we took over. I trust them all with this company's secrets. I'm going to tell them what's happening, in a roundabout kind of way."

I frown. "How are you possibly going to explain this shit to anyone?"

"Hey, if I managed to sell the fact that Cunningham was a glorified terrorist, I can convince them that I suspect large-scale corporate espionage. Don't worry about it. I'll gloss over your involvement, obviously. I just need to make sure this company stays strong and focused while I'm gone. Big picture and all that."

"Okay." I look around the spacious office, feeling a little awkward and suddenly out of my depth. "So, what should I do now?"

He smiles. "Just wait here and try to stay out of trouble. I won't be long."

He leaves the office, closing the door behind him. I walk over to the window and stare out. The first shades of pink tinge the sky as the sun thinks about calling it a day. Spread out below is a sea of organized chaos. I mean, this place never stops. It isn't a typical nine-to-five gig. There are groups of soldiers, dozens of vehicles in various sizes, and even helicopters, all buzzing around here twenty-four-seven. It puts New York to shame.

For the first time in a few weeks, though, I'm feeling like myself again. A lot of what happened recently still feels raw, but I'm putting those events to one side for now. I'm not dismissing them or burying them without dealing with them, like I used to. Kaitlyn had a bigger effect on me than I think even *she* realized. I just know that now isn't the time to start arguing with myself about guilt, nor for grieving over the people I've lost.

In the few hours since I called him, Josh and I have made good progress. There's still nothing solid on The Order, but this Sterling Group looks as if it's a good place to start. Once he's finished doing whatever he's doing, we'll hit the road, just like old times.

I feel terrible. Look at everything Josh has accomplished without me. He was always destined for great things, and I always felt like I was holding him back. I know he would never look at it that way, but that doesn't mean I'm not right. It's as if I'm making a son move back home with his parents after living alone for twenty years. I'm restricting him, cramping his style. That said, his life's in danger. We're in for the biggest fight of our lives, and all this technology and fire-power he's surrounded by can't protect him.

I look down at my cast and sigh.

I just hope to God that I can.

7

We're doing eighty along I-5. The burnt-orange sun is sinking slowly behind us, and the road ahead is clear. Josh's car is a convertible, and it's still pleasant enough to justify having the top down. I lean back, close my eyes, and enjoy the wind on my face.

I still haven't been able to shake this feeling of freedom.

Josh and I haven't spoken much in the twenty minutes we've been on the road. He looked stressed after his meeting. I think he's struggling with the idea of stepping away from his work, entrusting it to others while he's with me. I haven't been able to come up with any words of comfort, either. The silence isn't awkward, but I still feel I should say something, and I'm annoyed at myself because I can't find the words.

It's a straightforward run to Seattle. I think we're hoping to make it as far as Sacramento before stopping for the night, which is roughly four hours away. Josh insisted on doing all the driving. He said he wouldn't trust me behind the wheel of his car with two good hands, let alone one.

Asshole.

I glance sideways. He's relaxed, staring almost absently ahead. He looks at me quickly, then double-takes and stares at me. "What?"

I shake my head. "Nothing. Just... I dunno, checking you're all right."

He raises his eyebrow and turns back to the road. "I'm fine. Just trying not to think about all the things I hope other people don't screw up for me while I'm gone."

"You didn't have to come, y'know. I know you have a lot going on right now."

"Yeah, I did, Adrian. All that stuff I've got going on... all the important work GlobaTech is doing around the world that I oversee... it's hard to manage all that if I'm dead. Besides, you're useless without me. I mean, look how royally screwed we are right now. And why? Because you were left to your own devices. You're like a kid left home alone while his parents are away, trying to clean up after a party he was expressly told not to have."

I burst out laughing. "Kiss my ass!"

He laughs with me. "Seriously, you're like a dog off its lead that just runs around, sniffing other dogs' shit, maybe nibbling it a little until its owner shouts at it and makes it heel."

My cheeks ache. "How d'you figure that?"

"Well, look at your track record when I'm not with you. You pissed off a terrorist network and then the U. S. Government, which resulted in you being hunted by the CIA. Then you managed to piss off a secret organization comprised of the best assassins in history, resulting in us both being marked for death."

I shake my head. "And how would any of those situations have been different if *you* were there?"

He shrugs. "I dunno, exactly. But I know I wouldn't have let things get as bad as they did. You're like a planet, and your gravitational pull just gathers all the shit in the universe in one place, with you at the center."

"Okay, seriously, have you been working on all these metaphors for a while? Storing them up in case the day of my resurrection ever came?"

He laughs again. "No, they're just coming to me. You make it easy to do."

"All right, d'you know what..." I unfasten the cast on my right arm and gently slide it off, being careful not to move my hand. I raise my arm, showing Josh the tattoo on my inner forearm. "You see this?"

He glances at me and frowns. "Since when did you get a tattoo? Or find religion?"

"WWJD doesn't stand for *What Would* Jesus *Do*, man. It stands for *What Would* Josh *Do*."

He's silent for a moment. "Are you serious?"

I nod. "I got it soon after starting over with my new life, courtesy of The Order. I needed something to keep me grounded and sane. I needed you, Josh, as my guide and my voice of reason. But you weren't around, so this was the best I could do. I would ask myself the question all the time, to help me make the right decision."

He falls silent for a few moments. "That's... ah... damn, Adrian, that's made me feel bad about all those metaphors."

I smile. "Sorry."

"I'm actually honored you would do something like that."

"What can I say? I agree with you. I usually *am* screwed

when you're not around. It was scary as hell being on my own."

I carefully slide the cast back in place and fasten it securely.

Josh looks over again. "Listen, Adrian, I gotta ask. You haven't got my name tattooed anywhere else, have you?"

I laugh.

"It's just... y'know... it's a nice thought, and I know you were lonely, but if you have my initials on your ass cheeks or something, I'm not sure I'm okay with that, mate."

"Screw you, Josh."

We bump fists, and he reaches for the stereo. He presses a few buttons and turns the volume dial all the way up. Straight away, the opening riff of *Thunderstruck* by AC/DC blasts out. I smile and think about the last time it was just me, Josh, and the open road. It's been way too long.

We both look at each other.

"Thunder!" we say in unison.

Josh starts tapping on the steering wheel.

"Thunder!" we say again.

I pat his shoulder, laughing. "I'm telling you, Josh, with the dream team back together, those bastards don't stand a chance."

He doesn't respond. Instead, he frowns and leans forward, turning off the music. "You hear that?"

I listen intently. There's a noise. It's faint, but it must be close if we can hear it over the rush of the wind and AC/DC.

I nod. "Yeah, what *is* that?"

"I dunno. It kinda sounds like..."

"A helicopter gunship?"

He looks at me. "That was worryingly specific..."

I turn slightly in my seat, looking back along the interstate. "That's because there's a flying tank about a half-mile behind us."

In the distance—and closing fast—is a large, black helicopter, with rotary cannons attached to the underside of each wing. Josh quickly looks over his shoulder, and his eyes go wide. "Holy shit!"

"I've seen it before. In Abu Dhabi, after I killed the prince."

"Wait, *that* thing is what made the news by destroying the top floor of the Etihad Tower?"

I nod. "That's the one."

"Bollocks!" He looks ahead. "Adrian, we have no cover."

I turn to stare at the road. Straight as an arrow.

Shit.

"Well, at least there's no—"

Shit!

The lightning-fast stutter of automatic gunfire erupts behind us. The noise is deafening. I slide down in my seat and glance back as a thick line of fire moves toward us like a laser, tearing up the surface of the road.

"Josh!"

He swerves instinctively, keeping the car under control as he fishtails away to the left, trying to avoid being ripped apart by the chopper's impressive arsenal. I look around again. The stream of bullets strafes left, following us, tracing its mark across the interstate.

I tap his arm. "Go right!"

He slides back across. The sound of the screeching tires is barely audible over the hail of bullets chasing us. I glance through the windshield. Thankfully, there aren't any other vehicles close to us, but that's a small comfort right now. We need to—

Wait... there's a sign.

47

Without thinking, I point to it. "Turn off here."

Josh yanks the wheel to the right, and we slide around the bend at speed. We shoot past a small-town fire station and follow the road around as it takes us along the overpass, back across I-5. I look back at the road, the way we came. The chopper is close, but at least it's stopped firing for now.

I sit straight again. If that's the same helicopter as back in Abu Dhabi, that means Pierce might be on board.

I owe that sonofabitch big time.

I take a deep breath, subduing the instant thirst for vengeance. It's not the time. Not yet. If it *is* him, then I know he won't care about any of these innocent people driving around here. The Order is only secretive about the shadowy, behind-the-scenes string-pulling they do. When it comes to front-line shit, like taking people out or cleaning up after one of their pet assassins, they're brazen to the point of arrogant because they can cover up anything they want.

We need to distract him.

The overpass leads us to a junction, which splits left and right. Tall, thin trees line the near edge, separating it from the interstate.

I point and say, "Go right."

Josh guns the engine and makes the turn.

I look over, through the trees, and see the chopper flying parallel to us, a good distance above the road. It doesn't appear to be looking for an opportunity to re-engage. It's just keeping pace with—

Josh swerves again as a bullet hits the side of the car. The impact is loud and high-pitched, and my ears are ringing slightly, despite the speed. I quickly slide back down my seat, covering the side of my head with my cast. "For fuck's sake!"

Another two rounds punch into the side of us but thankfully don't penetrate the bodywork. I can tell from the time between shots that whoever's shooting at us is using a bolt-action, mid-range rifle. I really want to put the roof up for extra protection, but slowing down enough to do it will cause more harm than good. Staying fast will make us harder to hit, which is far more important.

We just passed a car rental place on our left. There are houses up ahead and a sign that says, *Welcome to Lebec. Please drive safely.*

Josh glances at me. "Adrian, it would appear we're leading the chopper straight toward the good folks of Lebec, California."

I sigh. "Yeah, I noticed. Just keep going. How big can this place be, right?"

He slows a little to navigate around a car in front of us but quickly hits the gas again once we're past it. The needle's pushing ninety.

I glance at the back seat, then at Josh. "I don't suppose you have any weapons in this thing, do you? I was hoping to see a black bag of goodies behind us, but..."

He gestures behind him with his thumb. "I actually have a couple of things that belong to you in the trunk."

I arch an eyebrow. "You've got my Berettas? Are you serious?"

"Yeah, they were among your possessions that were taken when Schultz hauled your ass off to be executed. I asked if I could hang onto them—y'know, for posterity."

"And you keep them in your car?"

He smiles briefly. "In a hidden compartment, along with your holster and a few magazines."

"Sonofabitch... I wondered what happened to my babies. Thanks, man."

I look over at the chopper. It's banked farther away from

us but is staying level. Whoever had the rifle has stopped taking potshots at us too, which is nice of them. The tree line is getting a little denser now, so we'll be harder to see.

I reckon we've covered a mile or so, easily. We just passed a church, and the landscape is opening up and expanding ahead, separating us from the interstate. Thankfully, we're still protected by the trees. There's a hill on the opposite side of us that's partially blocking the sunset. The streetlights are sparse, but Josh wisely keeps the headlights off.

"Now what?" he asks.

"I'm thinking..."

I stare ahead, my vision blurring slightly as I retreat into my mind, searching for a plan. Assuming that *is* Pierce, we don't stand a chance against him like this. He's a vicious sonofabitch. He'll waste us and anyone who happens to be near us in a heartbeat. The only way we get out of this alive is to force him out of that chopper. But how do I—

I refocus and see a sign stating that there's a power plant up ahead.

Perfect!

The road veers right, and it comes into view on our left a moment later. It's surrounded by a chain-link fence, with a padlocked entrance at the end of a low ramp.

I point to it. "Josh, in there."

He nods. "I see it."

The road splits up ahead, carrying straight on and splitting left. The entrance to the plant is diagonal between the two, at our ten o'clock.

He eases off the gas slightly as we approach the turn. He grips the wheel with both hands as he aims the car at the fence. I grab the top edge of the windshield, bracing myself against my seat.

We plow through the gate with a loud, metallic crash and slide to a stop on the gravel. We both jump out and rush around to the trunk. Josh opens it and lifts the false floor up, revealing a compartment housing my custom Berettas. I take one out, holding it lovingly in my hand for a moment. These bad boys have gotten me out of more shit than I can remember.

Let's hope they can do it again.

I hold it out for Josh. "Here. I can't use both, and you're the only other person I trust to use this. Be nice to it."

He takes it, works the slide, and flicks the safety off. "It's an honor. Thanks."

I take the other, and he closes the trunk. I look around. The power plant isn't huge, but I guess it doesn't need to be if it only services Lebec. The compound is almost square, with the main building roughly central. It's a long, low structure, with cooling towers at either end. There are also four generators, one in each corner. Floodlights shine down, making every inch of the plant visible, but that doesn't matter. It was still a stroke of luck finding this place. It's perfect because of how many powerlines are running over-head. The chopper can't come close without the risk of hitting one. Plus, I doubt even Pierce would be reckless enough to destroy it. While he wouldn't care for the loss of lives, blowing up a large part of a small town, right next to a busy stretch of road, and blacking out a noticeable chunk of California wouldn't be easy to cover up, even for The Order.

I point to the main building. "Come on. We'll get into position over there."

Josh looks at me as we set off walking. "You sure this is a good idea?"

I shake my head. "No, but it's the only one we've got. The way I see it, they either land and storm us on foot, or they cut their losses and leave. Whichever way it plays out, it'll be better than trying to outrun those Miniguns in your sports car all night."

"Fair point."

We make it to the building and press ourselves against the wall. I look over at the busted gate and the road beyond. The chopper is some distance away, circling impatiently, like a predator stalking its prey. After a moment, it banks left and disappears along the road that leads away from Lebec.

"You think they're giving up?" asks Josh.

I scratch my forehead with the barrel of my gun. "No, I think they're looking for somewhere to land."

"Great."

"Come on. Let's head around the other side and wait. We still have the advantage."

We move past the door at the end of the building. Stuck to it is a sign with a big yellow triangle on it, outlined in black, with a lightning bolt in the middle. It says *Warning— Danger of Death*.

You'd better believe it.

8

I'm kneeling around the corner of the main building, watching the entrance intently. I'm gripping the gun in my hand a little tighter than I usually would. I'm confident in my abilities, despite my stronger hand being out of action. I'm just... I'm finding it hard to suppress everything I'm feeling right now. I've always prided myself on being able to keep emotion out of what I do. I stay focused on the task at hand and simply walk away when it's done without looking back.

But that was before all this. That was when life was simpler. Don't get me wrong. It was darker back then. *I* was darker. I was... troubled, I guess. But looking back on it now, my job was so much easier. The last few months of my life have turned everything I ever worked for upside-down and opened my eyes to a whole new world of emotional pain. I just can't shut it out anymore. I don't feel I can maintain the

53

clinical approach I once had. I just have a desire to rip apart everything and everyone that's hurt me. Starting with—

Pierce.

He's just walked through the damaged gate, accompanied by four men who are all armed with automatic rifles. He doesn't appear to have a weapon, which just makes me hate the arrogant, over-confident dickbag even more—thinking he doesn't need a gun because he has some kind of power over me. Looking at him now, all I can think of is seeing Yaz murdered in front of me and hearing Kaitlyn scream as the blood of her young neighbor sprays over her.

I want to kill him. Not as an assassin. Not as a professional. I want to wrap my hands around his neck and choke the fucking life out of him. A bullet's too good for him. He deserves to suffer for what he's done. I want to see his eyes bulge in their sockets. I want to hear him gasping for breath. I want to see the moment he realizes he's dying and there's nothing he can do about it.

I'm fighting to keep myself in check. I need to remember what we're up against. The only way I'll get to Horizon is by thinking like him. I need to be smart, plan ten moves ahead, and keep the big picture in the forefront of my mind at all times. I glance over at Josh, who's standing behind the generator across from me, out of sight. We exchange a small nod.

Showtime.

I step out, holding my gun by my side, my finger resting gently on the trigger. Pierce's men slow to a stop. He carries on alone toward me. The only sound is our footsteps, crunching on the gravel, loud in the palpable silence. We stop a few feet from each other.

He looks around before resting his gaze on me, smiling.

"You really haven't learned anything from your time in The Order, have you?"

I shrug. "Oh, I dunno. I've learned you're a terrible shot, even with a helicopter."

"See, I've been telling Horizon since the day he saved your ass that it was a mistake to bring you in," he replies, ignoring me. "But he didn't listen to me. He insisted he knew best. He said he had a grand plan and that you played a big part in it. But he's finally seen sense. Finally decided to cut his losses. That's where I come in. You're going to die today, Adrian. I hope you understand that."

I smile. "You keep telling yourself that, douche-monkey."

"It's your call, Adrian. Do you want a bullet? Or..." He reaches in his pocket and takes out the detonator for the tracking device. "...is it off with your head?"

"Pierce, if I had a shit, I still wouldn't give it, all right? Do whatever you want."

He paces idly back and forth in front of me. "I'm curious, though. What made you think you'd managed to mask the signal from your tracking device this time? It was a much better attempt than that kid made for you, but you must've known we would still find you?"

I grip the gun tighter in my hand, feeling the color drain from my knuckles. I bite my tongue, swallowing back the instinctive reaction. I'm not giving him the satisfaction.

He smiles. "He died because of you. Y'know that, right? You kept pushing, kept asking questions, kept looking for a way out. You never grasped the fact that once you're in The Order, that's it—they own your ass. Lily understood it. And... wow, I mean, what an ass to own there, am I right?"

He laughs, staring straight into my eyes. He's trying to get under my skin, and I'm not going to let him.

Bastard.

I step forward, closing the gap between us. "And look where it got her. Nobody owns me. Nobody can control me. Think what you want. Say what you want. You need to understand something, Pierce. I'm gonna tear it all down. The Order, Horizon, everything. It's all gonna come crashing down around you, and when the dust settles and you're surrounded by the rubble of what used to be your life, the only thing you'll see is me, standing over you, pointing a gun at your face.

"Then you'll know why Horizon chose me. He saw past my authority issues. Past the moral compass. Past all the bullshit and bravado. He saw the real me. He understood that I'm more than just a man. I'm a goddamn tsunami— and it'll be my story people tell for years to come. No one will care about The Order and how they operated from the shadows like ghosts. They will only know the legend of how Adrian Hell burned them to the ground... how he could take anyone out... how nothing could stop him... and how his quest for vengeance and justice brought the world to its knees—starting with you."

I raise my arm and aim the gun at his head.

He laughs again and holds the detonator up in his hand, waving it side to side. "Nice speech. But it was wasted breath. You're like a dog refusing to be trained."

I roll my eyes. "Oh, don't you start with the goddamn metaphors..."

"Any last words, Adrian?"

"You mean besides *fuck* and *you*?"

He shrugs. "Have it your way. You brought this on yourself. It's a real waste of talent, but it needs to be done. Maybe I'll pay that therapist of yours a visit when I'm finished here and break the news to her that her favorite patient is dead."

He smiles, waves, and ceremoniously pushes the button.

...

...

...

Nothing.

Obviously.

I wave back at him with my cast, adjust my aim slightly, and squeeze the trigger twice. The two shots echo around the otherwise silent power plant, followed a moment later by two more. Pierce spins around in time to see all four of his men drop to the ground with a dull thud, staining the gravel with their blood. A thin, crimson mist slowly evaporates above them.

He turns back to face me, his eyes wide. "How did you..."

I smile. "How did I... what? Keep my head on my shoulders after you pressed your little button? Or manage to kill four men when you only saw me fire two bullets?"

I take another step toward him and see his gaze shift to my right. A moment later, Josh appears beside me, holding the other Beretta low and loose. I gesture to him with my head without taking my eyes off Pierce. "He's a good shot, isn't he? Four headshots between us in a matter of seconds, without any coordination. You gotta admit, we're pretty awesome, right?"

Pierce takes a step back, his eyes wide. His gaze darts around with uncertainty. "You're both dead."

I snap my gun to him and fire, hitting him in his left kneecap. The detonator goes flying away to the side as he drops, clutching his leg. He lets out a guttural scream, partially muffled through gritted teeth. The kneecap is one of the most painful places you can be shot. It's made worse because it's not lethal, so you know there's no reprieve coming from the agony you feel, just the knowledge that you won't ever walk properly again.

I pace slowly toward him. He raises his head slightly to look at me. "H-how are you still alive?"

I crouch beside him and rest my arms on my knees, letting the gun hang loosely over him. "This is Josh. You might recognize him. He runs GlobaTech. He's also my best friend, and Horizon made a drastic error in judgment when he sent me to kill him. See, it turns out, he's a lot smarter than you. That little tracking device bomb thing you stuck in me? He disabled it and removed it."

"Th-that's impossible!"

I smile. "I did say you didn't control me." I look up at Josh. "Didn't I say that?"

He nods. "You said it. I heard you."

I look back at Pierce. "See, your problem is that you never listen. You just live in your own little bubble, thinking that, because you're in The Order, the rules somehow don't apply to you."

"But we... we were tracking you..."

Josh crouches next to him, across from me, holding a small device between his thumb and index finger for Pierce to see. "This is a tracking device of ours. I configured it to the same frequency as yours and piggybacked your signal, so you could still see us without knowing you couldn't blow Adrian's head off. Pretty simple, really."

Pierce spits on the ground beside him, breathing heavily. "You're both finished. Once Horizon finds out, he'll—"

I shake my head. "Nah, we'll be long gone by the time word of this reaches him. Don't worry about that."

He rolls side to side, clasping his hands over the hole in his leg.

I nudge him with the barrel of the gun. "I'll tell you what. You help us, and I'll make that pain stop."

He starts laughing, but it degrades into a cough. "Screw you, Adrian."

I look at Josh. "What do you think? Is it worth trying to get anything out of him?"

He shrugs. "I dunno, man. He seems pretty adamant. Maybe just leave him lying here in agony? We'll get everything we need from Grant Sterling anyway."

Out of the corner of my eye, I was watching Pierce for any reaction when we said Sterling's name. I saw a flicker of... something. He's expertly trained, and he hid it well, but I saw it—that *oh, shit* look when you find out someone knows something you didn't think they knew.

I pat him hard on his injured knee. "What's the matter, Pierce? D'you not like the idea of being left here to suffer?"

He doesn't say anything.

Josh stands. "Come on, Adrian. You're wasting your time. This guy's been drinking from the Kool-Aid too long."

I watch him pace away, then stand slowly. I go to follow him.

"W-wait."

I smile to myself, then look back down at Pierce. "What?"

He's gasping for breath. I bet it's hard fighting to stay conscious in so much pain.

"How... how do you know that name?"

"Who? Sterling? Oh, that was easy. I just asked the right questions. You know how inquisitive I can be."

He closes his eyes briefly and then lifts his head to look at me. "It's no use. Whatever you... think you know... whatever you're planning, it's... futile. The Order is bigger than you can imagine. There's no... stopping them."

Josh moves back over to us and stops beside me. He looks down at Pierce. "*Them*? What happened to *us*?"

I chuckle. "I think someone's starting to realize that they've backed the wrong horse."

Pierce shakes his head. "I'm just accepting the fact I... I won't be here to see you two fail. You don't stand a... chance, and if you think otherwise, you're even more... stupid than you look."

"Uh-huh. So, what's the big deal about Sterling, anyway? You didn't seem happy that we knew the name."

He relaxes his head on the ground for a moment, staring wide-eyed at the evening sky.

Josh nudges him with his shoe. "Hey, don't clam up on us now. You were doing so well."

Pierce lifts his head to stare at Josh. "Just kill me. Get it over with."

I crouch beside him again. "Look, this is your only shot at redeeming yourself. After all the shit you've done to me, it's taking all my self-control to refrain from beating you to death. It wouldn't be quick or pleasant. You would hurt, and you would suffer, and you would spend your last moments on this mortal coil wondering how it was possible to experience so much pain. You see, I'm the personification of every childhood nightmare you ever had, Pierce. You can't fathom what I'm capable of putting you through. But you have one chance and one chance only, right now, to avoid all that unpleasantness. You just have to tell us what you know about The Order. How they operate, what they're planning —everything."

He holds my gaze for a few moments. I can tell he's searching for any hint that I'm lying. I stare right back, unblinking, knowing he won't find anything.

Finally, he looks over at Josh. "He... talks a lot, doesn't he?"

Josh smiles and nods. "Yes, he does. And the frightening thing is, he means every word."

Pierce sighs and leans back again, gazing back up at the sky. I notice his grip on his knee loosens. "How did you find out about Mr. Sterling?"

I frown. "It's *Mr.* Sterling now, is it?"

Josh crouches opposite me. "We know The Sterling Group is trying to buy Fuelex, which is why Horizon wanted Sayed bin Mawal taken out. What we don't know is why."

"The Committee..." he manages.

My eyes narrow. "What about it?"

Pierce sighs. "Sterling's on it."

Josh and I exchange a glance, filled with surprise, excitement, and apprehension. Not only are we on the right track, but we just hit the goddamn jackpot.

9

His words hang ominously in the air. I remember Horizon saying these Committee members are the sonsofbitches who run the show. If Sterling's one of them, this is a big opportunity for us.

"What does his conglomerate want with Fuelex?" asks Josh.

Pierce shakes his head. "I... I don't know."

I press my gun against his temple. "Now isn't the time to be vague, asshole."

He casually bats it away with his hand. "I'm not. You know someone like... like me wouldn't know... something like that. I don't even know who else... is on... the Committee."

"How do you know Sterling is?"

"I heard Horizon mention him... when we were looking at... bin Mawal as a target."

Josh shrugs. "Okay. We'll get more information out of Sterling, anyway. At least we know we're on the right track." He looks over at me. "Adrian, we should think about getting out of here."

I ignore him, instead pressing the barrel of my gun into Pierce's knee. "Where's Horizon?"

He screams, his face contorted with pain. "I don't know!"

"Don't lie to me."

"I'm... I'm not. He left Dubai two days ago, after he... sent you to kill... your friend. He didn't... say... where."

I believe him. It was a long shot, anyway. Besides, Horizon is just one battle. The war is with The Order, and Sterling might be the break we need to get ahead of the enemy for once.

I stand and hold my gun out to Josh. He straightens up too and takes it, looking confused.

"Go wait in the car," I say to him.

He frowns. "Why?"

"Because you're a public figure and a respectable citizen. You don't need to see what's about to happen."

He raises an eyebrow. "Adrian? Don't do anything stupid. Just—"

I shake my head. "Walk away, Josh."

We hold each other's gaze for a moment, then he sighs, nods once, and turns on his heels. He walks back over to the car. He knows me better than anyone, which means he can tell when I'm already fixed on doing something that's either stupid or violent.

This is going to be the latter.

I look down at Pierce. "I've had a lot of things to think about these last couple of days. One of those things is what I would do to you if I ever saw you again. I know you're dangerous and good at what you do. You see, where your arrogance blinds you, I give credit where it's due. I know from experience that you're a mean sonofabitch. The Order has some of the world's best assassins working for it, and you were the one Horizon sent to help them. That says a lot. But I'm not among the best... I'm *the* best. I'm going to stop The Order, and I'm going to lay waste to every single one of them. I want you to know that."

He smiles weakly, barely able to lift his head. "No one man can stop... The Order, and you're delusional if you... if you think otherwise. There's only one way this will end."

I take a deep breath. "Maybe you're right. But I'm not *one man*. I have Josh. And between us, we're unstoppable. But as for how this will end, you're right. There is only one way. See, at first, I figured if I ever got a hold of you, I would just shoot you, right between the eyes. But when you chased us in here, and I realized it was going to come down to you or me, I decided a bullet was too good for you. Too merciful. Like I said before, it took a lot of self-control to stop myself from beating you to death before I'd gotten any information from you."

He shifts uncomfortably on the ground, as if he's trying to scramble away from me but can't. "You... you said if I helped you... you would—"

"Spare you the unpleasantness of suffering... yes, I know. I was there. The thing is..." I kneel beside him, then slam my cast down across his face, as hard as I can, like a hammer. "I lied."

He grunts from the impact and brings an arm up in a desperate attempt to protect himself.

There's no protection from this.

From me.

I lean forward and grab his throat. I have a strong grip.

The only way you get out of it is if I let you. I pin him to the ground and bring my cast down once more across his face. I feel his nose give way beneath the impact. A thick, dark red spray covers his shirt and the gravel beside him.

He gasps for air, unable to breathe through his nose now, but the hand I have around his throat is making it difficult for him.

I hit him again, with as much brute strength as I can. His left eye swells almost instantly, forcing itself shut. A large welt rises on his cheek, and what remains of his nose spurts more blood over him. He clutches my wrist, desperately trying to relieve some of the pressure on his throat, but he can't. He seems insistent on leaving one hand over his leg wound, choosing to limit his own chances of survival.

I hit him a fourth time, and his cheek splits. Blood pulses from the wound, running freely down his face and chin. I lean close to him. "I don't care if you were a willing soldier or nothing more than Horizon's puppet. I don't care how helpful you've been. Bottom line is, you killed Lily, you killed Yaz, and you tried to kill me. This is just the beginning. What I'm going to do to you is nothing compared to what Horizon and anyone else involved in The Order has coming to them. You should be thankful you won't be around to see it."

I hit him again. And again. And again. The muscles in my face ache from gritting my teeth. I snarl as the full extent of my wrath is slowly unleashed, little by little, with each furious blow. My arm and shoulder begin to throb from the exertion, but I don't stop. I can't. Not now. I just need to keep swinging. To keep hitting him. To punish him and make him suffer.

I bring the cast down for the eighth time and feel his jaw unhinge. I pause, breathing heavily. He's a mess. His eye is swollen completely shut. His cheek isn't just split open. The bone has been exposed and crushed, leaving a large dent in his face. His mandible is badly dislocated, hanging loose on one side. I can't see any skin—he's fully hidden beneath a mask of deep crimson. I think he's unconscious. He's not dead because his chest is still rising and falling, but it's hard to tell if he's conscious or not.

He groans and moves his lips silently, revealing the gaps where he's now missing some teeth. I can't tell what he's trying to say, but honestly, I don't care.

I hit him again and feel more bone cave beneath the impact. My breathing is heavy and loud. Each exhalation is laced with fury. I move to hammer the cast down one more time but almost overbalance as the weight of me pushing on his throat finally proves too much. I feel his windpipe collapse under my hand, which is now almost flat against the ground. It killed him instantly.

I sit back on my haunches, taking deep breaths to slow my heart rate. Sweat runs freely down the side of my face. I stare at Pierce. His head is little more than a puddle of shattered humanity, and his throat is black and contorted. I hold my cast up in front of me and watch as thick blood oozes over it, dripping slowly to the ground.

"Holy shit!"

I look up, feeling the blank, numb expression on my face. Josh is standing there. His mouth is hanging open with shock, and his eyes are wide, transfixed on the horrific sight before him.

I quickly shake my head, snapping myself back to the here and now. I check Pierce's pockets and retrieve his billfold and cell phone, then get to my feet.

"Get the assault rifles his boys brought with them," I say to Josh. "They might come in handy."

I walk away, toward the car, leaving him standing there in silence.

That felt good. It felt satisfying, as if the memories of Lily and Yaz had finally seen justice. And I'm just getting started.

10

We made it to Sacramento shortly before one a.m. and found a motel with vacancies just off the interstate. It's nothing fancy, just a twin room with a shower and basic cable. The walls and carpet are straight out of the seventies. And judging by the faint, stale odor that's lingering in here, I wouldn't be surprised if this room had featured in more than its fair share of crime scene photos. Still, we needed somewhere to lie low and get some sleep, and this place was as good as any.

I'm staring out the window, watching as the sun rises slowly in the pale morning sky. Behind me, Josh is still asleep, sprawled half-dressed on top of his bed. We haven't spoken much since last night. All that with Pierce was... intense, to say the least. I'm used to all that—as much as anyone *can* be used to a heavily-armed gunship chasing them and beating a man to death, anyway. But Josh... he's been away from this life for a long time. Aside from all the

68

GlobaTech stuff, he's got my shit adding to his stresses *and* the fact that there's a price on his head. I left all my troubles back in Lebec, staining the ground with their blood, but I can't imagine what's going through his mind right now.

I take a deep breath. We have a long day ahead. It's another twelve hours to Seattle, and I have no idea what will happen when we get there. Sterling has gone from being a person of interest to basically running the whole damn show. And you can bet your ass he knows we're coming.

"Do you mind brooding a little quieter?"

I turn around and see Josh sitting on the edge of the bed, scratching the back of his head. I smile. "Sorry. I didn't mean to wake you."

"You didn't. Sadly, lying down with your eyes closed isn't the same as being asleep." He stands, puts his shirt on, and begins fastening the buttons. "You okay?"

I shrug. "I'm fine."

"Uh-huh..."

I roll my eyes. "What?"

He shakes his head as he disappears into the bathroom. I lie on the bed, sitting up against the headboard, and stretch my legs out in front of me. I massage my temples, trying to ease the dull ache pulsating behind my eyes. I need some aspirin. Everything is sore. I look down at my cast, desperate to ball my hand into a fist. I hate feeling handicapped like this, and the timing sucks.

Josh reappears, sits down on his bed facing me, and leans forward, resting his forearms on his knees. He looks at me and cocks his head slightly. "All right, here's the deal. If you want me to carry on watching your back, being your voice of reason, and all the other crap I do for you, we need to get something straight. Now isn't the time for deflecting questions. You've worked so hard at talking about shit that needs to be talked about, so don't stop now. When I asked if you're okay, it wasn't an invitation to dismiss me. It was an invitation to tell me how you're feeling after beating a man to death with your bare hands. Especially one who did the things that prick did."

Hearing him say that brings back so many memories of how things used to be. I breathe through the wave of nostalgia, suppressing it. He's serious and has a valid point.

I nod. "That's fair. And you're right. I *am* getting better at talking about things that weigh on my mind. It's just not as easy with you because I've never needed to do it. It used to be that we both knew what the other was thinking, so a lot of things could go unspoken."

"Yeah, that's true. But that was also a long time ago. Right now..." He sighs. "You gotta talk to me, mate."

"I know, and I'm trying, Josh. I was open with you on the mountain..."

He gestures to me with his hands. "So, tell me how you're doing. Last night couldn't have been easy for you. You can't honestly expect me to believe you feel fine after that?"

I think about it for a moment. "D'you know what? I kinda do. It felt good, man. I rarely feel any kind of pleasure from a kill. Satisfaction, yeah, but that's not the same thing. That's more like professional pride. But beating Pierce to death... I enjoyed it. It gave me something I should never get from what I do. I've never once received it in the past, from any of the hundreds of people I've killed."

Josh frowns. "What's that?"

"Hope. Hope that whatever shit is going on right now, it'll get better. I looked at Pierce as if he represented everything that was messed up about my life. And not just from the last few weeks, which he *was* involved in. I'm talking about everything. I took something positive from arguably the most negative thing a person could do, and yeah, that worries me. I hardly slept last night, despite being so tired, because my mind was racing, thinking about what I did and what lies ahead."

Josh nods, staring blankly at the floor.

I smile faintly. "Is that weird?"

He looks up at me and shakes his head. "What's weird is *that* isn't weird. Maybe I've known you too long. I dunno. But you... I don't think the rules that govern regular people really apply to you. You exist beyond convention, in a world inhabited by few others and understood by almost no one. I don't think you can be held to the same standards as everyone else. In your position, after everything you told me you've been through... everything you've seen and done... it makes sense that you feel driven by a desire for vengeance. You were like that once before, when you went after Wilson Trent. Do you remember?"

I nod. "How could I forget?"

"You embarked on a crusade that took years out of your life. And do you remember how you felt when you finally killed him?"

I nod again. "Empty."

"Yeah, you felt empty. *Hollow and unsatisfied*, I think were the words you used. Yet, this time, you felt a sense of justice and closure. What's different, do you think?"

I frown, running both past and present scenarios through my mind repeatedly. What *is* different? What's changed since Pittsburgh? It's probably easier to think about what hasn't changed. Look at the world nowadays. Look at how messed up and chaotic everything is. I was involved in the chain of events that led to the world being the way it is today, but I'm working hard to stop blaming myself for it, and I'm getting there.

Maybe that's it?

I look at Josh. "I don't feel guilty anymore."

He snaps his fingers and points at me. "Exactly. Even though Trent killed your family, you always felt that your life—your decisions—were the true cause of their deaths, as if you pulled the trigger yourself. It took you a long time to move past that. But with Pierce, you don't blame yourself for the things he did, so seeking revenge no longer feels selfish. Because you're not feeling guilty, you can see it for what it is: justice being served... in your own unique way."

I shake my head and smile. "I thought I was the new Dr. Phil?"

He laughs. "I just know people. And I know you. But remember, Adrian, what we're doing is not going to get any easier. From what you've told me, I think I know this Horizon asshole well enough to know that he's going to try messing with your head. You need to keep focused on that freedom you have... that sense of justice. It won't always be this straightforward to deal with. I need you at your best."

"Yeah, fair point. Anyway, speaking of things not getting any easier, what do you think about Grant Sterling being on The Order's Committee?"

He lets out a low whistle. "Yeah, that's a stroke of luck, isn't it?"

"Maybe. It's good that we have an opportunity to find out more about them at the highest level, but it also makes getting into Seattle a lot harder. There's no way they don't know we're coming."

He shrugs. "I dunno. We might just be a mistake Horizon's trying to keep quiet from his superiors..."

"I don't think our luck will stretch that far. The impression I get is nothing happens in The Order without this Committee's approval. He'll know we're coming."

"If that's the case, how are we gonna get anywhere near him?"

I smile. "We're going to walk right through the front door and ask for him, as if nothing's wrong, like we would've done originally."

He frowns. "You think that'll work?"

"I dunno, but if he knows we're coming, why try to hide it? It'll just—"

There's a noise outside, which is getting louder with every second that passes. Josh and I stare at each other, both stunned to silence as the sound of sirens gets ever closer.

After a moment, we refocus, jump to our feet, and rush toward the window. There are six black Chevrolet Suburbans parked in a loose semicircle in the lot, covering the only exit. The flashing lights built into the grill just below the hood are reflecting in the glass.

We look at each other, our eyes wide with shock and uncertainty.

"Friends of yours?" I ask.

Josh shakes his head. "They're not GlobaTech."

"Shit."

I turn and take a step toward the door but stop as it bursts open. The room and hallway beyond are flooded with Sig Sauers, Remingtons, and dark suits. I stay where I am and slowly raise my arms. I have no urge to run, fight, or antagonize. No desire to ask questions. These guys swept in with frightening precision, from out of nowhere, and secured the entire hotel within thirty seconds of pulling into the lot.

I know a losing battle when I see one.

If this were The Order, both Josh and I would be chalk outlines already. But these guys aren't shooting on sight. They're here to take us, not kill us, so I'm guessing whoever sent them either has questions to ask or answers to give. Best thing right now is to go along with it.

I glance at Josh, who's reacting the same as I am, and nod. "I'm guessing somebody knows I'm alive..."

One of the dark suits steps forward, holstering his gun. "Sir, I'm going to need your full cooperation."

I shrug. "Sure. So long as you don't shoot me."

"My orders are to bring you in, but I *am* authorized to use lethal force if necessary."

I smile. "I'll behave, promise."

Josh steps to my side. "I'd like to speak to the person in charge of this."

The guy turns to him. "That would be me, sir."

"Good. Do you know who I am?"

"Yes, sir, Mr. Winters. My apologies, but my orders are to bring you along and extend you no special treatment."

Josh sighs and glances at me. "All the promotions I've had lately, and I still haven't seen one benefit."

I smile as the guy gestures both of us out of the room. "I'm just impressed you worked the phrase *Do you know who I am?* into the conversation without expressing any shame."

"Please... like you haven't said that before?"

"I can get away with it. I talk shit for a living and shoot the people who say *No* when I ask."

"True."

The guy behind us shoves my shoulder. "No talking."

I let it slide, offering no resistance as we step out into the throng of matching suits filling the hallway. They surround the pair of us, then escort us out of the hotel via the rear entrance and across the lot, toward the group of vehicles. The guy from the room guides us both into the back seat of the nearest one and slams the doors behind us.

We're not restrained, which is a good sign. They clearly

know who we are but aren't here because we're deemed a threat.

The front doors open and close in unison. The driver starts the engine, and the passenger shifts in his seat to look back at us. He tosses two black cloth bags onto our laps. "Put these on."

Josh frowns. "Is this really necessary? I work for—"

"We know who you are, sir. Please, put the bag over your head."

We exchange a glance and do as we're asked. It's hot and airless inside. A claustrophobic smell of must surrounds me. We settle back in our seats, and the car drives away.

"If you reach for those bags before you're told to, I'm authorized to shoot you."

That was the passenger. His voice sounds slightly muffled from inside here. Man, I hope I don't have to wear this for long. I can barely breathe.

We take a right out of the lot, stay straight for a couple of minutes, then take a left and another right. We go left again, and I feel the road get smoother. We also pick up speed. I'm not familiar with the layout of the city, but I'm guessing we're on the freeway.

After maybe twenty minutes, I feel us slow down as we veer right. We pass sections of noise—horns beeping, people shouting, et cetera. It comes and goes, which is weird. Are we going to a protest rally or something?

Finally, we slow to a stop. I hear more voices. Someone outside asks for ID. We set off again, slowly, and drive around for about five minutes, with seemingly no intended direction. Then we stop. I hear the front doors open, and a second later, ours do too.

"Let's go," says the passenger.

I feel his hand on my arm, guiding me as I step out of

the car. I shrug it free and take a moment to stretch. Man, that feels—

Ah!

Sonofabitch.

Someone just whipped the bag off my head. I squint in the sudden influx of light. I look away, rubbing my eyes until they adjust. I look across and see Josh being escorted to my side, reacting much the same way as me.

I nudge his arm with my cast. "You okay?"

"Yeah."

I gaze around. There's a strong, cool breeze hustling around me. Lots of people are standing about who look just like the guys who took us from the hotel. And there's...

Oh.

In front of me is an enormous airplane, standing alone on the vast runway. It's quite distinctive, with its blue nose and matching stripe that runs along the side, all the way down to the tail. I sigh and turn to Josh, who's already looking at me, with a mixture of regret and concern on his face.

Without a word, the passenger and two other matching suits start walking toward the plane. We follow them without needing to be asked and begin climbing the steps of Air Force One.

11

We're greeted just inside the plane by a Secret Service agent, who frisks us thoroughly. Neither of us is armed. Everything happened so quickly back at the hotel, we didn't have a chance to grab our bags. Luckily, all the guns were back in the trunk of Josh's car, which is still parked in the lot.

The agent finishes patting us both down and gestures to his right, along a wide, carpeted corridor. "Follow me."

He leads us past some offices and seating. As we're walking, Josh looks to me. "Maybe let me do the talking?"

I raise an eyebrow. "Why?"

"Because you're *you*. That's why. This isn't just Schultz anymore. It's *President* Schultz. You need to either be nice or be quiet."

"Hey, I'm always nice!"

"No, you're not. Right now, I have no idea how the Secret Service knew where to find us, but the fact that you haven't been shot on sight is a good thing. I think it's safe to assume the president is aboard, and I doubt he'll be happy to see you. Or me standing beside you, for that matter. He'll want answers, which will make for a difficult conversation, so please try not to make matters worse by treating him like you normally do."

"You mean like he's an oversized, wheezing crapsack?"

"Yeah, like that."

I hold up three fingers on my left hand. "Scout's honor."

"Pretty sure you have to salute with your right hand for it to count..."

I shrug. "Whatever. So long as I'm not executed again."

We pass the leather seating area usually assigned to the press and head through a curtain, into another section of offices. The agent stops outside a light wooden door and raps firmly on it with his knuckles. Not waiting for a response, he opens it for us but remains where he is. I nod a silent *thank you* and step inside the room. Josh follows me, and the door is closed behind us.

It's compact yet feels spacious. Two windows fill the room with light. To our right, a cream leather sofa runs the full width of the room, with a coffee table in front of it. A corner desk takes up almost the entire left side, with just a narrow space beside it to walk around. Sitting behind it, staring at us through bloodshot eyes, unblinking above bloated red cheeks and a clenched jaw, is Ryan Schultz.

Or *Mr. President*, as he likes to go by these days.

Josh steps forward and clears his throat. "Sir, if I can—"

Schultz points a finger at him. "I'll deal with you in a moment, son." He stands, makes his way around his desk, and stops in front of me. He tilts his head a little as he stares up at me. "Now, I'm a God-fearing man. When I was younger, I went to church each and every Sunday. Hell, I even sang in the choir. I studied my Bible, and I believe in the Lord Almighty. In all my years, I've only ever known one person to have risen from the dead... and son, your hair ain't long enough for you to be Jesus. So, can someone please tell me how this is possible?"

Josh glances at me before I can answer, probably to make sure I don't. He looks at Schultz. "Sir, I know this is a lot to process, but—"

"A lot to process?" He points to me. "I watched that son'bitch die with my own two eyes, after personally signing his execution order. Hardest goddamn thing I ever did, but I did it anyway because it was the right thing to do for the people of this country. They wanted justice, and I gave it to 'em. But despite watching as he was pronounced dead by a state-appointed doctor, here he is, alive and well, standing on my goddamn airplane! *A lot to process* is a fucking understatement, Josh!"

Josh sighs. "We can explain, but you need to take a moment to calm down, sir. Getting angry isn't going to help anyone."

Schultz glowers at me, then pushes past to sit back down behind his desk. He leans back in his chair and gestures impatiently with his hands. "Okay, I'm listening."

Josh clears his throat. "To start with, sir, how did you find us?"

He smiles humorlessly. "Are you kidding me? First of all, a gunship tore up a stretch of interstate lined with security cameras. Next, you broke into a small-town power station in California, and left five dead bodies behind you—one of which was mutilated beyond recognition, I might add. I'm assuming one of the others was the pilot because we found the gunship abandoned on a school football field a half-mile away. Believe it or not, people tend to notice those sorta things.

"Local PD got the call about the bodies, and the FBI analyzed the security footage. You weren't exactly hard to spot in that ridiculous car of yours. Thankfully, the director of the FBI contacted me personally, and we had it all locked down before word got out that the most infamous assassin who ever lived had come back from the grave. I wanted to speak with you both myself before deciding what the hell I'm going to do."

Josh nods. "Okay, fair enough. So, here's the thing, Mr. President. And please, bear with me on this, all right? There's a myth in certain *unsavory* circles about an organization of assassins known as The Order of Sabbah. Most people in the business know the story—someone disappears while on a job, never to be heard from again, or a contract has mysteriously been carried out before you arrive. It's basically a campfire tale for professional killers."

Schultz takes a deep breath. "What in the blue hell does that have to do with anything, Josh?"

"Well, it turns out, it's not a myth. The Order actually exists, and they've been using their near-unlimited resources for God-knows-how-long to infiltrate every aspect of our society. They recruit the best assassins in the world and use them to kill whomever they deem necessary, to further their own cause."

"Are you being serious?"

"I am, sir."

"Josh, this sounds... far-fetched at best. You make them sound like the goddamn Freemasons."

"They're along those lines, I guess, but is it more far-fetched than a sitting president being at the center of a terrorist plot to wipe out half the planet?"

There's a slight pause.

"Touché. Okay, I'll play along. What evidence do you have to back this up?"

"Right now? Not much. We're still piecing it together, but we know for sure that they were behind the assassination of Sayed bin Mawal a few days ago."

"The Saudi Prince who owned Fuelex?"

"That's him. Twenty-four hours after he was killed, Fuelex's stocks crashed. Twenty-four hours after that, The Sterling Group announced their takeover bid."

"The Sterling Group is one of the largest conglomerates in the United States. It's hardly front-page news that they're buying up another company, Josh."

"You haven't been away from GlobaTech *that* long, sir. Mergers and takeovers involving companies the size of Fuelex don't happen overnight. You know that."

"Well, no..."

"Except this one did, and it was conveniently announced the day after Fuelex's value dropped by eighty percent. We know, with absolute certainty, that The Order had bin Mawal assassinated. We also have it on good authority that Grant Sterling, CEO of The Sterling Group, is a member of The Order's Committee—an inner circle consisting of five people who oversee everything. We believe he could have information critical to stopping them."

Schultz frowns. "And how can you be so sure bin Mawal was killed by this Order?"

I step forward. "Because I was the one who killed him."

He shifts his gaze to me. "Of course, you were. I was wondering where you fit into this shit-show."

Josh shoots me a glance, which I recognize as a plea to keep my mouth shut. I nod once, and he addresses Schultz again. "Unbeknownst to him at the time, Adrian was recruited to The Order while awaiting execution. They subsequently helped fake his death, so he could start a new life working for them. As with most situations where Adrian's required to follow someone else's rules, it didn't really take, but he felt he had no other choice at first, so he went along with it. He killed bin Mawal, as per The Order's instruction. But a couple of days ago, everything changed."

"How so?"

Josh takes a breath. "Because they sent him to kill me."

"Jesus H. Christ..." Schultz spins counterclockwise in his chair to stare out the window and rubs a hand over his face. After a moment, he turns back to face us. "Well, I guess that explains why you two are on the road, leaving bodies behind you."

"They need to be stopped," says Josh.

Schultz looks at me as if he didn't hear what Josh had said. "I sat and watched you die..."

I smile. "Was it a good show? I'm waiting for the DVD."

He ignores me. "How did they even do it?"

I absently stroke the gristle lining my jaw. "They substituted whatever shit I was supposed to have injected into me with some other shit that makes you look dead, called TTX."

He shakes his head. "Well, I'll be damned. So, where the hell have you been for the past six weeks?"

I shrug. "The Middle East, mostly. Look, I'll tell you about it over a beer sometime. Maybe I'll put on a slideshow or something. But right now, we all have bigger problems. The Order want Josh and me dead. They sent someone to kill us. One of their best. We survived this time, but it's only gonna get worse."

Schultz looks at each of us impassively. "Tell me why I should care. Tell me why I shouldn't just have both of you thrown into a goddamn hole somewhere, never to be seen again. I'm the president. I know where all the holes are now. It'd be easy."

Josh steps closer to the desk. "Sir, if you wanted to do that, you wouldn't have gone to all the trouble of tracking us down and bringing us here. I think you saw me with Adrian on that security footage, and when the shock wore off, your instinct was to get some answers. We could've easily fought off the Secret Service agents you sent for us, but we came along willingly. Please, hear us out. What if The Order want me dead because they have plans for GlobaTech? When you think about all the things we're doing right now, this could be the biggest threat we've ever faced." He pauses to glance at me. "I guess, seeing as the cat's out of the bag now anyway, we could use your help…"

I look at him questioningly, but he ignores me.

Schultz gets to his feet and leans forward on his desk. "And why should I help you?" He points to me. "*He* got you into this mess by shooting Cunningham, instead of allowing him to be arrested and put on trial. I already gave you GlobaTech, Josh. I don't owe you a goddamn thing."

I shake my head and smile with a scoff. "Some things never change. You're still the same stubborn, narrow-minded asshole."

He returns the gesture. "And you're still the same arrogant son'bitch who thinks the rules don't apply to him."

I take a deep breath, trying to subdue the rising fire inside me, but it's not working. I roll my eyes. "This isn't about rules, you piece of—"

Josh puts his hand on my arm. "Adrian…"

I shrug him off. "No, Josh. Helping us is the least he can do, but this prick wants to turn his back on me again, and I won't stand for it. Not when there's so much at stake."

"Again?" Schultz looks pissed. He's scowling at me, and

his cheeks are so red, they're almost glowing. He points his finger angrily. "I bent over backwards trying to help you, you ungrateful bastard. I did everything I could to protect your ass while you went on a goddamn killing spree to get to Cunningham. After all those NSA agents you took out, how dare you—"

I frown. "Sit down, Ryan, before you collapse beneath the weight of your own bullshit."

He shakes with rage, glaring at me. He leans closer over the desk. "You better start showing me some goddamn respect, son. You're addressing the president of the United States."

I nod. "I know. I got you elected, remember?"

He goes to speak but stops himself.

I don't move an inch. I just hold his gaze. "Everyone who came after me was working for Cunningham, so as far as I'm concerned, they were just as guilty as he was. But after everything that happened, you knew *why* I did what I did better than most. You stood beside me in what was left of my bar, back in Texas. I know you stuck your neck out for me, for all of us, after Atlanta. I'm not saying you weren't there for me in the days before and after 4/17, *Mr. President*, and I understand you felt your only option was to give the American people justice, to maintain the cover story you fed them, pinning everything on me.

"What I'm pissed off about is the fact that you could've quite easily done what The Order did. You could've helped me disappear, given me a new life. You could've shown a little fucking gratitude for me stopping this country from tearing itself apart and for getting you a promotion. But you didn't. You played by the rules dictated to you and left me to die. But, like a wise man once said, it's better to be pissed off than pissed on, I guess.

"So, here I am, telling you that the people who saved me are trying to steer civilization in a direction we probably don't want to go in. They're sitting in the shadows, killing everyone who disagrees with them, and pulling the strings of people in positions of power. And d'you know what? Just once, it'd be nice if I didn't have my own government as an enemy while I'm trying to help."

He's breathing heavily, staring at me hard through a deep frown. After a few moments of silence, he flicks his gaze to Josh. "Well?"

Josh shrugs and nods to me. "What he said, sir. Only, y'know, less aggressive."

Schultz sits down heavily in his chair and spins around again. He stares thoughtfully out the window and strokes his chin.

Josh leans in close to me and whispers, "Very respectful. Well done."

I glance across at him and shrug. "What? I tried."

Schultz spins back around and looks at us both. "Okay, let's get a couple of things straight. Adrian, if you talk to me like that again, I'll see to it that you're charged with treason and locked away for the rest of your life, our past be damned. And Josh, running around with this maniac? If you ever give me cause to doubt your commitment to your job and to this country again, I'll have you deported back to England."

I can't tell if he's serious, or if he's just flexing his muscles to save face. If it's the latter, I think it's a little unnecessary. The fact we're standing on *his* plane proves that he's in charge, no matter what we say.

Schultz sighs heavily, as if in resignation. "Now, that being said, if this job has taught me anything, it's to stay objective. Adrian, these Order of Sabbah assholes... in your opinion, how big of a threat do they pose to this country?"

I shrug. "Right now, I have no idea. I know how big of a threat they pose to *me* if that helps?"

He shakes his head. "Not really. Josh?"

Josh clears his throat. "We know Grant Sterling is one of the highest-ranking members of their organization. Our plan was to travel to Seattle and speak with him. That's where we were heading when you had the Secret Service pick us up."

"That sounds like a smart play." He takes a deep breath. "Okay, I gotta ask—who were the five bodies you two left in Lebec?"

"Four of them were hired guns," I reply. "But one of them—the guy with no head—was called Pierce. He was the right-hand man of the asshole who recruited me. He's the man The Order sent to help their pet assassins with whatever they needed. He killed someone who meant a lot to me, as well as an innocent kid who had no idea what he was involved in. He murdered them in cold blood, right in front of me. I've been carrying their deaths on my shoulders through this whole thing, and when that bastard came after me... ain't no way I was allowing him to leave that power station. Simple as that."

Schultz nods. "So, he had it coming, huh?"

"Like you wouldn't believe, *sir*."

"Tell me, Adrian, is this just another one of your self-righteous crusades for blood and vengeance? Or are you actually looking to help, for the greater good?"

I pause to think how honest I should be but quickly decide not to hide anything. "Ryan, The Order is dangerous. They've killed a lot of people, some of whom I cared for. They held me hostage, made me kill for them—which I was against from the start. They offered no justification, no reasoning for their targets, and that didn't sit right with me. I asked enough questions to become their enemy, and now here I am. Whatever their intentions are, I doubt they're good, and someone needs to stop them. Yes, I want revenge. I want to kill every last one of them and tear the whole organization to the ground. But I want to stop them because it's the right thing to do, and I'll do whatever it takes, with or without your help."

He falls silent, rests his elbows on the arms of his chair, and bridges his fingers together in front of his face. He stares blankly ahead of him, rocking gently back and forth. After a few moments, he looks up at us.

"Okay, I've known the two of you idiots long enough to know that I should listen when you tell me about things like this, no matter how ridiculous they might sound. Josh, meet with Sterling and report back to me directly. If you can find evidence of a threat that will allow us to go after these assholes legally, then so help me, God, I will use every resource at my disposal to protect this country. You have my word."

Josh nods. "Thank you, sir."

Schultz turns to me. "And you..."

I hold his gaze but say nothing.

"I'm willing to move forward and put the past behind us. For now, anyway. But I won't tolerate you racking up another body count because the urge takes you."

"You can't fight a war without casualties, Ryan."

"I'm well aware of that, but this isn't a war. Not yet. If we find ourselves with armies of trained killers on the streets, I'll put a gun in your hand and turn you loose myself. But until then, you keep your psycho in check and follow Josh's lead. Understood?"

I glance at Josh and then shrug. "Fine. Whatever. But if anybody tries to kill me in the meantime, Mr. President, I won't be diplomatic about it just to keep you happy. I'll leave their corpses where they fall. Is *that* understood?"

He smirks. "Well, I can understand almost anyone wanting you dead at any given moment. You have that effect on people."

I smile sarcastically. "Nice to know."

He takes a deep breath and glances at his watch. "I should get going." He looks at Josh. "I'm trusting you with this because we're friends, but make no mistake—mess this up, and it's both your asses."

He turns to me, regarding me silently. I raise an eyebrow. "Yes?"

He pauses and then smiles. It's forced, and his awkward expression betrays how uncomfortable he is right now, but it's a smile nevertheless.

"It's... ah... it's good to see you back among the living, son. I'll never like who you are, Adrian, but for what it's worth, I'm glad we both have a second chance. Bottom line, if the shit's about to hit the fan, I want you on my side."

I smile back and nod a respectful acknowledgement of what I'm sure will forever be the closest Schultz comes to saying something nice to me.

"Thank you, sir," says Josh as he makes for the door.

I follow his lead. We leave the room and head back along the corridors, down the steps, and out onto the runway. We're shown into one of the Suburbans, and an agent drives us all the way back to our hotel. We travel in silence and only speak to each other once we're standing in the parking lot, on either side of Josh's sports car.

I look around, taking in the fresh air and enjoying the light breeze on my face. "So... Seattle?"

Josh nods. "Yeah, just gimme a sec to grab our things."

He heads inside, then returns a few moments later holding our bags. He throws them in the trunk before climbing in behind the wheel. I slide in beside him and shift in my seat to find a comfortable position.

I look across at him. "I'm assuming you have something appropriate to listen to for the ride?"

Josh looks at me as if I'm from another planet. "Why do you even ask me these things? It's insulting."

He reaches over, opens the glovebox, and takes out a CD, which he feeds into the stereo. He hits play. A moment later, the opening chords of *Turn the Page* by Bob Seger blast out.

I smile as he reverses out of the lot and guns the engine, heading to rejoin I-5.

12

20:57 PDT

We just entered Seattle on the interstate, shot past the airport, then exited at Yesler Way. The roof is up on the car. Seattle's naturally cooler than anywhere in California, especially at this time of night, as it's closer to the North Pacific. It's currently in the low sixties, which suits me fine.

We turn onto 6th Avenue and slow to a stop as we hit some light traffic. Josh sighs. I think frustration is setting in now, which is understandable after such a long drive. Seriously, the guy's a machine. We only stopped once since leaving Sacramento, and that was out of necessity, to take a leak at a rest stop and grab some food to eat on the way here. He's still alert, still focused on the road. The music's probably helped. We blasted out some real classics on the way here, falling seamlessly back into our old routine of using time on the road to forget about what we're doing.

It amazes me how he always seems to know where he's

going too. I never see him read a map or use a GPS. It's as if he has Google Street View running through his mind at all times.

"You wanna grab a drink before we find somewhere to stay?" I ask him. "I think you've earned one after all that driving."

He smiles faintly, distracted. "Yeah, maybe. Keep your eyes open for somewhere."

The road ahead clears a little, and he navigates the streets as if he's lived here his whole life. We—

Huh?

A phone has just started ringing.

We exchange a glance, frowning with the same confusion. "Have you changed your ringtone?" I ask.

He shakes his head. "Nope."

"Well, it ain't mine."

"Why, what's yours?"

"*Black Betty* by Ram Jam. Has been since Pripyat a couple of months back."

"Ah, nice. So, whose phone is that?"

I look around. It's coming from the back seat. I turn and stare at my jacket. Then it occurs to me.

"It's Pierce's cell. I took it from him before we left. It's in my pocket."

I retrieve it from my jacket, put it on speaker as I answer, and hold it out between us. I don't say anything. It could be anyone, so I need to be careful here.

"What took you so long to answer the phone? Is it done?"

Wait a second. I know that voice...

Josh raises an eyebrow. I point to the phone and mouth *Horizon*.

"Pierce? What the hell are you playing at? Why aren't you back here yet? I have the chopper on radar, and it's not moving."

I take a breath. Time to do what I do best.

I lean close to the speaker. "Hey, Colonel Sanders! Pierce can't come to the phone right now. Can I take a message?"

There's a moment's silence.

"A-Adrian? It's, ah, good to hear from you. I'm happy to hear you're alive and well. I was beginning to worry."

"Aww, ain't that sweet. I'd be more touched by the sentiment if you hadn't just tried to have me killed."

Another pause. "What are you talking about? I haven't tried to kill you. I thought we had come to an understanding. Why would I want to eliminate one of my top assets when they're in the middle of a job?"

I roll my eyes. "Cut the shit, Horizon. Feigning innocence doesn't suit you."

He lets out a tired sigh. "So be it. Where's Pierce?"

"Dead."

"That's... unfortunate. Not altogether unexpected, I suppose, but a shame, nevertheless. Tell me, Adrian, are you any closer to finishing the task I assigned you?"

"Sure. In fact, I'm with my target right now. Say hi, Josh."

Next to me, Josh leans close to the phone. "Hey, asshole."

I smile. "That was Josh. He doesn't like you because you sent me to kill him."

Horizon sighs, and his breath is distorted on the line. "This is disappointing, Adrian. But again, not a complete shock. Tell me, why are you in such a rush to die? What have you got against living? Surely, any life is better than nothing at all?"

Oh, man, this is going to be good. For once, he doesn't know something. Okay, play it cool...

"There's an old saying: it's better to die on your feet than live on your knees. Being in The Order isn't any kind of life, and it's certainly not good enough to warrant killing my best friend for."

Horizon chuckles. "How poetic. But yes, it seems I misjudged your enthusiasm for what we're trying to accomplish here. Such a shame. Such a... waste of talent."

"And what exactly are you trying to accomplish? I'm assuming you're getting ready to kill me, right? So, why not tell me?"

I exchange a glance with Josh and shrug. Worth a shot.

"Oh, I see. This is the part where I divulge everything to you, so you can escape my evil clutches, exact your revenge, and stop my plan in the process?" He laughs. "Adrian, you embarrass yourself. This isn't a movie. Real life doesn't work like that. You won't live to find out what goal The Order is working toward, and neither will your friend. Mr. Winters, I assume you're listening? I'm afraid you have become an obstacle that needs to be removed. If you have any last words for our mutual acquaintance, I would say them now. He'll be dead momentarily, and you won't be far behind."

Josh leans toward the phone again. "You really like the sound of your own voice, don't you? Listen, dipshit, killing me isn't going to stop GlobaTech from doing all the good work we're doing. We're not Fuelex."

"Mr. Winters, I'm not interested in your little company or the charity work they're doing. Whatever you think you know is irrelevant. It won't change anything. Nothing we do is without purpose, and eliminating you is no exception. Now say goodbye to your friend."

There's silence on the line.

We look at each other, shrug, and yell in unison, "Bang!"

We start laughing, and I almost drop the phone. I hear a noise on the line. "That's impossible!"

I shake my head. "Apparently not. Now here's the inside scoop, Buttercup—your device doesn't work. You can't kill me, you have no clue where I am anymore, and your days are numbered. I'm coming for you with everything I've got. Do you understand? I'm going to kill you and anyone else associated with your pathetic little club. I'm not gonna stop until you're all dead."

Horizon sighs. "If you two need to tell yourselves that, go right ahead. But you should understand this: The Order of Sabbah has existed for centuries with good reason. Our reach extends far beyond what either of you can comprehend. The fact you have disabled your implant changes nothing. You cannot stop us. Many have tried, all have failed, and you two will be no different. I'll see you soon, Adrian."

The line clicks off. I buzz the window down, throw the cell phone out of it, and turn to Josh. "Well, what do you think?"

He shrugs. "There's no denying the guy's a tool, but he's probably right about most things. You do know that, right? This is an uphill struggle whichever way you look at it."

I nod. "I know. But we've stared down shit like this before and managed. This time is no different."

Josh raises his eyebrows. "I wish I had your optimism, man. I really do."

I pat his shoulder. "It'll be fine. Trust me. Just concentrate on finding us somewhere to drink."

We fall silent, and I stare out my window at the city outside. The streets are well lit, and the sidewalks are still busy. Life goes on. No matter what happens, the world will always keep turning, and people will always find a way to carry on with their lives. That's what we're fighting for here, and that's how I know we'll beat this.

Because we have to.

13

This bar is way too upmarket for me. The table is smooth and polished, the chairs are comfortable, and the carpet is clean. There are paintings on the walls and indoor plants everywhere.

I hate it.

There isn't even a jukebox, for God's sake!

Josh is opposite me, looking relaxed, sipping his ice water with a slice of lemon like a big girl. I have a beer. I think. I don't recognize the name, and it's from Belgium, apparently. It tastes good, though, which is what matters.

We're sitting in a small booth against the far wall. The layout of the place resembles an inverted L-shape. There's a line of seating just inside the entrance on the right, which stretches all the way to the opposite corner. More seating runs along the back wall, where we are, with a small gap on the right that leads to the kitchen area. Most of the left side is taken up by the bar, with tables scattered across the space in the middle.

It's pretty full, with the constant low babble of multiple conversations resonating throughout. Most of the people in here are smartly dressed—mainly couples, with a few small groups here and there.

A young waiter just walked past our table, barely breaking stride as he collected our empties. Josh glances at him and then stares blankly at me.

"You okay, man?" I ask, arching my brow.

He nods. "Yeah. I'm just trying to figure out how much you hate this place."

He smiles. I laugh. "It wouldn't be my first choice. I'll be honest."

"Mine neither, truth be told. But I have to go to places like this for meetings sometimes, and they've kinda grown on me."

I roll my eyes. "You've changed, man."

He laughs.

"Seriously, there isn't even a pool table. What kind of ass-backward place is this?"

He finishes his drink. "It's nice to see you haven't lost your sense of humor."

I shrug. "You gotta laugh, man. If you don't, well... y'know, you get sick or something."

"Amen to that. What do you make of what Horizon said to us before?"

I take a swig of my beer. "I dunno. I think a lot of it was hot air. As powerful as he is, a lot of what he does is smoke and mirrors. He plays mind games, which means he bluffs just as much as he genuinely threatens. He'll be running scared now that he knows Pierce is dead and he can't kill me whenever he wants."

"I think *running scared* is a little optimistic. I know people like him, Adrian. He'll already have six contingency plans in place to deal with us. I'm worried you might be underestimating him."

"I'm not. Relax. I've dealt with him—and people like him —before. Trust me."

He finishes his drink and gets to his feet. "I need a piss. All this water is killing me."

I smile to myself as I watch him disappear behind the bar, searching for the restroom. He was skeptical when I was positive. It's usually the other way around. He might have a point, though. Am I kidding myself, thinking Horizon isn't prepared for this? Killing Pierce doesn't mean shit when there's an army of trained killers lining up for their chance to come after me. Besides, Horizon himself has said many times how resourceful The Order can be. How can we possibly compete with that?

You know what? No. I should trust my gut. I'm the only one to ever truly get away, which counts for something. They won't know how to handle it because they've never had to before. If we can—

What was that noise?

I snap my head left and look out across the restaurant. I feel time slowing down around me. It's instinctive... reflexive... and nothing good ever happens when it does. It means something bad is either happening or is about to, and I'm not paying attention, so my subconscious is spelling it out for me.

It's a useful skill to have.

I heard a high-pitched ping, and now I can hear people screaming. Directly in front of me, a woman is falling. She hits the floor hard, and her head lolls to the side. Her lifeless eyes stare up at me. My gaze is drawn to the bullet hole between them, leaking a thin trickle of blood down her face.

What the hell is going on?

People are scrambling to their feet, rushing around with no direction or purpose, lost in panic. I follow the path I know the bullet must have taken and see a small hole in the front window. That would explain the ping. Beyond that, the street and the sidewalk are quiet. There isn't any traffic passing by—just a large, rusty panel van parked across the street, with its side door open. Even with the low, atmospheric lighting in here and the slight glare on the window, I can make out the rifle and the man kneeling just inside, holding it steady, aiming at the building. At me.

Aiming... right... at... me...

Shit!

Time resumes its normal pace. I dive out of the booth, to the floor, keeping low. There's another ping, followed by more screaming. I look around, but I can't see another—

Someone else just hit the floor, dead. A man this time. Another headshot.

I close my eyes briefly. "Goddammit!"

I scurry over to the bar and crouch behind it. I take out my gun, struggle to work the slide, flick the safety off, and peer around the side. I can't see the shooter from here. Everyone is still running around, although a few of them seem to have realized there's a door, and they're rushing out onto the street.

Josh appears, wiping his hands on his legs. He sees me and stops. A split-second later, he hits the deck, pressing himself against the bar beside me. "What's going on?"

I quickly peer around the corner again. "Sniper. In a van across the street. Two dead. Both headshots."

I hear him rack the slide back on his gun, chambering a

round. "For Christ's sake, I leave you alone for two minutes!" He sighs. "Horizon must've traced the call earlier, when we answered Pierce's cell. That must be how he tracked us down so quickly. Shit!"

"I don't care how this happened, Josh. The woman over there, by our table... the bullet she caught was meant for me. It was on target too. I never would've seen it coming, Josh. She's dead because she decided, in that moment, to leave her table and walk in front of ours."

He nudges my arm, a small gesture of comfort. "Not your fault, man. Fate can be a bitch, but don't put that on your shoulders, okay? Other people's destinies are definitely not your problem."

I nod. "I know. But the fact that you're right doesn't make me feel any better."

"I can imagine. But right now, we have slightly more pressing matters to attend to, wouldn't you say? What's the plan?"

I look past Josh, toward the back, where the restrooms are. "Is there a back way outta this place?"

He nods. "Yeah, there's a door that leads out into the alley where the trashcans are. I just passed it."

"Okay. You head out there, circle around, and see if you can take him out from his right flank."

"What are you going to do?"

I take a deep breath. "Give him a target."

14

22:03 PDT

I step out from cover, aiming my gun directly at the van across the street with as much steadiness as I can muster. I'm not used to fighting the effects of adrenaline with my weaker arm, so this isn't as easy as it usually is.

Focus, Adrian, come on...

I walk quickly through the restaurant, ignoring the confused looks from the people who have finally figured out that it's beneficial to not move. I'm almost at the front entrance now.

Why hasn't this asshole fired at me yet?

The door is standing open. Just outside, another body is sprawled face-down on the sidewalk, leaking blood from a hole in the side of its head.

Oh.

I put my back to the strip of wall between the door and the window, holding my gun loose and ready at my side. I take some deep breaths as I struggle to keep my heart rate steady. In a moment, I'm going to pop out and drop to one knee. I should have enough time for one shot, which is all I need. I don't know who the shooter is, but I think it's safe to say they're one of The Order's finest.

You should have seen this coming...

Yes, I know.

I bring my gun up and rest the top edge of the barrel against my forehead. I close my eyes for a few seconds, playing out my next move over and again in my head, planning for every eventuality to ensure the other guy ends up dead.

"Hey. Are you a cop?"

Hmm?

I open my eyes. A few feet in front of me, a young couple are crouching beneath the table of their booth. The guy is looking up at me expectantly.

I smile awkwardly. "Ah... no. But I *am* the guy that maniac out there is trying to shoot, so I figured I'd try shooting him first... see if I can put a stop to this before anyone else gets hurt. Sound like a good idea?"

He nods hurriedly, his eyes wide. The poor guy's scared out of his mind. But he has his arms around the woman he's with, holding her close, shielding her.

Good man.

I pat the air with my hand, gesturing for him to stay where he is. "That asshole is a good shot, but I'm better, okay? Just keep doing what you're doing, and you'll be fine. You all will. Let me—"

Shit!

I instinctively tilt to the side as a bullet punches into the wall where my head was a moment ago. I look ahead and see a man pointing a gun at me. He must have come out of the kitchen area on the right.

"Oh, come on! There's *two* of you? That's cheating!"

I snap my aim to him and fire twice. I miss the mark both times, but I was close enough to force him back inside the kitchen. People start screaming again, shocked by the sudden gunfire.

I hope Josh is going to shoot that asshole in the van because this prick is mine.

I set off running back through the restaurant, keeping as low as I can. I make it to the back wall without getting shot at, which is something. I turn right and see the double swing doors that lead to the kitchen. There's a large partition next to me, wide enough to have fake plants inside it. I crouch with my back to it and rest my shoulder on the nearest door. Using my cast, I gently push it, cracking it an inch.

No sign of him, but that doesn't mean shit.

Staying low, I switch sides and rest my shoulder against the left door. I lean forward and push the right door open hard. Two gunshots sound out, echoing slightly from inside, and punch into the door about halfway up as it swings back. They don't go through because it's made of thick metal, but they cause indentations on my side. I can tell from the shape of them that the rounds were fired on a slightly downward angle, which means this bastard is standing directly ahead, in line with the right-hand door.

Still crouching, I shove the left door open and step inside. I fire off four shots in the direction I think he's in. I see movement but no shooter. He must have ducked away, farther inside the kitchen. I stand and make my way around the left side, moving past the large ovens and grills, still hissing away. There isn't anyone here. They probably all took off when the screaming started.

The kitchen is laid out in an S-shape, with the walkway running between all the cooking surfaces. A variety of smells, both current and stale, fill the air. The floor is clean, but the tiles are discolored from years of grease. I navigate through the area, stooping slightly and keeping my finger lightly on the trigger.

Still no sign of anyone.

Where the surfaces finish, it opens out into another area. Two large sinks, side by side, are filled with water and foam. Beyond that, it branches off to the left and right, which leads to an exit and a storage room. I doubt the guy would have split, so I follow it to the right, and—

Uh!

—walk into a heavy punch that connects with the side of my head. It catches me off-guard, and I stagger backward slightly, dropping my gun.

Shit, where did that go?

I recover quickly and bring my cast up for protection. I throw a left hook, hitting the guy on the side of his ribcage, just below his armpit. He creases over but manages to swing his gun around like a dead weight, striking me squarely on the forehead.

"Fuck!"

I stagger backward again, except this time, I can't recover as fast. A lightning bolt of agony shoots across my brow, pulsing like a sick heartbeat. The pain can wait. I'm just glad it didn't re-open my wound.

I turn back around as the guy is striding toward me, raising his gun. I whip my cast up and to the side, knocking his arm back across him. Then I push my foot into his leg, just below the inside of his knee, to send him off-balance. As he falls forward, I throw another hook, which connects with his jaw on his way down. I didn't hit him as hard as I usually would, but it'll do for now. He crashes to the floor, still awake but stunned. His gun disappears under one of the ovens.

I wish I'd seen where *my* gun went...

I head over to get it but hear movement behind me. I spin around to see what this guy's—

Ah!

Never mind. It would appear he's recovered.

I fall back against the side, reeling from the straight punch to my face, but I manage to get my cast up to block the follow-up shot. He leans over me, and I push him away with my leg. He takes a couple of steps back, but it does little to slow him. I don't know who he is, but he's a tough sono-fabitch. I'll give him that. He just keeps coming.

I move forward and bring my cast down hard like a hammer. He blocks it but still reels slightly from the effects. I follow it up with a jab to his nose, hoping to do enough with it to at least make his eyes water. He shrugs it off, grabs me by the throat with both hands, and spins me counter-clockwise into the next surface along. He pins me down, forcing my back to arch over the edge as he tightens his grip, restricting my ability to breathe.

Just relax, Adrian. Don't panic. Focus.

I tense my neck and jaw as much as I can, fighting against his grip. I push back against his throat with my cast and fumble for his hand with my left, trying to grab a finger or two to break.

Holy crap, it's getting hot...

I flick my gaze to the side and see a deep fat fryer, bubbling away furiously.

That might be why—shit!

I grit my teeth, still struggling to take a breath. I shuffle my hips into position, swing my leg up, and catch him hard between the legs with my shin. You can be as tough as you want, but you get kicked in the balls, and it'll make you think.

He loosens his grip enough for me to wriggle free. I push him to create a little distance, then swing my cast again, connecting with his temple. He didn't see it coming and caught the full brunt of it. The blow didn't drop him, but his eyes are glazing over.

I don't pause for a second. I slam the inside edge of my good hand into his throat, which makes him cough as he gasps for air. I hit him again, this time in the gut, to knock the wind out of him. He instinctively doubles over, and I grab the back of his head, dragging him over to the fryer.

Another hammer blow to his head with the cast for good measure.

"*That's* for shooting at me, you sneaky bastard."

I stamp on the back of his leg, so he buckles beneath his own weight, and then shove his head forward, completely submerging it in the boiling oil of the fryer. I lean back, trying not to get splashed. I feel him push against my grip, and his arms flail wildly for about ten seconds.

Then he stops moving.

I give it a few more seconds to be sure, then pull him up slowly, trying to avoid—

Holy shit!

Oh, man, that's disgusting! His skin has *dissolved*. The bits of flesh that remain attached to his face are still festering. His eyes have...

You know what? Never mind. It's too horrific, even for me. The guy's dead. Let's leave it at that, eh? All I'll say is that if Freddy Krueger ever needs a stunt double, this guy is now top of the list. He wouldn't even need make-up.

I let his body drop to the floor and lean forward on the surface in front of me, trying to catch my breath.

Man, that sucked.

Okay, where's my gun?

I crouch and look around near where I was standing when I got punched in the face the first time.

...

...

...

Got it. It was under the sink.

Right, where's Josh?

I head out through the back door, which leads to an alleyway. I turn right and follow the damp, gritty, weed-covered path until I reach the sidewalk at the front of the building. I press myself against the wall and peer around the corner. I reckon I'm maybe ten feet from the main entrance. I can see the van across the street and have a much clearer view of the guy with the sniper rifle.

I kneel, bring both my arms up, and rest my gun on my cast to steady my aim. There's enough panic around here that one more gunshot isn't going to make much difference. Besides, this guy needs to be taken out before he decides to take another potshot inside the restaurant.

I line up my shot, aiming for—

A single gunshot echoes loudly. I watch the sniper slump to the side, fall out of the van, and land face-down on the road.

What the hell?

I stand and walk out, looking along the street. I see Josh appear from the opposite side of the building, his gun aimed low but ready.

I roll my eyes and sigh with relief. I make my way over to him. He sees me and meets me in front of the restaurant window.

I nod. "Nice shot. What took you so long?"

"Some people followed me out the back, so I was trying to get them to safety first. Then I..." He trails off as he looks me up and down. "Jesus, Adrian! What happened? You look... interesting." He sniffs the air beside me. "And you smell of deep-fried chicken."

I roll my eyes. "Yeah, I'm never eating at KFC again..."

"What do you mean?"

"Nothing. There was a second gunman. He's dead. That smell of chicken is actually the guy's head. I drowned him in a deep fat fryer."

"Holy shit! That's disgusting!"

"Correct. Beats being killed, though."

He's lost a little color in his cheeks and keeps grimacing, as if he's struggling to keep his lunch down.

We walk over to the van. I can hear sirens in the distance. Josh crouches beside the body and flips him over, revealing his face. He looks up at me. "You know him?"

I shake my head. "Never seen him before. He had to be with The Order, though. He was a good shot."

Josh stands. "That would be my guess too. Come on. It's probably time we weren't here. I'll make some calls when we get to a hotel. If Horizon mobilized a two-man team so quickly, he must be rattled. Maybe you were right."

"Maybe. But this might have been nothing more than a show of strength from Horizon. A shot across the bow, so to speak. He got a team to intercept us within a half-hour of speaking to us. That's scarily impressive."

Josh nods gravely. "True. Plus, this basically confirms that Sterling will be expecting us tomorrow."

"Well, let's worry about that tomorrow. We should move." We jog back over to the parking lot around back and climb inside Josh's convertible. He puts the key in the ignition, but I reach over and put my hand on his wrist before he turns it. "Wait a second."

I climb back out, bend down, and check underneath the car. I run my hand under the wheel arches.

Nothing.

Satisfied, I get back in. Josh is looking at me. "Everything all right?"

"Just checking for explosives. Having been blown up by a car before, I'm naturally paranoid during times of crisis."

He smiles. "It must be crazy inside your head, man."

He starts the car and eases out of the lot. We head away from the restaurant and are soon lost in the sea of anonymous traffic. Every kind of emergency service races past us, sirens blaring. I hope everyone in that place is okay. I'm thankful we are too.

I have a feeling this is just the beginning.

15

Not to sound paranoid, but I feel justified in thinking every single person I see right now could potentially try to kill me. I'm not scared. And even though I only have one useful hand, I'm confident that I'll kill anyone who comes at me, without prejudice or hesitation. The problem is that my years of training and the instincts I've honed through many years of killing people for money won't allow my mind to rest when my life could be in danger. Consequently, I had zero sleep last night.

Josh, on the other hand, still managed to get a few hours, despite everything that's happening. I don't know how he switches off like he does, but today, he's wide awake, refreshed, and his usual loud, cheery self.

It's irritating the piss out of me.

After we left the chaotic scene outside the restaurant last night, we found a low-key hotel to spend the night. Most parts of my body were—and still are—aching from the fight

I had in the kitchen, so I've been taking painkillers like they're candy to help take the edge off. But fatigue and the fact I only have one coffee inside me has shortened both my temper and patience dramatically.

We're standing on the sidewalk, staring up at the steps leading to the large glass building on the corner of 7th and Union, which serves as the North American headquarters for The Sterling Group. It's one of many buildings that towers over the city of Seattle.

"You ready?" asks Josh.

I shrug. "I'd feel better with some more caffeine inside me, but I'm as ready as I'll ever be."

"If this guy's on the Committee, there's no way he's not expecting us. Especially after the welcome party last night. We need to approach with caution. Maybe let me..."

I stop listening. Heading down the steps toward us are five men, each wearing suits and earpieces. Their arms are crossed low and awkward in front of them, which suggests they're preparing to reach for weapons they have holstered inside their jackets.

I take a breath, steeling myself for whatever comes next.

"...you even listening? Adrian?"

I turn to him and point to the men. He looks ahead and sighs. "Oh. Right."

"So much for approaching with caution."

Four of the men quickly surround us. The fifth stops in front of me, blocking our way. He stares at each of us in turn. "Mr. Sterling is expecting you."

I raise an eyebrow, acknowledging the obvious. "I figured. Are you boys the tour guides?"

He turns his body to the side and gestures to the steps. "Follow me. And try not to cause a scene. This is a respectable business."

I exchange a glance with Josh. *Try not to cause a scene.* Is he being serious?

The men usher us up the steps and lead us through the revolving door of the main entrance. Inside, the lobby is spacious and minimalistic. The company's name and logo are emblazoned across the wall facing me, with a long desk just in front of it. We stop and the men fan out, forming a loose semicircle behind us.

Sitting behind a computer monitor is a young woman wearing a navy blue blazer. She's typing feverishly while talking into a headset. She looks at us and hurriedly gets to her feet. She makes her way around the desk, revealing the matching skirt that makes up her business suit and her long, slender legs beneath it. She's undeniably attractive, wearing minimal make-up and her dark hair tied up in a ponytail.

She smiles professionally. "Gentlemen, Mr. Sterling is—"

I hold a hand up. "—expecting us. Yeah, we get that. Just take us to him already."

She seems genuinely taken aback, and I immediately feel bad. Perhaps I shouldn't have assumed every single person in the building is drinking The Order's Kool-Aid. I shouldn't let my—

Ow!

She just slapped me across the face! What the hell?

She steps closer to me. The smile has gone. "You'll see Mr. Sterling when *he's* ready for *you*, you ignorant prick. And you would do well to watch your tongue."

I glance over at Josh and shrug. I must admit, I'm a little embarrassed—and not because I just got my bell rung by a woman. God knows I've come across my fair share of female badasses in my time. No, it's because it took me so completely by surprise and consequently threw me off my game. I felt bad because I snapped at someone whom I figured didn't deserve it. But in doing that, I ignored my instinctive paranoia. I should've assumed every single person in here works for The Order. Guilty until proven innocent. But once again, my emotions clouded my judgment.

Time to pull your head out of your ass, Adrian.

The receptionist takes a step back, and the professional smile returns, as if she just put on a mask. "Mr. Sterling's office is on the seventeenth floor. My colleagues here will escort you."

She gestures to the side of the front desk, where the lobby stretches back to a bank of elevators. The group of men surround us both once more and hustle us toward it. The clacking of our collective footsteps resonates all around.

"You okay?" whispers Josh.

"Uh-huh."

"That was a pretty mean swing she had..."

"Screw you."

I look over and see him smiling to himself. How is he still so upbeat? I either need more sleep, or I need to take whatever he takes in a morning. Jeez.

As we reach the elevators, the men behind us clamp their hands down on our shoulders. The two on either side of us move in front and turn to face us.

"Arms out to the sides," says the one in front of me.

"Move and we'll put you down," says the other.

Shit.

We do as they say, and they begin frisking us. Obviously, it doesn't take long for them to find the Berettas. They both hold them up to show us, dangling them on a finger looped through the trigger guard. The one in front of me tuts repeatedly and shakes his head. "Did you really think you could walk in here armed? Are you that stupid?"

I smile. "Worth a try, right? Now make sure you take good care of them. I'll be back to collect them when I'm done with your boss. And so we're clear, if I see so much as a scratch on either one of them, you and I are gonna have a problem."

He exchanges a look with the man beside him. Both raise an eyebrow with disbelief. They step to the side, and the fifth guy presses the button for the elevator. The doors slide open straight away.

Without a word, we step inside. The fifth guy files in after us, pushing his way to the back so that he's behind us. Josh hits the button for the seventeenth floor, and the doors slide shut. A moment later, we begin the smooth climb into the belly of the beast.

I roll my eyes to myself at the thought. If we're going up to the belly, it means we started at the ass. Figures.

Josh looks over at me, narrowing his eyes, staring as if he's trying to read my mind.

He's doing that because A... he's known me long enough that he probably *can* read my mind, and B... he's known me long enough to know that he doesn't need to.

I spin my body clockwise and whip my cast back, connecting with the guy's gut. His eyes pop wide with shock, and I feel the wind rush from his lungs. He bends over instinctively, wheezing. I continue turning my body as he does and bring my left elbow down hard on the back of his neck. He hits the floor, unconscious.

Easy.

I crouch beside him and quickly retrieve his weapon. It's a Glock 17. Nice. I eject the mag, allowing it to drop into the palm of my right hand. It's full. I slam it back in place and stand. Josh is still staring at me, almost impassively.

I shrug. "What?"

He shakes his head. "Oh, nothing. Just, y'know... wondering for the billionth time since the day I met you if you've lost your fucking mind. That's all."

I take a deep breath, tightening my grip around my newly acquired gun. "Look, we've established Sterling knows we're coming, but this could be a trap. For all we know, there could be a hundred assassins waiting for us when these doors open."

His eyes grow a little wider. "I... ah... I hadn't thought of that. Maybe I should be more insanely paranoid, like you."

I smile. "Good job I'm here, isn't it? If we sit down with this asshole, maybe get some answers, that's great. But if I'm right, and we're about to step out to face a firing squad, I'll handle it. Don't worry."

"Why, do you have a hundred bullets for that Glock?"

"Ah. No... no, I don't."

He raises an eyebrow. "Good job I'm here, isn't it?"

I laugh, then glance up at the display above the door. "Well, at least I'll go down shooting."

Fifteen...

I quickly lean forward and press the button for sixteen. The elevator starts to slow. I tap Josh on the arm. "Give me a hand, would you?"

He frowns. "With what?"

I gesture with my thumb to the unconscious security guard behind us. "We don't want everyone to see him, do we?"

There's a ding, and the doors slide open. Josh sighs and crouches next to the guy, hooking his hands underneath his arms. He hoists his body up and drags him out. The guy's heels drag on the floor. I peer out and see a deserted waiting area with some seating just to the left of us. Josh lifts the guy onto one of them, positioning him so that he's sitting normally, albeit with his head hung forward. He puts his hands on his shoulders, trying to adjust the balance of his weight so that he stays upright, which he manages.

Josh jogs back inside, and I press the button for the seventeenth floor again.

I tuck the gun in my waistband behind me and adjust my jacket to cover it. "Nice work."

Josh closes his eyes as he takes a deep breath. "God, I wish I knew what you were doing..."

I smile. "Me too."

The elevator stops, and the doors slide open once more. Standing in front of us is a woman. She's dressed similarly to the receptionist in the lobby, except her dress suit is light gray. She's smiling at us. "Gentlemen, if you would follow me, please, I'll show you to Mr. Sterling's office."

She turns and walks left. We exchange a glance, shrug, and step out. I take a good look around. No sign of any assassins, and the woman seemed unfazed by the fact that our escort was no longer with us. Sterling must really be looking forward to seeing us.

We follow her along a wide network of corridors until she stops outside a thick, wooden door. A brass nameplate on it says *GRANT STERLING, CEO*.

She knocks once on the door, then opens it and steps inside, holding it for us. Josh goes in first, and I take another look around before following him. The woman smiles politely and leaves, closing the door gently behind her.

In front of us, standing beside a huge, solid mahogany desk, is Grant Sterling. He's wearing a fitted, charcoal-gray suit, with shiny black shoes. The first thing I notice is his watch. It's thick and gold, and it looks as if he should have trouble lifting his arm when he wears it. He has thick, dark, styled hair; a chiseled, clean-shaven face; and a salesman's smile.

He flashes his whitened teeth. "Gentlemen, so nice of you to come. We have much to discuss."

16

He looks younger than I expected. His voice is smooth, and his accent is proper, as if he were Ivy League-educated. I get the impression he belongs to a yacht club. Y'know, when he's not trying to rule the world.

I move in and stand next to Josh, keeping my left arm by my side, ready to draw my weapon if I need to. I quickly look around his office, taking in all the details I need. Ahead and to the left is all glass, offering a panoramic view of Seattle. Along the right wall are some cabinets, with a safe in the corner by the window. His desk dominates the room, with several small stacks of paper piled up across it.

So, I have no cover from potentially being shot by a trained killer with a sniper rifle, but this guy is likely storing useful information in his office.

Every cloud, right?

Josh and I exchange a glance, and he clears his throat. "Mr. Sterling, I'm sure you're wondering—"

Sterling holds up a hand. His smile sits somewhere between friendly and smug. "Save it. I appreciate the gesture of innocence, but we all know why you're really here, so let's dispense with the pleasantries. I'd offer you both a seat, but I doubt you'll take it." He moves to sit behind his desk, resting comfortably back in his chair. "I'm actually impressed you made it this far, although Pierce's fuck-up made it easier for you both, I suppose."

I scoff. "Pierce didn't fuck up. I just beat him. Literally. To death."

"And I'm sure you're so *very* proud of yourself. I assume it was he who gave me up?"

"We were coming here anyway, but he told us you were on the Committee, yeah."

He shakes his head. "I really wish he hadn't done that. Horizon ought to keep a tighter leash on his pets."

"What does The Order want with Fuelex?" asks Josh.

Sterling laughs. "Straight to the point. I like it. But no, that's not how this works, Mr. Winters. You don't come here and demand answers from me."

With hardly any movement, I whip the gun out from behind me and aim it unwaveringly at Sterling's face. "Actually, that's *exactly* how this is gonna work."

He smirks. "Adrian, please. Do you think I'm afraid of you?"

I shrug. "I think if you were as smart as you'd have us believe, you'd know that you should be. Josh, get the door."

He moves back and clicks the lock in place.

Sterling's gaze flicks between Josh and myself for a moment, then he smiles again. "Okay, I'll play along. But please, understand that whatever you do here is nothing more than a futile attempt to delay the inevitable."

"Duly noted."

He nods. "Okay. We bought Fuelex because The Order wants to control the flow of crude oil into the parts of Europe and the Middle East that Sayed bin Mawal was helping with his... charity work."

"Why?" asks Josh.

"To control those regions, of course. Without resources, they can't rebuild in the aftermath of 4/17. Fuelex was giving them those resources at practically no cost. But now The Order controls how much they get, which means we control how they rebuild."

I frown. "So, that's it? It's a power play?"

Sterling nods. "What were you expecting?"

"It must be part of a bigger plan, surely?" says Josh. "What's your endgame?"

"I suppose it is, depending on how you look at it. But the acquisition of Fuelex *was* the plan, and it was executed almost to perfection." He turns to me. "Obviously, Lily involving you prolonged the intended outcome and created an additional problem we would've preferred to do without, but nevertheless, mission accomplished."

Josh paces away. I watch him as he stares at the floor, putting some more pieces of the puzzle together. After a few moments, he stops and looks over at Sterling. "So, The Order are nothing more than power-hungry thugs. There's no elegance or intricacy to you. You're not some Illuminati types hell-bent on changing the world. You just want power..."

I see where he's going with this.

I gesture with my gun. "And you're using your influence to make subtle changes here and there to get what you want. Nothing too major, nothing that draws too much attention to you, but enough that the right people control the right things. Sonofabitch."

Sterling frowns, as if he's confused. "You sound almost... disappointed?"

I shake my head. "Not at all. I just think Horizon exaggerated The Order's aspirations a little."

He laughs. "Yes, he does get carried away sometimes, but the man's a believer and cannot be faulted for his work ethic and dedication to the cause. He's good at spotting opportunities to expand our reach and scouting men of talent to help us. Men such as yourself, Mr. Hell. Such a shame you didn't work out."

"Oh, I'm gonna enjoy killing every last one of you arrogant bastards."

"No, you're not. You'll be lucky to survive the next hour. Besides, the little... tweaks we make to this world do serve a higher purpose. A purpose far greater than you and your empty threats. You're not the first person to try to stop us, and while some of my fellow Committee members may disagree, I personally doubt you'll be the last. It's human nature, after all. Most people crave the security and simplicity of being controlled, so long as they're allowed to remain ignorant of it, while a small minority think they're better off navigating their future alone. Make no mistake— over the years, we have become *very* adept at dealing with that minority."

Josh walks over to the desk and leans forward, resting both hands on the surface. "So, why me? What purpose does killing me serve? GlobaTech won't go the same way Fuelex did just because I'm dead."

Sterling waves a dismissive hand, frowning as if offended by the question. "I'm not interested in what GlobaTech do. It's great that your company is helping people who need it, and—for now, at least—the way you're going about it doesn't concern us."

"So, why send me to kill him?" I ask.

Sterling tilts his head slightly. "Your friend has more than one job."

I look over at Josh and watch his expression change as a realization dawns on him. "You want influence on the White House," he says finally.

It wasn't a question.

"The new president isn't as... open-minded as the last," replies Sterling. "Of the entire National Security Council, he holds your opinion in the highest regard. Someone in your position could do great things for The Order."

I shake my gun at him. "Whoa, back up. Cunningham was in The Order?"

He laughs. "God, no. That man was a lunatic. However, we did have someone high up in his administration who proved useful."

"Unbelievable..."

"I hate to break it to you," says Josh, "but it's *my* opinion he holds in high regard, not the opinion of whomever is in charge at GlobaTech. My replacement probably wouldn't even be appointed to the Security Council. Killing me wouldn't help you in the slightest."

"Perhaps. But we believe the person who runs Globa-Tech would be capable enough to command the same respect you do and would, therefore, be afforded the same responsibilities you are. It's a chance we're willing to take. Schultz doesn't share The Order's vision for the United States, nor its wider view of what's best for every country on this planet, and we intend to influence him to see our way of thinking."

I frown. "This might be stating the obvious, but why not just take him out?"

"Because, Adrian, The Order is a scalpel, not a sledgehammer."

"Ha! You could've fooled me. You're, like, the most indiscreet secretive organization ever."

He smiles humorlessly. "Only when necessary. Killing Schultz would have an adverse effect on this country, especially so soon after the last president's demise." He pauses to stare accusingly at me. "A subtler method is needed this time, and we intend to do that by installing someone in Mr. Winters's position whom we can control."

"What for?" asks Josh.

"Because it serves our greater purpose."

"Which is..."

"None of your concern. I've humored the pair of you long enough. It's time to do what Horizon should've done days ago. This entire building is being evacuated as we speak."

Josh frowns. "What for?"

Sterling smiles that type of smug smile people use when they know things you don't. "Because not everybody who works here belongs to The Order. We're not monsters. We run legitimate enterprises all over the world. It's the perfect cover. So, the people who aren't involved in this are being asked to leave."

I scoff. "There you go again, being as subtle as a tank..."

"Hardly. To them and any casual observers, it will simply look like a fire drill." He checks his watch. "However, *entering* the building right about now is a unit of our top assassins, who are under strict and simple instructions to come to this office and kill both of you."

I do my best to ignore that for now and simply shrug. "So, why not tell us about your greater purpose? C'mon...

I'm curious. What's all this about? What did I get dragged into?"

He stares at me for a moment. "The Order exists to do the bidding of the man who created us and will lead us toward a better future."

"The head of your Committee?"

"No, Adrian. Even the leader of our great organization answers to someone."

"Who?"

He smiles. "Why, God, of course."

17

10:16 PDT

Josh shakes his head. "You're kidding me, right? You're saying *God* is running The Order of Sabbah? Are you out of your freaking minds?"

Sterling nods patiently. "The Order was created in His name, to carry out His will."

He turns to me. "Can you believe this shit?"

I think about it for a moment. "Actually, yeah."

Josh frowns. "Huh?"

Even Sterling looks surprised.

"I mean, it's hardly the first time people have killed in the name of religion, is it? I guess I'm a little disappointed, though. The Order has been a legend to people like me for years. When Horizon revealed himself to me a couple of months ago, I admit there was a part of me that felt excited about the prospect of working for you. What assassin wouldn't be, right? But to find out you're nothing more than a group of religious fanatics with a big bank balance... that's kinda sad."

Sterling jumps to his feet. "We are *not* fanatics!"

I emphasize the gun in my hand by stepping toward the desk, leaning over slightly, and placing the barrel against his chest. "Touched a nerve, did I? Sit the fuck down."

He hesitates but takes his seat once more, although I note he isn't sitting quite as comfortably as he was a moment ago.

I step back again and lower the gun. "This is where you start talking, asshole. By all accounts, I'm dead anyway, so I have no qualms about killing you before I check out. It's not as if I have anything to lose..."

He waves his hand dismissively. "Threaten me all you want. I'm prepared to die for my beliefs."

I smile and walk around the desk. He spins in his seat, following me, a bemused expression on his face. I stop in front of him, place the gun against the top of his kneecap, and look him right in the eye. "See, assholes like you are quick to say you'll die for your cause. You might be one of those people who actually *are* prepared to, and if that's the case, good for you. But there's a big difference between dying... and suffering."

He swallows as I press the barrel harder against his leg.

"See, dying is easy. It's fast, and you don't even know you've done it. But *suffering*... that can go on a while, man. And it hurts. A lot. Are you prepared to suffer for your beliefs too?"

His breathing has grown notably quicker in the last few moments. He's gripping the arms of his chair tightly, so his knuckles lose some of their color. He's sweating. He's afraid. "No, please. I... I'll tell you whatever you want."

I smile. "I figured. The pricks who run the show tend to

be the most cowardly. Now what does God have to do with anything?"

He sighs, relaxing a little, but he's still tense because my gun's still pressing into his leg. "The church has shaped mankind's destiny for centuries. The Knights Templar began this mission. As generations passed, they evolved, and The Order was born. We have adapted throughout the years, learning to seamlessly blend in with society, to carry on the church's true mission."

I raise an eyebrow. "Which is?"

"The betterment of mankind. We understand that people don't always know what's best for them."

"And I suppose you do?"

"Yes, we do. We determine the best course of action for the greater good, no matter the cost. We use our positions and our influence to make the tough choices no one else wants to make. We're not bound by politics or diplomacy. We act on the word of God, and you, you... *heathen*, are not going to stop us."

I frown. "Heathen? Oh, right... the Adrian *Hell* thing. I see. I must admit, listening to your religious babbling has made me question why you would bring someone like me into the fold in the first place. I'm not exactly a poster boy for clouds and halos."

"As I said, no matter the cost."

"You're delusional."

"And soon, you'll be sent straight to Hell!"

I smile. "Been there, bought the T-shirt. Besides, you say that like it's a bad thing. If the man supposedly running Heaven needs to hire people like me to do his dirty work, how bad can Hell be?"

Sterling shakes his head. "You're missing the point. We're

doing this for the righteous, so all the people on God's Earth can live free from tyranny."

"From *other people's* tyranny, you mean? They'll still be living under yours, whether they know it or not."

"There is a responsibility to guide those people, yes, and that's The Order's burden to bear."

"Okay, you gotta stop, man. The stench of your bullshit is killing me."

"I understand you're not a believer, and that's okay, but please don't insult me because I am."

I frown. "I'm not insulting you because of your beliefs. People should be free to believe whatever they want, so long as they don't force it on the rest of us. No, I'm insulting you because you're full of shit. You say you want what's best for people, yet you go around killing whomever you choose in order to achieve it. You can't have it both ways."

He smirks. "Says the assassin..."

"Yeah, someone *you* recruited to kill for your cause. I'm under no illusions about what I am, and I accepted it a long time ago. But I don't go around saying I'm fighting for the good of mankind."

"So, why do you kill, Adrian? What's your cause?"

"I don't have one. I just think I have a duty to use my exceptional talents to help rid the world of bad people. For a modest fee, of course."

"Then you're no different than us. Not really. Such a shame you can't commit to what we're fighting for."

"See? There you go again with your bullshit. You're not fighting for anything except more power. You certainly don't care about the masses or the *good of mankind*. You say you're doing God's work, yet you kill for your own gain. How is that something He would want?"

Sterling shifts in his seat again. His expression hardens.

"Look, as much as I could sit here discussing morality with you all day, I have things to do. And you... both of you, are done. If you go quietly, you'll be disposed of quickly and mercifully. That's the best you can hope for right now."

I turn to Josh. "How are we looking?"

He nods. "Door's secure enough for now. No sign of anyone yet."

"Good." I look back at Sterling. "I'm going to put an end to The Order, once and for all. That's a promise."

Sterling chuckles. "You have no hope against us. We're too big for anyone to overcome. That's why we've existed for so long and will continue to exist long after the three of us are gone."

He's getting some of his confidence back, despite me still pressing the gun to his leg. His breathing has slowed. Why is he...

I close my eyes.

Shit.

Shit, shit, shit!

Adrian, you're an idiot.

I know.

You got so caught up arguing with him, trying to get information out of him, you didn't realize he was keeping you busy. He was buying himself time, so his minions can show up and save him.

I know.

He needs to be afraid of you, Adrian. He needs to understand he's going to lose. He needs to understand what The Order is up against.

...

...

...

I know.

I open my eyes again and fix him with the dark, emotionless gaze I've spent years perfecting. Intimidation starts with the eyes. I don't need weapons. I need a cold, dead stare that shows beyond any doubt that all humanity has gone and instills fear in whomever I look at. That tells people that I'm the worst kind of evil there is.

I lean close. "You say all this is in God's name? Well, here's a quote from His biography: *Never avenge yourselves, but leave it to the wrath of God, for it is written, vengeance is mine, I will repay.*"

I pause for a moment, letting the words sink in. I let the meaning of them register in his mind.

"D'you know why people call me Adrian Hell? It's because the one time I fought for a cause, I swept through my enemies like a biblical plague, and what I left in my wake was unholy. So, you can summon whomever you want to protect you. It isn't going to do you any good. I'm telling you right now, asshole... Lucifer himself ain't got shit on me."

I squeeze the trigger, and the room is filled with the sound of his screams.

18

The bullet drove down through the top of his patella on an angle, eviscerating flesh and bone with frightening ease. With his leg bent from sitting, it continued its deadly journey, plowing through the top of his calf muscle and exiting below his kneecap. Consequently, the shot obliterated the top of his shin and nearly severed his leg in half.

He's clutching desperately at the wound, forcing his screams through gritted teeth and a locked jaw. I take a step back. I must admit, I wasn't prepared for how much blood there would be. I'm impressed with the shot. I must remember it for future use. It all but destroyed his leg, beyond any chance of repair.

That'll teach him.

Dick.

I hold the gun out toward Josh. "Here, take this."

He steps over and does so without question. He'll argue

most decisions I make, but he knows better than to say anything when I'm working.

I move behind Sterling, clamp my hand over his mouth, and force his head back against his chair. "Now listen to me, ass-clown. I'm guessing we don't have much time, so I'm gonna need you to do two things. First, I want you to tell me who decides what happens in The Order, how the message gets to all the *Horizons* in the world, and most importantly, where I can find all the other pricks like you. Second, I want you to open that safe. I'm guessing there's some shit in there I might find interesting. Do those things for me and maybe you'll get to just suffer for your cause, instead of dying for it too."

I remove my hand and spin his chair around, so he's facing me. His eyes are glazing a little, which I'm guessing is due to the pain and blood loss he's experiencing. He's fighting it, though, with an impressive stubbornness.

He glares up at me, his jaw still clenched. "Why should I? You're just going to kill me, anyway, aren't you?"

I shrug. "Honestly? I haven't decided yet. It depends how helpful you are, but right now, my offer stands. Help me and maybe you'll see tomorrow."

"You don't scare me, Adrian. You can't even fathom how important I am. I'm far more than just a CEO."

I nod. "So you keep saying. But here's what I know— nothing happens in The Order without the say-so of your little Committee. So, for Horizon to approach me, he must have had your approval, which means you must know exactly who I am and what I'm capable of. You only recruit the best, right? With that in mind, I think this stubborn, high-and-mighty act is just that—an act. I think you're shit-ting your pants because you can see all that power you had slipping away. No more secret handshakes, no more influence, no more money... It's all going to come tumbling down around you. Because of me. Now, if you're as smart as you say you are, you'll tell me what I want to know and maybe save your own ass."

Sterling shakes his head rapidly, as if in denial. He forces his chair around, grimacing from the effort. He looks over at Josh, who is leaning against the door, peering through the window beside it, holding the gun ready to shoot. "You... you can't be a part of this. Look at who you are. If you get out of here, and people found out you were involved in something like this, it would destroy GlobaTech's reputation!"

Josh smiles. "Maybe. But we're here with the president's blessing. We've already begun to expose you. You're losing, and you don't even know it, dipshit."

Sterling's eyes grow wide with panic, and he seems momentarily distracted from the agony he's in. He looks back at me. "I... I don't understand. Surely, if the president learned you were still alive, he would have you executed again? If the public found out, there would be an outcry."

I smile. "Given half a chance, I think he still might. But we told him everything, and he knows us well enough to listen to us when we tell him something's important. We get enough evidence on The Order to prove you all exist, he puts the full weight of the U.S. Government behind trying to expose you. Saves me the job of hunting you all down."

He shakes his head. "You won't find anything. No one knows *everything*, only the head of the Committee, and you won't get to him."

"Oh, yeah? And why's that?"

"Because he's too well protected."

I shrug. "So was the last president, but it didn't stop me then..."

"No one can touch him. No one even sees him. Hell, *I* don't know where he is. The other three members of the Committee and I meet in person, but the Head always video conferences in."

"But you know who he is, right?"

He nods.

"So, tell me that, and let me worry about finding him."

"Fine. Okay. I'll... I'll tell you what I know. But you have to promise not to kill me. You have to protect me."

I nod. "I'll do what I can, so long as the information's good. How this plays out for you is in your hands now, Grant."

Sterling lets out a long, heavy sigh. He opens his mouth to speak, but the only sound I hear is a muted crack. A split-second later, his head explodes, vanishing in a thick, crimson cloud, which sprays across the ceiling above him. A chunk of his mandible bone lands on the desk. It's as if someone just smashed a watermelon open with a sledgehammer.

Josh and I both jump with shock. Sterling's body slumps sideways, resting awkwardly against the arm of his chair.

"Jesus fucking Christ!" yells Josh. "What did you do?"

I feel my eyes bulge with shock. "Me? I didn't do anything! I'm good, but I can't make people do that!"

He shakes his head. "Shit, they can see us. Adrian, The Order must have eyes on us right now."

I drop to the floor on instinct and scurry around the desk, trying to keep out of sight of the windows. Josh crouches, alternating his gaze between the windows behind me and the one next to the door. I look down at my T-shirt and jacket. I'm covered with Sterling's blood.

Josh slams his fist against the floor. "Damn it! We were

this close to getting something out of him. To getting an advantage."

I nod. "Yeah, close enough that The Order chose to detonate the chip inside one of their leaders' necks."

"And now we're back to square one." He lets out a heavy sigh. "Adrian, we need to think about trying to get out of here. If what Sterling said was right, we're about to have a bad day."

Josh seems to be more bothered about this than me, which is strange. Maybe, on some subconscious level, I kind of expected it to go this way. A combination of experience dealing with The Order and my own shitty luck. But for once, I'm being the positive one.

I look over to my left, at the safe. "We're not done yet."

I crawl over and kneel up in front of it, resting back on my haunches. These things aren't my area of expertise, but I recognize the biometric lock on it, which is opened by placing your thumb against the small scanning pad just above the handle.

I look back across at Josh and gesture to the safe. "If we can open this, we might get lucky and find something that would make this trip worthwhile."

He seems uncharacteristically hesitant. "Maybe, but we'll only have one chance at opening it. I'm familiar with that type of lock because we manufacture something similar. It has a security failsafe, which seals the entire safe permanently if you don't get it right first time, rendering it useless. You can still crack it, but you need a seriously big drill and about six hours. It's pretty high-end stuff."

"Shit. Okay."

I stand but keep low, glancing out the windows as I move over to the body, watching out for the glint of a rifle scope from the neighboring buildings. I look at both of Sterling's hands to figure out if he was left or right-handed. After a moment, I grab his right hand by the wrist and drag him over to the safe. I place the thumb on the scanner. The lock whirrs and clicks, and the door falls open.

"How did you know which hand?" asks Josh.

"There was a small indentation on the outside of his right ring finger, which would've been caused from holding a pen. I noticed the amount of paperwork on his desk, so I figured he would have been writing recently. If he wrote with this right hand, chances are he was right-handed, so that's the hand he would've instinctively used to code the safe."

Josh looks impressed but says nothing.

Inside, there are some loose papers, a cell phone, and a flash drive. I take everything and stuff them inside my jacket. "We'll check all this later. Now we can think about getting out of—"

The glass next to the door shatters as a hail of automatic gunfire erupts from outside the office. I duck, bringing my arms up to cover my head. "Fuck me! Josh, are you okay?"

I look over and see him doing the same. The door is thin and won't offer much protection from an onslaught like this. He slides the gun over to me. "Get us out of here, Adrian."

I take it and crouch behind the desk. I rest my hand on the surface, taking aim. The firing's stopped for the moment. I just need to wait for them to show themselves, so I can shoot them.

I take a deep breath and try to focus my mind. Sterling's out of the picture, which must be a huge blow to The Order, regardless of how or why. After speaking with him, we know more about them than we did before we got here, which is a bonus. We've emptied his safe, so we're done, and I can forget about him now.

I need to concentrate on getting the pair of us out of here in one piece. Sterling didn't have the chance to mention exactly how many people are coming for us. I only have sixteen rounds in this Glock, after putting one in his leg, so I suspect every shot will have to count.

At least there are no innocent people to worry about.

Through the space where glass used to be, I see a man appear at the end of the hall, level with the elevators. He's wearing a suit and walking slowly toward us, carrying a machine gun he's in the process of reloading.

Rookie error. You don't show yourself until you're prepared to fire your gun.

I take aim and squeeze off two rounds in quick succession. Both find their target, punching themselves into the guy's chest. I hear the faint thud as he collapses to the floor. I hold my aim a few seconds longer to make sure he's done moving and breathing.

Yup. He's dead.

"Josh, let's go."

I spring to my feet and head for the door. Josh stands and moves to follow me but stops himself. Instead, he heads back over to the desk.

I look over my shoulder, frowning. "What are you doing?"

He starts frisking what's left of Sterling's body. After a moment, he retrieves a wallet out of his inside pocket. He holds it up to me. "Might come in handy."

I smile. "Check you out, pillaging corpses. I'm so proud."

We step out of the office and look around. Ahead of us is clear now, as far as I can tell. The corridor stretches to our left and right too. I look right and see no sign of anyone. I look left and—

Oh.

There are four men about forty feet from us. Two are crouching and two are standing behind them, all holding guns, which they have trained on us. They're not dressed the same, so it's not an official unit, like the kind Pierce used to run. These are assassins, like me. And they have the drop on us.

Shit.

Josh sees them. "Oh, bollocks."

I sigh. "Maybe you can throw that wallet at them?"

19

10:59 PDT

No one moves. Time hasn't slowed down for me; it's stopped altogether. My arm is frozen to my side, rendering my borrowed Glock temporarily useless. My mind is rushing toward multiple conclusions and quickly analyzing each one for plausibility.

I'm fairly certain we're screwed.

These assholes in front of us have most likely been there for a while. Everyone knew where we were, so there was no need to rush. The guy I killed just then... his job would've been to draw us out. Josh wouldn't have seen these guys by looking out of the office, not from the angle he had.

We were played.

Shit.

I lost sight of the bigger picture and dismissed Sterling's threat of The Order's finest descending on us. Now we're trapped because I didn't plan ahead.

Double shit.

I'm losing perspective. It's taken me until this moment, right here, right now, to realize I've been going about this all wrong. I'm trying to stop The Order, but I've been giving them too much credit. Showing them too much respect.

Maybe Josh was right when he said I sounded afraid of them.

Maybe I was.

But why? They recruited me because they recognized my talents. They know how dangerous I can be. And they also sent a lot of manpower after me when I turned my back on them, which tells me they're more threatened by me than I should be by them.

So, no... there's no *triple shit*. Not this time. See, I've got this situation all wrong. I'm not trapped on the seventeenth floor of a building with a bunch of assassins.

They're trapped here with me.

The scene unfreezes. I push Josh back into the office as I spin counterclockwise. I whip my other arm up to quickly take aim and squeeze off four deliberate rounds. I react much faster than anyone else and watch with some degree of satisfaction as each bullet buries itself between the eyes of its intended target.

Josh reappears in time to see them drop to the floor as the collective thud fills the hallway. He looks at me, his eyes wide. "Holy shit..."

I look back at him. "It's about damn time these people find out exactly who the fuck I am."

We bump fists. "Amen, brother."

We walk side by side toward the elevators, with renewed urgency and purpose in our steps. I don't know how full this building is getting with trained killers and have no wish to find out. A moment of epiphany can work wonders, but it can't magically create more ammunition when we're outnumbered twenty-to-one. Those four back there were nothing. But this isn't the time to get cocky. It's time to be smart.

As I pass the corpse in the suit, I hand the Glock to Josh. I crouch to take the assault rifle this asshole was reloading when I killed him. I eject the mag. It's full. He was ready to start shooting at me but was just a fraction too slow.

We reach the elevators, and I press the call button on the wall between them. I watch the display screen above each one, but neither whirrs into life.

"You think they've disabled them?" I say to Josh.

He shakes his head. "They wouldn't usually be able to do that without cutting some of the power to the building. Maybe they've got a separate—"

Shit!

A cacophony of gunfire erupts to my left. I instinctively drop to one knee and level the rifle, ready to fire. As the shooting stops, I take a breath, steeling myself. I see an arm and a leg appear, then a torso, as someone makes their way around the corner, coming from the right side. I see the gun they're holding...

I've seen enough.

I fire two bursts in quick succession, adjusting my aim slightly between each one. Bullets strike the middle of their thigh, then, a second later, the stomach. I watch the body drop and see the gun slip from their hand.

Easy enough, but we're not out of the woods yet. That was a mixture of auto and semiauto gunfire a moment ago. Whoever I just killed dropped a handgun, which means there are more people waiting around the corner. I look back at Josh, who's crouching against the wall opposite the elevators, his gun held expertly in both hands. I point two fingers at my eyes, then back along the corridor, at Sterling's office—a silent instruction to watch our ass.

I move quietly toward the edge of the wall and lean against it. I slow my breathing, then snap my head around the corner, affording myself a split-second glance. The flash will tell me all I need to know.

More gunfire sounds out, chasing me back into cover.

Holy crap!

I saw six people, but there could've been more. They were taking cover in the doorways of the offices lining the corridor. I'm sure I recognized one of them—a member of the unit Pierce used to run.

I don't like these odds.

We need to leave.

I stand and set off running back toward Sterling's office. Josh hastily follows.

"Where are we going?" he asks.

"Not that way. That's for sure." I look both ways once we reach the office. To the right is the group of dead guys. To the left... "There. The fire exit."

We rush through the door and into the cold, concrete stairwell. Fluorescent wall lights buzz on every side. I peer over the metal railing that winds around the outside edge of the steps, looking both above and below us.

"Josh, we need to get out of here and get the information we took from Sterling's safe to Schultz."

He nods. "Yeah, but that's easier said than done. How many more floors are likely to be filled with highly trained hitmen?"

I shrug. "Honestly? Probably not that many. The Order might have a vast array of resources, but they don't have hundreds of men to spare on a moment's notice. If I had to guess, I would say they've sent people directly to us, as well as a team on the roof and a team waiting for us in the lobby. Maybe thirty men in total. And we've already taken out six."

"So, how do we get out?"

"You tell me. What's the logical move?"

"I don't know. To go down and out through the main doors, maybe?"

I nod. "That's what I would say too. We can't stay here because we'll never fight everyone off at the same time. And there's no sense heading for the roof because... what? We jump twenty-odd stories to safety? That's insane, right?"

"What's your point, Adrian?"

"My point is that's how logic dictates we're going to think, and a dollar for ten says that's how Horizon thinks we're gonna think."

"So, you're saying—"

"We head for the roof."

He nods. "We head for the roof. I knew you were going to say that. You know logic usually prevails, don't you?"

I smile. "Not when I'm around."

He scoffs. "No shit."

"It'll be fine. There'll be less people on the roof than in the lobby. Besides, you're going to have a chopper meet us up there."

"I am?"

"Yeah."

"Ah, right. I am. I can do that."

I roll my eyes. "And I thought I was guilty of forgetting myself in a crisis. Jesus..."

He takes out his cell phone and dials a number as we start running up the flights of stairs, taking two steps at a time. We pass the door for the eighteenth floor. A few moments later, we pass the nineteenth.

I couldn't tell what Josh was saying behind me, but he's just hung up and drawn level with me. "The chopper's en route, but it's thirty minutes out."

"That's no use to us, Josh. We need it now."

"I know, but at least it's carrying a team of my best men, all heavily-armed and ready for a fight. That's better than nothing."

"I guess if we don't make it, they can always clean up afterward and get the information out of here." I lean out over the rail and look up. "How many floors does this place have, exactly?"

"Twenty-four, I think."

I take a long, deep breath. "Man, I'm out of shape."

We turn the corner at twenty, but as I step onto the next flight, I hear a noise above me. I snap my cast up, signaling to Josh to stop. We step back, plant ourselves against the wall, and wait, listening intently.

I hear boots. Multiple, heavy footsteps stamp on the concrete, getting louder with each second that passes.

Josh nods toward the sound. "Logic's a bitch, isn't it?"

"Shut up."

I tighten my grip on the rifle and rest it on my cast, ready to fire. It's hard to tell how many men are coming. You can bet your ass the ones we left on the seventeenth called ahead to their friends above us. Probably below us too, although it'll take them longer to reach us. They're going to pin us down and either wait us out, knowing they have more ammunition than we do, or swarm us, guns-a-blazing. They'll take the hits but ultimately get the job done.

I nod to his gun. "How many bullets you got left?"

He checks the magazine. "Ten, plus one in the hole. You?"

"Not enough."

We're cut off from the roof, twenty floors up, with a significant number of skilled assassins closing in on us from all sides and not enough bullets to kill them all.

Okay, fine...

Triple shit.

20

11:12 PDT

I yank open the door leading onto the twentieth floor and step through, quickly checking both sides to make sure we're alone.

It's eerily quiet, save for a desk phone ringing somewhere on the other side of the office. Josh looks around. "The only ways out of here are this door and the elevators, which weren't working before. We're trapped in here. You do realize that, right?"

I let out a heavy, frustrated sigh. "Yeah, I know. I'm thinking."

I head left, following the layout until I reach the elevators. I hook the strap of the rifle over my head and arm, so it rests comfortably on my right shoulder.

I press the call button again.

Nothing.

Josh gestures wildly with his arms. "Great! We need a plan, Adrian."

I raise an eyebrow at him. "Will you relax? Jeez. I thought you were supposed to be the rational one..."

"It's hard to be rational when you're being hunted. We're not all accustomed to shit like this, y'know?"

"Yeah, I know. But you used to be. It's just like riding a bike, man." I pause a moment and smile, trying to lighten the mood and maybe lift his spirits, but it doesn't work. He's just staring blankly at the wall ahead of him. "What's going on with you, Josh? Since Sterling exploded on us, you haven't had your head in the game. Kinda like Sterling, thinking about it..."

He turns to me, his eyes wide. "Oh, I'm sorry! Sorry I can't remain calm when shit like this is going on! I was *never* used to this, Adrian. You seem to forget, I spent most of our mutual career behind a desk, miles away from the bullets. I know I can take care of myself, but this is insane. The shit you do, the shit you get yourself in the middle of... it's a world away from the things I did for this country and for my own. I'm not you! You brought me along on a suicide mission, and you can't understand why I'm a little fucking concerned! I have a lot more to lose than you do. No offense."

"None taken." I regard him quietly. Adrenaline must be pumping double-time right now, and he's not controlling it. He's panicking. "Y'know what? You're right. You're not me. You're *better* than me. Yeah, you have more to lose, but that just goes to show how you've accomplished so much more on your own than you ever did booking my Greyhound tickets. But you're still the same guy I've known over half my life. The same guy who steered me through the darkest of times... who is single-handedly responsible for my success. And that guy wouldn't be acting like a pussy at a time like this."

His lip curls with anger. But I don't care. I'm right and he knows it.

I step toward him. "At first, I thought maybe you were still a little pissed with me about the whole *faking my death* thing, but that's not it. Truth is, you've gone soft on me, Josh. The things you've been doing with GlobaTech are staggering, and I have no doubt you've earned your place in history because of them, but you've grown so accustomed to being invaluable, you've forgotten what it's like to take risks. To put it all on the line. This isn't about what we have to lose. It's about why we have to win."

I slap him across the face. The crack of the impact lingers around us in the silence. He steps back, his eyes wide with shock, and puts a hand on his cheek. I set my jaw in case this doesn't work and he hits me back.

"Now find your balls, Josh, and find them fast. We're up shit creek without a paddle here, and I can't do it alone."

The silence now is deafening and a little awkward. I hold his gaze, waiting.

After some tense moments, he looks away, sighing heavily. "Okay."

Phew.

I move in front of the elevator doors. "Gimme a hand, would you?"

I place the fingertips of my left hand on the crack between the doors, pressing in as much as I can. Josh moves next to me and does the same with both of his. Between us, with a little effort, we force them open. I lean in and look up and down the shaft. I can barely see the carriage below us, so it must be near the first floor.

"What are you thinking, Adrian?" he asks.

I turn to him and smile as I point to the wall of the

elevator shaft facing us. He looks over at it and then back at me. His expression is deadpan. "No..."

I nod. "Yes."

"But I thought you hated heights?"

"Not as much as I hate being shot."

He lets out a long sigh through loose lips. "This is a stupid idea."

I flick my eyebrows and smile. "Probably, but until a better one presents itself, this is what we're going with."

On the back wall, across from the opening, is a service ladder built into the brickwork. Just above each doorway is a gantry that runs around all four sides of the shaft. I think we should climb up the ladder, onto each gantry, and make our way to the top floor. There should be a staircase there, leading to the roof.

Josh steps slowly to the edge and peers over. "Okay, how are we getting to the ladder? It's at least eight feet away. There's no way I'm jumping, Adrian! There are risks, and there are *risks*..."

I can't believe I'm suggesting this.

I clear my throat. "We don't need to jump. We simply step out, grab a hold of the cables, and use them to climb over."

"That's actually insane."

"Yeah, I know, but I reckon we have about two minutes before God-knows how many more of The Order's assassins arrive and start shooting at us. I don't know about you, but I don't have that many bullets left. So, it's either this, or we take on a small army of killers with nothing to help us except sarcasm and a winning smile. Your call."

He leans in again. He looks up and down, over at the ladder, then finally back at me. "All right, fine."

I step to the side. "Good man. Now you're going to have to go first."

"What? Why?"

"Because I only have one hand, which means I can't hold the cable and grab the ladder. You need to be over there, so I can hold the cable in my left, and have you help me across by grabbing my cast."

Josh sighs. "Shit, man. I hate you."

He tucks the Glock in his waistband behind him and shuffles apprehensively to the edge of the shaft. He leans in, stretching a little, and wraps his hand tightly around the cable. He tugs at it, testing for sturdiness, then swings his front leg out. He hooks his foot around it, and I see his arm muscles tense. He takes a couple of quick, deep breaths, then steps out over the abyss, quickly grabbing on with his other hand. He lets out a grunt of exertion as he brings his back leg out and right across, placing it firmly on the bottom rung of the service ladder.

He glances down and immediately closes his eyes. "Holy crap."

"Focus on your breathing, man. You've got this," I say to him.

Josh adjusts his grip, hugging the cable close to his chest with his left arm while he reaches out with his right. His fingertips brush against the ladder, stretching to get a hold.

"Almost..." he mutters.

...

...

...

His hand wraps around a rung of the ladder. He pulls himself across, linking them to hold him steady.

I punch the air. "Nice!"

He climbs up and steps onto the gantry, level with the

top of the doors. It's not wide, but he crouches and then lies flat, keeping one arm hooked on the ladder. "Right, your turn."

Okay, here we go.

I start the same way Josh did. I lean in and grip the cable with my left hand. Then I bring my front leg out and hook my foot around it.

So far, so good.

Don't look down, Adrian. Don't... look...

I look down.

"Oh, sweet Jesus!"

Above me, Josh hisses, "Why did you do that?"

"I don't know!"

"Come on. Sooner you're over here, sooner we can get to the roof."

I grit my teeth until my jaw aches, forcing back the rising dread in my mind. I tense my muscles and swing myself out, simultaneously wrapping my back foot around the cable and raising my arm, searching for Josh's hand.

...

...

...

I feel his grip on my cast, which causes swift and immediate pain in my hand, but I can live with it, under the circumstances.

"Got you," he says. "Just step over and grab the ladder."

My arm's aching, and my feet are slipping. "I'm... trying..."

I reach over with my right foot and hook it around the ladder, which takes some of the strain. As I transfer more of my weight to my right arm, a bolt of pain shoots through my hand.

I breathe through it, trying to block it from my mind.

It's now or never.

I push off with my left hand and step over to the ladder. My full body weight pulls on Josh's grip as, for a split-second, I dangle precariously over the pit yawning ominously below me.

"Ugh!"

Christ, it's excruciating!

...

...

...

I wrap my left hand and foot around the ladder, and Josh immediately releases his grip, allowing me to hook my right arm around it too.

I made it.

I take a moment to compose myself and let the agony subside, then steadily climb up and step onto the gantry across from Josh. We press our backs and heels to the cold brick, our feet only a couple of inches from the edge of the metal platform.

I look over at him. "You okay?"

"Not really. You?"

"Peachy."

We look across. The bottom of the door on the floor above is maybe three feet above my head. Too far to reach from beneath. I steel myself and look down. The top edge of the elevator doors below us is maybe a little over a foot below the gantry.

I gesture to it with a small nod. "We'll have to climb up to the gantry for the twenty-fourth and then reach down to pry the doors open for the twenty-third. We'll get off there and take the stairs the rest of the way."

"Okay, let's get this over with."

I shuffle to the side, step back onto the ladder, and start

to climb. I hear Josh below me doing the same. It's completely vertical and hard to make our way up, especially with one hand. I'm having to hook my entire forearm around the rungs, which takes more time. Still, it's not something I want to rush.

I draw level with the next platform, just above the doors to the twenty-first floor, and stop. I hear something below me. I look down and see Josh staring up at me questioningly.

"Did you hear that?" I whisper.

He nods slowly, and we both hold our breath, listening.

It sounds like footsteps. Lots of them.

We exchange another glance and both look down, over our shoulders, at the open elevator doors below us. I see a head poking out and a face staring back at us, smiling.

Oh, shit.

"Josh, we gotta move!"

I start climbing again, passing the gantry just as gunfire breaks out. The bullets whizz and clatter against the metal and brick at our feet but luckily avoid us. I climb as fast as I dare, ascending the ladder with renewed urgency.

We soon draw level with the gantry above the twenty-second floor. The angle should be too steep for anyone to get a shot off now.

"I think we're clear," I call down. "It's just a little farther."

I step out onto the metal platform, taking a moment to catch my breath. Josh appears next to me. "Do you wanna make the joke about us being shafted right now, or shall I do it?"

I smile. "Be my guest."

He's quiet for a moment. "Nah, I'll save it. It'll be funnier when we're telling this story back to people."

"Damn right. Come on."

We start the climb again. It only takes us a few minutes to reach the gantry above the twenty-fourth floor. There's not enough room to stand on it, so we crouch and shuffle around until we're positioned on either side of the elevator doors below us.

I look at Josh. "You're gonna need to climb back out onto the cables, shuffle down so you're level with the doors, and try to force them open yourself. I can lean over the edge, but I doubt I'll be effective one-handed."

He flicks his eyes sardonically. "Yeah..."

Without any hesitation, he reaches over, secures his grip, and pulls himself out once more over the shaft. He wraps his legs and feet around the cables and moves himself slowly down, his knuckles white with tension. As he draws level with the door below, he leans out and presses his fingertips into the crack. I hear him grunt with effort, but he sees no success.

"Let me try to help." I lie flat and hook my right arm around the top rung of the ladder, then reach down with my left hand. It's a stretch, but I can just about reach, firmly pressing my own hand against the doors. "Okay, go."

We both struggle and pull, desperately trying to separate the doors. A small crack of light appears. More effort, and the gap widens enough for us to both fit our hand in.

"Almost... got it..."

The shaft below me is bathed in light as the doors slide apart.

I close my eyes and breathe a quiet sigh of relief.

"Good work," says Josh. "Now let's get out of here, and—"

A mechanical whirring echoes around us, cutting him off. The sound of gears shifting follows.

What's that?

Our eyes meet, and I can see from his face that we've reached the same conclusion at the same time. Those bastards must've overridden the system somehow and reactivated the elevator!

The cables creak as they begin to move, and Josh is suddenly dragged upward.

"Shit!" he yells. He begins climbing down, although the motion simply keeps him in the same place.

I look up. The ceiling isn't far above us. If he stays on those cables, he'll be crushed!

"Josh, you gotta move! Now!"

He begins climbing down faster, inching closer to the open doors. He keeps looking below him, checking the distance of the approaching carriage. He draws level with the gap and heaves himself off the cables, diving head-first out of the shaft, disappearing from my sight.

I'm glad he's safe, but what about me? I can't stand where I am, and looking at the elevator, I won't make it onto the gantry below me in time.

Shit! Shit! Shit!

It's closing fast.

Think, Adrian, come on!

I peer down again. It's only a few floors below me.

Shit!

...

...

...

I look at the cables.

Screw it.

I push myself up into a crouch and jump off. I hook my right arm loosely around the cable and use my momentum to spin myself clockwise as I descend rapidly toward the oncoming carriage. As I complete the turn, I unhook my arm and fly feet-first through the open doors below. I land heavily on the carpeted floor, rolling toward the wall opposite. I come to a stop and stare back wide-eyed as the elevator shoots past the doors.

Holy shit!

My heart's hammering so fast, I can hear it.

"Jesus! You okay?"

I look to my right and see Josh sitting on the floor nearby, his arms stretched out behind him, his legs flat out in front. He's breathing hard, and his brow is glistening with sweat.

I nod silently. Not sure I have the ability to form words just yet.

That was crazy!

But there's no time to rest now. We may have passed everyone once, but that means they're now all below us. They'll be heading up here to see if we're pancakes or not, which means we need to move.

We both scramble to our feet and head across the floor of the office building, toward the fire escape. Josh checks his watch. "The chopper should be here any minute."

I open the door. "First piece of good news we've had all day."

We both step back inside the concrete stairwell. The cool breeze is refreshing after everything we've just been through. As we begin climbing the steps, heading for the twenty-fourth, I risk a peek over the railing. Maybe three floors below us, a group of men are racing toward us.

"They're coming," I say, picking up the pace, taking the steps two at a time.

Past the door for the twenty-fourth is a final set of steps, leading to the roof. We sprint up them and come out in a narrow, damp corridor, with a metal door at the end. We burst through it, out into the blinding glare of the midday sun.

I slam the door closed behind us, squinting as my eyes adjust to the sudden influx of natural light. The wind whips around me, much stronger and colder all the way up here. A venting system traces itself around the roof. The oblong metal piping is close to three feet tall, maybe the same across, and it snakes around the door and the small space behind it.

A large, hexagonal helipad dominates the far end of the roof. Josh has moved out into the open, standing a few feet from it, scanning the horizon for any sign of the chopper. I stand beside him and look out at the Seattle skyline sprawling out around us.

Before I can take it in, I hear the door slam open against the wall behind us. I spin around to see armed men filing out, their guns raised as they move into position, seeking cover behind the vents.

I look around. We don't have any.

Shit!

We both level our weapons and fire preemptively. We walk backward, using the valuable seconds it buys us to move across to the far side of the helipad. It's raised slightly, only by a few steps, but it's enough to duck behind.

The hammer of my borrowed rifle clicks down on an empty chamber. I'm out. I unhook the strap from around my neck and throw the weapon aside. As we reach the other side of the helipad, Josh fires his last bullet too.

We crouch beside each other as The Order's hit squad opens fire, retaliating with a carefree spray of bullets that ricochet off the ground all around us. I peek over the top and see seven men walking slowly toward us, shooting indiscriminately, without any obvious aim. They have the advantage here, so there's no need to be shy with their ammo, I guess.

I duck back and look at Josh. "I'm sorry, man. This is my fault."

He nods. "I know it is. But you have nothing to apologize for. If we don't make it, I want you to know that—"

He stops talking. We both turn in unison as we hear the repeated thudding of helicopter blades suddenly drown out the howling wind. Sweeping into view, circling high behind the men, the chopper slides to a hover. The side door opens. Two men appear, dressed in GlobaTech fatigues, and—

Holy shit!

—open fire on the roof! They mowed down all seven of these assholes in seconds. They barely had time to turn around. As the last of the men hit the ground, the chopper banks toward us and touches down gently on the helipad ten feet from us. We make our way up the nearby steps, stooping as we pass under the blades, and climb aboard.

Facing us are five GlobaTech security operatives, sitting along both sides. Another two are kneeling in the middle of the floor, facing the seats, positioned with their backs to the cockpit. Both Josh and I sit in one, and he puts a headset on. He says something inaudible, presumably to the pilot, and we take off a moment later.

One of the men in front of us slides the door closed and extends his hand to me, which I shake gratefully. He then looks at Josh. "Sorry we're late, sir," he yells.

Josh smiles and shouts back, "All is forgiven. Now get us the hell out of here."

We look at each other and bump fists.

"Nice work," he says to me.

I nod. "Let's not do that again, though, yeah?"

He laughs. "Agreed."

21

I'm pacing back and forth in the hotel room, tracing the same route past the beds, down the side of each one, and back again. Josh is sitting at the small desk, tapping feverishly away on his laptop, analyzing all the information on the flash drive we took from Sterling's safe.

It's not going well.

The chopper dropped us off near the parking lot of our hotel. We got our bags, checked out, and drove north on I-5, crossing the border into Vancouver. We're working on the assumption that The Order can see us and have all their assets following us as best they can, so we drove aimlessly around the city for almost an hour before parking in an underground lot and walking to the nearest hotel.

It's nice but expensive. Given Josh's GlobaTech credit card is paying for it, we went all out and rented a suite. It's a single main room but spacious. The two queen beds are against the left wall, with a large bathroom opposite, furnished with an exquisite marble décor. Two large windows running floor-to-ceiling face the double doors of the entrance, providing plenty of natural light. To the right of the bathroom, a TV is mounted on the right wall, level with the gap between the beds. A lightwood desk is positioned beneath it, where Josh is sitting right now.

The left corner is a living space, with an L-shaped sofa dominating the area, and a small coffee table in the middle.

I walk behind him for the hundredth time. "What's taking so long?"

He sighs impatiently. "It's encrypted, and it's a bitch to hack into. Plus, it doesn't help you asking me why it's taking so long every five minutes."

I roll my eyes. "Yeah, yeah."

Man, I need to get out of here. It's only been an hour, but it feels like six. I guess it has been a long day. I haven't eaten anything, and I'm thoroughly pissed off that I had to leave my Berettas behind in Seattle. Especially because Josh took the liberty of caring for them when he thought I was dead. I loved those guns. They were a gift from an old friend who isn't around anymore, who understood the significance of giving me something like that.

While I've been pacing around this room, waiting for Josh to work his magic, I've had a lot of time to think. We had to have made at least a small dent in The Order's manpower after we met with Sterling. And him losing his head would've been a major blow for them, regardless of how necessary they might have deemed it. That's twenty percent of their upper management... gone. I'm sure everyone knows by now, and there's no way they're not concerned.

And let's not forget Horizon. He's the bastard sending all the men after us. He still has an advantage, simply because he has more guns than we do. But I'm not sure whether anyone's realized we robbed Sterling before we left and have all the shit from his safe. Granted, we haven't been able to decrypt any of it yet, but that's only a matter of time.

Hopefully.

I glanced through the papers we took, but there was nothing significant in there. A few financials, but it all looked legitimate, relating to The Sterling Group's overseas holdings. The real jackpot is going to be on that flash drive. It has to be—why else would they protect it so well? It must be good if Josh has been at it for an hour and hasn't gotten anywhere.

But including killing Pierce, who coordinated The Order's clean-up crew, we've dealt them some serious body blows in the last forty-eight hours, and that's a big win for us. I know there's still a long way to go, but we're on the right track. The next step is to figure out exactly what their endgame is. We know they wanted to kill Josh and ensure his replacement was one of their own, with the intention of using their guy to influence the National Security Council. I personally don't see how that would work, but Sterling was confident, and I know enough about The Order to know that any issues I see with the plan probably won't stop them.

But then what?

All this shit about God and the Knights Templar has really thrown me a curveball. At no point did I expect religion to factor into a secret society of assassins, but I suppose it wouldn't be the first time. Even so, it all creates more questions than answers.

"Got it!"

I look over at Josh. "You in?"

"Yeah, cracked the bastard. Right, let's have a look..."

I move behind him, looking over his shoulder at the screen

as I lean on the back of his chair. He navigates the files quickly, scanning over the contents, quickly determining the relevance before moving on to the next. He can read a lot faster than I can, and with time being a constant factor, I'm glad he's here. Windows pop up and close down. Documents open and close. Images flash up. He's working his way through the entire drive.

He stops on a spreadsheet. "This looks interesting."

"What is it?"

"It looks like... Shit, it is!"

"What?"

"It's a bloody personnel list!"

"Are you serious?"

He scrolls down a few screens. "Yeah, this lists every asset The Order has, where they're based, and which Horizon is looking after them. They literally give them numbers. Look." He points to the screen. My name is listed beneath a subheading of *Middle East*. Next to it is a brief but detailed biography, the number of kills I've completed for them, and *Horizon 7*.

I frown. "*Horizon 7*? It makes him sound like a fucking space shuttle. No wonder he leaves off the number when he's flapping his gums. Why would they even write this shit down?"

Josh shrugs. "I'm guessing it's not easy to keep track of. Someone's got to manage the books, I suppose, and it certainly explains the level of encryption. What is worrying is *this*." He points to a figure at the bottom of the screen. "*That's* how many assassins they have working for them."

My eyes widen. "Are you kidding me?"

"Nope. That number is how many cells are populated with names on this spreadsheet, which means, in total, they have close to fifteen thousand assets."

"Jesus. Okay, can you, like, filter it by location?"

"Sure can." A couple of taps on the keyboard and the list shortens. "There we go. They have nearly four thousand based in North America."

"Holy shit."

I take it back. The fourteen we killed earlier today probably weren't that big of a dent after all.

He turns and looks up at me. "We have to assume they're all coming for us, don't we?"

I nod slowly. "Uh-huh."

He sighs. "We might need some help."

"Uh-huh."

Silence descends, and I zone out a little as the gravity of it all sinks in.

"Hold up a second..."

"Hmm? What is it?"

"Look at this. I've unfiltered the list again and scrolled down to see if Sterling's name is on here."

"And?"

"It is. But it's in a different color than the rest."

"To highlight he's special?"

"That's what I thought, so I filtered the list again to only display names in that color. It found five."

I lean forward. "Are you saying you've found all five Committee members?"

He nods. "I think so, yeah."

I look at the list of names. Each one is in a different continent. Sterling, we can ignore. Three of the remaining four mean nothing to me. But one of them, I recognize. I point to it. "Where do I know that name from?"

Josh shrugs. "Dunno. Let me Google him. Hang on..."

I pace away while he does his thing. I'm torn right now

as to whether I should be glad or worried that we've found this list.

"Oh, shit."

I walk back over to Josh and lean forward again. "What? Who is he?"

He silently points to the screen. I look at the image displayed there and read the paragraph of text beneath it.

...

...

...

I swallow hard. "Oh, shit."

My mind starts racing, picking up all the individual pieces of this puzzle, trying to connect them. Some things slot together. Some things don't. The things that don't are at least starting to make some sense, even if I can't see how they're relevant just yet.

Things Sterling said to us begin running through my head, over and over, until they take their place in the giant jigsaw, helping to reveal that all-important big picture.

But one thing's for sure: if we weren't convinced as to how screwed we were before... we are now.

The image on the screen is of two men. Our guy is the one on the right. There's no doubt in my mind that he's the head of the Committee. The man in charge of The Order. He looks older than he is but younger than the person he's standing next to. The caption below explains who he is and where he is in the photo.

His name is Antonio Herrera Martinez. He's the current camerlengo of the Catholic Church, and the man he's standing next to is the pope.

22

Josh gets to his feet and moves over to one of the beds. He sits down heavily. I start pacing again, still fighting to put everything together.

"I don't understand..." he says, lying flat.

I sigh. "I think I do. Martinez is the leader of The Order. Sterling said himself that their mission is God's will, and their leader is incredibly well-protected."

He sits up again. "Yeah, but he also said he didn't know where his leader was and that he conferences in whenever the rest of the Committee meet."

"He had to have been lying. If he knew *who* he was, then it's obvious there's only one place he's going to be. He was protecting his boss."

"But... Adrian... he's basically the pope's secretary!"

"That explains The Order's vast resources. Doesn't the camerlengo handle the Vatican's finances? He's probably cooking the books and filtering off whatever he needs to fund The Order's missions."

Josh gets to his feet and stands in front of me. "But that's not all he does..."

He hurries over to the laptop, sits down in the chair, and starts typing urgently.

I move next to him. "What are you thinking?"

"I think I've just figured out how The Order works." He brings up the spreadsheet with all the assets listed on it. "See this date, next to the name? I noticed it before but didn't pay it much attention. I think that's when each asset was recruited. It certainly matches with you. Now, if I'm right, what do you notice?"

I look at the dates on the screen twice over and shrug. "Not much. They're all pretty recent..."

"Exactly. On this entire document, across all fifteen-or-so thousand assets, including the Committee and all the Horizons, not one of them has been a member of The Order for more than six years."

I frown. "That's strange, given how long they're meant to have been around."

"I know. Now the current pope was elected three years ago, when the previous one died. What do you know about the election process?"

I shrug. "Only what I've seen in the movies."

"Well, that's probably pretty accurate. All the cardinals are locked away until they decide among themselves who should be the next pope. Until they make that decision, the camerlengo assumes control of the Catholic Church..."

"What are you saying?"

"I'm saying, ol' Antonio here has been camerlengo for... you guessed it... six years. He was appointed by the previous pope. Now how's this for a theory? He gets the new job, gains access to everything the position affords, and discovers The Order of Sabbah hidden away in the Vatican archives. He sees an opportunity and resurrects them, but they need funding. When the pope dies, he sees his chance. While temporarily running the show, he uses his influence to somehow make sure the new pope is someone who won't ask too many questions."

"So, you think the pope's involved?"

He shakes his head. "Probably not, but maybe he's a little naïve. I remember reading about it in the paper. People were shocked that he was elected over some of the other cardinals, who were favorites for the job. Maybe this is why?"

I nod. "With someone who is easily manipulated in the big chair, Martinez would be free to siphon whatever funds he wants from the Vatican, so he can finance The Order."

"And he has likely been doing so ever since, allowing The Order's reach and influence to grow to what it is today."

"So, all the talk from Horizon and Sterling about the all-powerful Order being around for centuries is just bullshit?"

"Kinda. It's probably true that it's existed for centuries in some form, dating back to the Knights Templar, but it's not necessarily been an active organization. Just something that used to be, which people still talk about. Probably how the ghost stories started for people like us—a bit of research online and lots of Chinese whispers."

"So, they use the attractive-sounding history as their sales pitch?"

"Maybe, yeah. If they recruit assassins, it explains how word of them began to travel around our circles."

"But what do they want? What are they working toward?"

Josh shrugs. "No idea. There's nothing on the flash drive detailing future missions. But Martinez has taken an old idea from Catholic history and turned it into the modern-day Freemasons, giving him a modicum of control over almost everything. He gets together with his Committee, and they figure out how to maintain control of what they have and how to gain more of it, then pass the message on to the Horizons, who use their assets to do whatever needs to be done."

"If you're right—and I see no reason to doubt the theory—then there's no question it's impressive. But we still have the full extent of their wrath on our asses, and we still don't know what they're planning next."

"Maybe not, but I reckon we have more than enough to take to Schultz. If we can work with the Vatican to expel Martinez, that might stop them in their tracks. We can then hand it all over to the FBI and begin cleaning up all the business assets they have. Maybe we can restore a sense of normality to everything."

I nod. "Okay. Make the call."

I move over to my bed and pick up my jacket. I throw it on, heading for the door.

"Where are you going?" asks Josh.

I glance back at him. "To make a call of my own."

18:22 PDT

Mmm! Oh, my God, this burger is amazing!

So, my phone call didn't quite go as I expected. I asked someone to help us, and she declined, somewhat impolitely. It was a spur-of-the-moment idea, and it didn't pan out, which pissed me off a little.

Then I remembered I hadn't eaten in almost a day, so I

found a burger joint and ordered this bad boy. It's a half-pound slab of beef with melted cheese, bacon, lettuce, and tomato on top of it. I can feel my arteries clogging with each bite, but I honestly couldn't be happier right now. Everything looks better on a full stomach. I even bought Josh one, although I can't guarantee it'll make it back to the hotel room.

We're finally making progress. We know The Order is embedded at the top of the Catholic Church. We also know the best-case scenario right now is that we *only* have four thousand assassins hunting us both down. That's assuming they're not being brought in from all over the world to ensure that we're taken out.

The Order will go all-out to make sure I'm dead. As the one that got away, I now pose the single greatest threat to their existence. I know enough to expose them, and I'm good enough to survive long enough to do it.

Now we just need Schultz to do his part.

I'm walking a long, indirect route back to the hotel. I haven't seen anyone I think might be following me, but it's better to be safe than sorry, right? Besides, it's still nice outside. The sun's just starting to drop, causing the temperature to do the same. The wind's picking up too, but it's still borderline comfortable for me. Plus, it gives me time to eat my cheeseburger.

I arrive back at the hotel after a half-hour round trip and make my way up to our suite. I open the door to the room and see Josh gesturing wildly with one hand, holding his cell to his ear with the other.

"Sir, you *have* to take this seriously. You have to act!"

Huh. Doesn't sound like it's going well with Schultz, does it?

I shut the door, and he looks over. "Hang on. Adrian's back. Let me put you on speaker."

I walk over to him and hand him the bag of food. He sets the phone down on the desk and gestures to it. "We're on with the president."

I roll my eyes. "Hi, Ryan."

He sighs, causing a little distortion on the line. "Josh has just been telling me what you've found out about these sonsofbitches."

I nod. "And?"

"And I can't get involved. I'm sorry."

Josh and I exchange a glance. I frown, and he shrugs with defeat.

"You mind telling me why?"

"Son, the fact that you even need to ask me that is proof enough you're not thinking straight."

I stroke my chin, feeling the coarse stubble grate on my palm. "All due respect, sir, but you need to pull your head out of your ass."

Josh steps forward and whispers, "Adrian, don't..."

On the line, Schultz scoffs. "Here we go again. Understand this, Adrian—there's absolutely nothing stopping me from sending a SWAT team to bring your ass in right now. I can put you in a hole for the rest of your days if I want to. You and Josh currently have the freedom to pursue this as a courtesy, out of respect for the things you've done for this country. But make no mistake, either of you... I can pull the plug on this in a heartbeat."

Josh holds his hand up to me, signaling for me to stay quiet. It's probably for the best, all things considered. "Sir, you said if we got you sufficient evidence of a credible threat, you would help us."

"I know what I said, Josh. But what you've told me isn't a

credible threat. It's a goddamn international incident waiting to happen! What do you want me to do? Send the First Battalion to knock on the Vatican's front door to subdue the pope? Vatican City is its own country, and we can't get involved in another nation's domestic issues."

I slam my fist down on the desk beside the phone. "That's bullshit, Ryan!"

"Adrian, I swear to God, you better watch your tongue."

"You say you can't get involved... Explain Iraq. Explain Afghanistan. Explain North Korea. There was no issue with our government getting involved then, was there?"

"That's because they were genuine threats to the rest of the world, and it's our responsibility to—"

"And how is this *not* a genuine threat? Jesus, Ryan. Two months ago, North Korea invaded our fucking country! Yeah, it was a half-assed attempt, and there were mitigating circumstances behind it, but after Josh's boys pushed them back, what did you do? You sent troops into their country to keep them in check, while the rest of us tried to rebuild our lives."

"And that was justifiable. A necessary precaution."

"So is this! We have proof that the leader of The Order has influence over the Catholic Church. Hell, if the pope dies, their leader will *run* the Catholic Church! His resources are near-unlimited as a result, and he authorizes the assassination of anyone he deems necessary, without just cause or provocation. Josh is a target. Who's to say their next target won't be you? Or another foreign leader? Who's to say their actions won't trigger more international crises? That might be exactly what they want to do. You *have* to preempt this, Ryan. We know who he is, and we know how he works. You have to stay one step ahead of these bastards and buy us time to shut them down permanently."

"Adrian, Josh has spent the last twenty minutes pleading the same case, and I'll tell you what I've already told him. I can't march into another country with nothing more than a theory and overthrow the head of state."

I close my eyes briefly. I know, I know... he's right. Obviously. But that doesn't change the fact that we're right too.

I'll keep trying.

"Ryan, it's not just a theory. We have proof..."

"No, you don't. The camerlengo's name is on a spreadsheet you found in a dead guy's office. That doesn't prove anything. I'm not saying your theory isn't sound. It's perfectly plausible, and given what we know and what you've told me, you're probably right. But that doesn't change the fact that what you have is circumstantial at best. I said if I were to help you, it would be in an official capacity, above board. There are next-to-no official channels with which to approach the Vatican about this, and the Swiss Guard are unlikely to want anyone interfering in their affairs, especially now."

I frown. "What do you mean, *especially now*? What's happening?"

"Do you not listen to the news, son?"

"I've been a little busy..."

"In two days, his Holiness is going to hold a special Mass in St. Peter's Square to pray for those still fighting in the aftermath of 4/17, as well as those who lost their lives."

"On a Saturday?" asks Josh.

"That's right. Security's going to be on high alert ahead of it. Now listen up, the pair of you. The official position of the White House is that we cannot and will not get involved in matters of foreign terrorism without solid intel of a credible threat to our own country. Now—"

I sigh heavily, losing what little patience I had to start

with. "Ryan, this isn't just about our country. It's about everywhere. Imagine for a second that the leader of a terrorist network took control of the Catholic Church. It would affect everyone. We have to—"

"Goddammit, will you let me finish? As I was about to say, my *personal* position on this matter is that I believe you boys are on to something, and I want you on the ground in Rome to verify it. If you're right, I want you to do everything in your power to stop it before it's too late. This world has faced enough adversity for one generation. It's on both of you to make sure they don't face any more. You do what you need to do. But Josh... keep GlobaTech out of it. Use whatever alternative resources you need to and keep a low profile. Just because I can't help you directly doesn't mean I want to stop you from doing this yourselves. Now is any part of what I just said unclear to either of you?"

I exchange a look with Josh, who leans toward the phone. "No, sir. We understand."

"Good. Oh, and Adrian? I know this is personal for you, and I know you can take care of yourself, but keep a clear mind, son. I want Josh back in Washington, safe and sound, for a de-brief first thing Monday morning."

I shake my head and roll my eyes. "Yeah, I'll look after him."

"Godspeed, gentlemen."

The line clicks off, leaving a palpable silence in the room. After a few moments, I point to the brown paper bag. "I brought you a burger. It's nice."

"Thanks," he replies, nodding absently. He takes it out and has a bite, then sits down heavily again on the edge of the bed. "So, we're going to Rome..."

"Looks like it."

I pace away toward the window, leaving Josh to his food.

I massage my temples with my left hand and take some deep, calming breaths. I'm pissed off at Schultz. He said he would help us if we got evidence and then changed his mind after we risked life and limb to do so. And I know our theory isn't really evidence, but it's sound logic, and what physical information we *do* have is enough to at least prompt further investigation. At least, I think so.

Though, apparently, I'm in the minority there.

I check my watch. We need to be in Rome tomorrow, and we need to plan how to essentially wage war on the Catholic Church twenty-four hours before the pope appears live in front of thousands of people and on TV in front of millions.

Easy.

23

***

It's been a long-ass day. I spent the morning getting shot at and the afternoon trying to figure out the inner workings of a secret society of assassins, led by the man who, it turns out, is the pope's assistant.

There's something to be said for being a cubicle slave nine-to-five.

After a pat on the back and a *fuck you very much* from our commander-in-chief, Josh and I decided it was time to get some help. He's good and I'm the best, but what we're going up against is simply ridiculous, and we know we can't do it alone.

Forgetting how many people are likely hunting us right now, we need to find a way to discreetly travel to Rome, get inside Vatican City, and take out the second most important person there.

This would normally be when I would remind myself

that, despite how shitty and impossible things seem, I've been through worse. But at the moment, I'm struggling to do that. Yes, I *did* infiltrate the White House and kill the president not so long ago, but that was pretty straightforward. He and the people around him were all bad people. I wasn't concerned about body counts, collateral damage, or even the moral implications of what I was trying to do. To me, that hit was about as black and white as I'm ever going to get.

But this is different. Sure, Antonio Herrera Martinez is a grade-one piece of shit, but as far as we know, no one else around him is. The population of Vatican City isn't. The pope isn't.

The *pope*.

I've said that word to myself so many times in the last couple of hours, it's lost its meaning.

Yet again, I've managed to negotiate my way into the middle of someone else's shitstorm, and I have no idea how I'm going to fix it. Not yet, anyway.

So, armed with nothing but Josh's laptop and a healthy dose of cynicism, we left the hotel to get some proper food, some beer, and to find a way to bury The Order of Sabbah once and for all.

We found an upmarket wine bar, which Josh dragged me into with the justification that they had Wi-Fi. Personally, I think he loves places like this now and will do anything to go in one. Gone are the days where he was content with a dive bar, listening to rock music and shooting pool, surrounded by women in their twenties with inhibitions lower than a rattlesnake's ass.

Goddamn sell-out.

It's not busy here, though, and the low music in the background is there more for atmosphere than to actually be listened to. The décor is soft leather with a dark wooden trim. Tables are spaced out, making full use of the sizable interior, allowing patrons a little more privacy for their intellectual conversations and wine tasting. The waitresses are friendly and unimposing. Hell, even this beer tastes as if it should cost twelve bucks a bottle.

Which it does.

Which is insane.

Anyway...

We both needed a change of clothes, so we detoured via the local mall on the way here. He opted for a shirt and loose tie, with jeans and boots. The modern CEO look. I've gone for the most generic, anonymous thing I could think of—a fitted sweater, dark jeans, and boots.

We scoped the place out before we came in and were both happy there wasn't an immediate threat. We haven't had much luck with bars since this shit started, so I'm not taking any chances now.

Josh is sitting opposite me. His glass of ice water with a slice of lemon is standing beside his laptop. He's just closed the lid after almost an hour of key-tapping.

"Right, I've put the word out on the dark web, so we'll see if we get any hits."

I frown. "The dark web? What's that? It sounds like where you would find those sites full of weird, Japanese cartoon porn."

He smiles. "You can get *them* on the regular web. Apparently. No, the dark web is..."

He trails off.

I gesture quizzically with my hand. "What?"

"Nothing, it's just... honestly, you're probably not gonna understand it. Just let me worry about it, okay?"

"Hold up a second. Don't assume I won't understand it. I'm an intelligent guy."

He nods. "When it comes to guns and killing people, yeah, I agree. But leave the tech stuff to me, all right?"

I narrow my eyes, watching him. He's shifting a little in his seat, absently scratching his arm... he's restless.

Wait a minute.

I point a playfully accusing finger at him. "You were about to reveal one of your secrets, weren't you?"

He shakes his head. "What do you mean?"

"Holy shit, you were! All the years we've spent together, and you've never told me how you do *any* of the amazing things you do for me. It's always been *magic*, and you've loved every second of having a little mystique around you. But this dark web thing, that's one of your big secrets, isn't it? And you don't want to tell me. Even now, at a time like this."

He goes to speak but settles instead for rolling his eyes and sighing heavily. "Fine! Yes, it's one of my trade secrets."

I clap my hands, laughing. "I knew it! Come on, spill!"

"Y'know, you don't have to enjoy this so much. I'm giving up some of my mojo here."

"Are you kidding? This is like finding out how they saw someone in half."

He rolls his eyes again. "Whatever. So, you know what the internet is, right?"

I raise an eyebrow but say nothing. The look I'm giving him is saying enough.

He smiles. "Well, that's something. Every website on the internet has coding embedded into it that allows search engines to find it, like its own unique ID number. It's kind of a prerequisite when setting them up. But what most people don't realize is that almost ninety-five percent of all internet content doesn't have that coding, meaning that everything you see online today is only a fraction of the actual content available. Sites without that coding make up what's known as the dark web. They're completely anonymous and therefore not subject to any restrictions or laws. You can't search for them, which means you'll never find them unless you already know where to look."

I take a swig of my beer and shrug. "Sounds straightforward."

"The principle is, yeah. But directly accessing those sites can be dangerous if you don't know what you're doing. You need special software and encryption tools to hide your online identity, to protect yourself from people who might use the resources in the dark web to attack you."

"How could they do that?"

"Well, off the top of my head... if you stumbled across an online forum for computer hackers, someone watching you could easily steal your ID, your money, your social security number—you name it. They could frame you for almost any crime. They could destroy your entire life with the press of a button."

I let out a low whistle. "Christ. So, what's on all the sites you can't see? Is it all computer hacking and political bullshit?"

"Not exclusively, although there's a lot of that about. But because your activities on the dark web are almost invisible, there's a lot of crazy shit on there. For example, there's an online marketplace dedicated solely to narcotics. You can literally add a kilo of cocaine to your shopping basket, like you would a DVD on Amazon."

I let out a chuckle. "Are you serious?"

Josh nods. "And then there's the websites we use."

"We?"

"Forums and social media platforms for professional killers and mercenaries."

"You're kidding me?"

He shakes his head. "You've heard of Facebook, right? Well, we have Bulletbook. Why do you think your reputation is as widely known as it is? A lot of unsavory types use the dark web, Adrian. Word spreads fast in those circles."

"So, do I have, like, a website or something?"

He laughs. "Not quite, but you're pretty famous on there. When we were first starting out, I put together a good marketing campaign for you to make sure the right people found you and paid the right money. Obviously, your skillset and credentials helped too. So, now you're the stuff of legend on there. Alongside The Order, naturally."

I finish my drink. "Huh. I had no idea."

"Feel free to add *PR Department* to my résumé."

I nod to his laptop. "So, what have you just been doing on there?"

"I posted that you have a big contract, that you're looking for a team, and to contact me for details. I've said payment is a million dollars, with a very high-risk factor."

"What, you just take out an ad and hope you get some interest?"

He shrugs. "Pretty much, yeah."

I shake my head in disbelief. It sounds really obvious and organized, but I would never associate it with what I do or the circles I move around in.

Still, it's nice to know some things in life can remain simple.

"Now what?"

"Now? We sit back and wait, I guess." He gestures to my cast. "How's the hand doing?"

I look at it, rotating my wrist to examine both sides of the plastic molding. "It's fine. Doesn't hurt much, but I know it still has some way to go before it's healed. Sure as Hell wish I had two good shootin' hands right now."

Josh smiles. "Don't we all?"

He silently points to my empty bottle. I nod, and he signals a waitress over to order another round.

I gaze absently around the place, discreetly putting eyes on every single person in here, checking for the tenth time that no one's getting ready to shoot us.

So far, so good.

Now we wait.

22:38 PDT

We're walking across the lobby of our hotel. The last hour or so was a bust. No hits on our personal ad, so it looks as if we're still doing it alone. We briefly talked about how we intend to get to Rome without attracting any attention from anyone but soon decided it's a problem that can wait until the morning. I need some sleep.

On the bright side, no one's tried to kill me in... what? Almost ten hours? That's some kind of record, surely.

Josh presses the call button for the elevator. After this morning, I'm always going to think twice before getting in one of these things again. Thankfully, I don't think there's much chance of me having to climb the cables on this one. The doors slide quietly open a moment later. Inside, the carriage is burgundy, with gold highlights. It's nicer than most places I've slept in. We step inside, and he hits the button for our floor. The doors close effortlessly, and we begin the ascent.

He turns to me. "Look, I've been thinking. When all this is over—and assuming we're still alive—how about I help you get a new life? One where you truly are free."

I raise an eyebrow. "You... you would do that for me?"

He shrugs. "Sure, if it's what you want. I mean, you tried it before."

"Yeah... and look how that turned out."

"I know the last few months have given new meaning to the phrase *having a rough time*, but for the two years before that, you were happy, right?"

I nod slowly as I feel myself inundated with memories from my life in Devil's Spring. Owning my bar, being a part of the town... running with Styx each morning... waking up next to Tori...

I feel his hand on my shoulder and snap out of my reminiscing.

"With the resources I have at my disposal, both at Globa-Tech and within the government, you can be whoever you want to be, wherever you want to be. I can even get you some plastic surgery."

I smile. "I might feel old sometimes, but I'm not ready for Botox just yet, Josh."

He rolls his eyes. "Not for vanity, you idiot. I mean to help give you a fresh start. We could remove those scars on your cheeks. Maybe adjust the shape of your nose a little. You'd look totally different."

"I, ah... I dunno, man. I appreciate you offering, but let me think about it. A new life is one thing, but a new face is something else."

"I know. Just a suggestion."

We slow to a stop, and the doors open on our floor. I can only assume that every floor looks like ours—as luxurious as a palace and as clean as a damn hospital. The walls are cream, with a wooden trim halfway up. The carpet is immaculate and feels as if we're walking on pillows. There are only a handful of rooms on each floor, simply because they're so big. I don't feel comfortable in places like this, but a part of me can't help wondering what my life would've been like if I'd spent my days staying in hotels like this, using the fortune I amassed from killing to enjoy myself a little, instead of staying in no-name, flea-ridden motels and drinking in dive bars.

Nah, I probably wouldn't have enjoyed myself. I'm a simple creature.

We head right and stop outside the first door on the left. Josh opens it with the keycard, and we step inside. There's—

Hang on.

The shower's running.

I put my hand on Josh's arm. He looks at me, and I put a finger to my lips. I point to the closed bathroom door and then signal for him to move over to the far corner, next to the bed nearest the window. From there, he'll have a clear view of whoever's in there once they come out.

He moves quickly and quietly across the room, draws his gun, and crouches in position. I take out my own weapon and edge forward, keeping my finger resting lightly on the trigger. I make my way along the near wall, past the desk, toward the bathroom door.

I freeze as the water stops. I hear movement. I glance over at Josh. He nods, signaling he's ready. With us on opposite sides of the suite, we can't both be targets, which gives us an advantage. I continue slowly toward the—

The door opens.

A figure appears, wearing a short towel and dripping water on the carpet.

I lower my weapon and frown. "What the hell are *you* doing here?"

Ruby DeSouza smiles at me. "Hey, baby. Miss me?"

24

I shake my head slowly. "But I thought you—"

"Was pissed with you? Yeah, I am." Her bright red lips curl into a fiendishly familiar grin. Then, in a flash of movement, her hand disappears beneath the towel, only to reappear almost instantly holding a gun. She snaps it to me, her aim unwavering. Her smile fades, and an expression of pure anger replaces it. "You abandoned me, you selfish, stubborn, egotistical... asshole!"

No one moves. No one says anything. The scene is frozen, locked in a bizarre stand-off. With my gun at my side, I alternate my gaze between Ruby's eyes and the barrel of her weapon—which looks like a Glock from here. I honestly can't decide if she's going to shoot me or not.

Across from us, Josh looks confused. He's slowly raising and lowering his arm, seemingly unsure if he should aim it at her or not. After a few moments, he tucks it behind him and walks over to us. He stands between us and eyes Ruby up and down, then turns to me.

"She seems to know you pretty well," he says.

I glance at him. "Stop sucking up just because she's armed and angry."

He steps away, and my eyes meet hers once again. Neither of us speak. I see a flicker of movement just below my eye line. I adjust my gaze to see Ruby's towel slowly unravelling from around her. She frowns and looks down at the exact moment it slips to the floor. She's completely naked, save for a small holster strapped to her thigh. She looks at me with a bemused smile and raises an eyebrow.

I roll my eyes and sigh. "Oh, for God's sake..."

Josh quickly turns his back to her. "Whoa! Okay, you're... ah... you're... wow, yeah. That's... that's pretty naked."

She stares at Josh. "What's the matter, Cowboy? Been a while?"

I fail to suppress a chuckle. "Oh, I can't believe she went there..."

Josh glances over his shoulder, as if he's trying to look at her without looking at too much of her. "What? No! I just... I don't know you. It's not appropriate to see, well, everything."

She looks at me, feigning surprise. "Well, what a gentleman! Why aren't you like that, Adrian?"

Okay, I think the danger's past.

I crouch to retrieve her towel and then rest it over her outstretched arm, covering the gun. "Because I've seen it all way too many times before. Now put some clothes on and sit down, will you?"

I walk over to the sofa, hoping to God I'm right about this and she doesn't shoot me in the back...

I sit down and breathe a quiet sigh of relief. A moment later, Josh appears and sits next to me, staring blankly ahead. Another minute or two passes, then Ruby walks into view wearing her towel and sits across from us. She rests her gun beside her and ceremoniously crosses her legs, bouncing her foot up and down over her knee.

Josh looks at her. "So, you're Ruby, I'm guessing?"

She nods. "Guilty."

"I've heard a lot about you. And now I've seen a fair bit too..."

She laughs. "You do a great *awkward Englishman* thing. Very Hugh Grant."

He frowns. "Thanks. I think."

I clear my throat. "Ruby, what are you doing here? When we spoke on the phone, you... well, you insulted me."

She nods. "Yes, I did."

"A *lot*."

She nods again. "Yeah, and it was no less than you deserve. Seriously, Adrian, how could you leave me like that?"

I shrug and let out a long sigh. "I dunno. I thought I was doing the right thing. I didn't want you getting dragged down with me if it all went wrong. I figured—"

"Well, you figured wrong, you sonofabitch. Everything we went through to get there, and you didn't think I deserved to see it through to the end alongside you? We went through Hell to get to Cunningham. We both fought, we both bled, and we both risked everything. How dare you take that away from me? What gave you the right?"

I stare into her eyes, trying to hide the guilt in my own. I see a whole range of emotions burning beneath the emerald surface—anger, sadness, disappointment...

"I didn't realize, Ruby. I'm sorry. I was trying to protect you."

She scoffs. "Do I look like I need to be protected? You know me better than that, asshole."

I hold my hands up. "Okay, fair enough. I messed up. Did you at least get your money?"

She's quiet for a moment and then nods once. "Yeah, I got it." Another slight pause. "Thanks."

"You earned it."

"I know." She sighs, leans back, and brings her legs up, tucking them under her and readjusting her towel. "So, how are you not dead? Your execution was well publicized. How did you do it?" She smirks. "Friendly with the new pres'?"

I hold her gaze, allowing her to see into my eyes, so she knows I'm telling the truth. "The Order of Sabbah recruited me. They're real, and they faked my death in exchange for me working for them."

She sits forward, her eyes wide with shock. "No way! Seriously?"

I nod. "Yeah."

"You're shitting me?"

"Sadly not."

She leans back, shaking her head. "Cool."

"No, Ruby. Not cool. That's why we're here. They're planning something. We're still trying to figure out what, but they're a large and dangerous adversary. They actually sent me to kill Josh."

"Oh my God!" She looks over at him. "So, how come you're still alive?"

He smiles faintly. I roll my eyes. "Because I was never *actually* going to kill him. I... *we* want to stop them, but they're too big for us to do it alone."

"So, you're asking for my help?"

I nod.

"Am I the only person you've asked?"

"Well, you're the only person I called, yeah. We placed an ad on the dark web too, apparently."

"Huh, makes sense. Lots of merc-for-hire forums on there."

I frown. "Wait, you've heard of all that stuff?"

She shrugs and looks at me blankly. "Yeah, of course. Haven't you?"

I shake my head. "Not until a couple of hours ago."

"You're such a caveman sometimes."

Josh tries to suppress a chuckle beside me but fails. I shoot him a glance, but it doesn't stop him from smiling.

"Has anyone responded yet?" she asks.

I shake my head. "Not yet. So far, it's just you who's crazy enough to track us down. How did you find us, by the way?"

She waves her hand dismissively. "I just got my guy to run a trace on your cell number."

I look sheepishly at Josh, who's shaking his head at me with a disapproving look on his face.

I know, I know... I never learn.

I shrug. "Whoops."

She gets to her feet and pads over to us. She turns to Josh, bends down suddenly, and kisses him on the lips. His eyes snap wide with surprise, and he holds his hands up, presumably to make sure they don't wander anywhere that might get him shot.

I raise an eyebrow. I'm not sure if I should turn away.

She stands straight and winks at him. "I *love* Hugh Grant. Just saying." She steps to the side, moving directly in front of me. "And you..." She raises her leg and places her foot on my chest, pushing me back hard against the sofa. "If you ever abandon me again or patronize me by thinking I need to be saved like some damsel in distress, I swear to all that is holy in this world, I will shoot your balls off. Are we clear?"

I look up, keeping eye contact with her. God help me, if I looked ahead, I'd see everything from this angle. Again.

I nod. "Crystal."

She puts her leg down. "Good. Now I'm gonna go finish getting ready. Then you boys can tell me all about the shit you've gotten yourselves into this time."

She whips her towel off and starts drying her hair with it. She waits a moment, standing casually, seemingly oblivious to the fact that she's naked, then disappears back into the bathroom.

Once we hear the door close, Josh turns to me and nods. "I like her."

25

23:19 PDT

It didn't take much to convince Ruby to help us. Between us, we've brought her up to speed on everything we've found out about The Order and everything that's happened since I spoke to Josh on a mountaintop nearly seventy-two hours ago. She was initially fascinated by The Order, which is understandable, but the moment I told her what happened to Lily and Kaitlyn's neighbor, she hugged me and said she was with us, no questions asked.

That's why I like her. The apparent obsession with nudity I can take or leave, but her unwavering sense of right or wrong is what makes her invaluable to me, especially now. I know I can trust her. We've been in the trenches together before, so to speak, and when it came down to it, she had my back. People like her are far too rare nowadays.

Ruby's sipping a drink she made herself from the mini-bar. She raises her eyebrows and sighs. "Well, you two sure know how to have a good time, don't you? Seriously, could you be any more screwed right now?"

I smile. "I'm sure we'd find a way if we put our minds to it."

"So, your plan is to... what? Go to Rome and kill this karma guy?"

Josh frowns. "You mean *camerlengo*?"

"Whatever," she replies, shrugging.

"Yes, that's the idea," I say. "If he's running The Order, we just cut the head off the snake. Simple."

She places her drink down gently on the table and looks at each of us in turn. "Adrian, nothing you do is ever simple. How many assassins does The Order have tracking you right now?"

"Ah... almost four thousand."

"Right. And how, exactly, do you intend to leave the country without at least one of them noticing?"

"Well, we're working on that. It's top of our to-do list tomorrow. But I need—"

"You need to get your ass to Rome. Right now."

I look at Josh, who shrugs. "She might be onto something, man. Maybe it *would* be easier to do it in the middle of the night?"

I shake my head. "Nah. If I were chasing me, I'd expect me to try sneaking out when it's dark. It's too obvious."

Ruby leans forward. "Yeah, but—and I can't believe I'm about to say this—you have to consider the fact that all those people might not actually be as good as you are."

I can't fight the grin creeping onto my face. I turn to Josh and nudge his arm with my cast. "See? I told you I'm the best."

He hangs his head for a moment, then looks at Ruby. "Now look what you've done..."

She holds her hands up. "Well, I'm sorry, but it's a fair point."

I nudge him again. "Yeah, Josh, it's a fair point."

He sighs. "Shut up."

"The thing I'm getting at, boys, is just because it's The Order of Sabbah—the big, scary secret society of myth and legend—don't make the mistake of giving them more credit than they deserve. All jokes aside, few people would argue you're the best in the business, Adrian. And few would disagree that I'm right up there with you."

I nod. "True."

"So, stop thinking how *you* would and start thinking how *they* would."

Josh gets to his feet and paces slowly back and forth, then turns to face us both. "Ruby's right. Think about it. Everything that went down at Sterling's offices wasn't precision. It was desperation. Martinez will obviously know what's happening by now. He's down one Committee member and however many hired guns. The single biggest threat to his organization has, so far, managed to thwart any attempt to silence him. He's panicking."

I don't say anything. My mind's already ticking over, formulating moves and contingencies.

"You said it yourself yesterday," he continues. "Horizon's running out of ideas, especially now that Pierce isn't around to do his legwork. He hasn't got the resources to stop you himself. That's why The Order has sent everybody they have, instead of just leaving it to him. I thought you were underestimating them, but maybe you weren't. Maybe Ruby's right, and this fight isn't as one-sided as we think."

I stay silent.

He might have a point. Maybe I *was* right to dismiss Horizon's threats yesterday. Sure, The Order has the numbers, but quantity doesn't mean quality. We survived Seattle, which is more than most people would've done. Maybe it's time to stop being so cautious. Maybe we should stop assuming we should be on defense and start trying some offense.

What do we know?

The Order has lost people. I've seen no sign of them tracking me in the last twelve hours. They're acting desperate. But is that all it is? An act? Despite their efforts to stop me, they'll still be focusing on their own agenda. Killing Josh will likely be tied in with killing me now, but there's still their endgame to consider. We don't know what it is and, consequently, don't know how to stop it. All we know for sure is that it's imperative we get to Rome and take out the camerlengo as quickly as possible before they can execute their game plan.

That being said, do we even have enough time to get to Italy? And if we do, how am I even going to get anywhere near the Vatican to take out Martinez?

...

...

...

That's it!

The inside of my head has been filled with noise and chaos, clouding my judgment. I was asking myself all those questions without giving myself the chance to work out the answers. But as I focused, I heard Ruby's voice repeating something she said earlier. Something important. But I didn't realize how important until right now.

Stop thinking like me and start thinking like them.

I get to my feet. "Josh, get on the phone to whoever works your magic at GlobaTech and arrange a flight from Vancouver to Rome, as soon as humanly possible."

He immediately reaches for his cell but hesitates before dialing. "Ah, Adrian... Schultz said to leave GlobaTech out of it."

I nod. "I know, but Schultz isn't here. And even if he were, do you know what I'd say to him?"

He thinks for a moment and then sighs. "You'd say he could kiss your ass."

I nod again. "I'd say he could kiss my ass."

Ruby gets to her feet and stands with us. "As exciting as this has suddenly become, do you actually have a plan here? What are you thinking?"

I look at her. "I'm thinking you were right. Fuck The Order. Let them come after us. They won't stop me from taking out the camerlengo, which is all that matters."

"So, you know how you're going to get to him?"

"I do. You see, there's no way I'll actually get to him. Not inside the Vatican."

She rolls her hand, urging me on. "But..."

"But I don't need to get to him. As luck would have it, I've had the means to kill the guy all along." I point to Josh. "And it's in his secure vault."

He stares at me blankly.

I'll give him a moment to work it out.

...

...

...

He slaps his palm against his forehead. "The Holy Trinity!"

I nod.

Ruby's eyes grow wide. "Hold up. You don't mean *the* Holy Trinity? The set of three rifles... rarer than Venus de Milo's arms... technically superior to any other weapon in its class and more expensive than the Hope diamond... that Holy Trinity?"

I smile at her. "One and the same. I had number three, but Josh confiscated it. If we can get that into Rome, I don't need to get anywhere near Martinez. I could shoot him from wherever I wanted."

"Oh my God! This just keeps getting more and more exciting! Can I see it? Can I touch it?"

I raise an eyebrow. "Please tell me you're still talking about the gun?"

She punches my arm.

Josh taps in a number on the screen of his phone. "I'll arrange for it to be couriered to Rome. It'll be waiting for us when we arrive."

I clap my hands together. "Excellent. Pack your bags, boys and girls. We're going to Italy."

26

June 9, 2017 — 13:12 CEST

I'm sitting at a table outside a café overlooking the River Tiber. The breeze is warm and pleasant. The sun is bright and hot, reflecting off the still surface of the water as it flows lazily under the bridge across the street.

We landed about three hours ago. We had no issues making it to the airport in Vancouver. As always, Josh had arranged a private plane for us. Despite it belonging to GlobaTech, we all checked it over ourselves to make sure there were no surprises. Having found myself in the unenviable position of either jumping or being pushed out of an airplane twice in the last couple of months, I'm in no rush to do it again. Consequently, I insisted on us all taking an extra few minutes to ensure there were no bombs attached to it.

The flight was smooth and uneventful. We all caught some sleep. Between us, we tried to piece together some more of the puzzle, although we're still clueless as to what The Order is working toward. We just need to focus on what we're here to do and hope we can put the camerlengo down before it's too late.

Straight ahead of me, on the other side of the bridge, is the Piazza dei Tribunali, home of Italy's Supreme Court. I stare at it, allowing myself a quiet moment of reflection as I take in the stunning European architecture.

...

...

...

And then I snap back to my shitty reality and look left, following the road. It heads west, disappearing behind the trees that line the street over there. But I don't need to see it to know where it leads. A little over a mile and a half that way lies Vatican City. The belly of the beast.

I take a deep breath. This isn't going to be easy.

An irritating noise registers in my head, distracting me from my musings. I look over at Ruby, who's sitting beside me, cradling her drink in her hands. It's some weird iced coffee, and she's sucking it loudly through a straw.

"Are you enjoying that?"

She turns to me and nods. "Yeah."

"It certainly sounds like it."

She tips the straw toward me, seemingly oblivious to my comment. "Want some?"

I hold up a hand. "I'm good, thanks. I dunno how you can drink cold coffee..."

She sighs. "Oh, don't start."

"What?"

"Complaining about shit. You were just the same when we went into that Dunkin' Donuts. Everything was weird or wrong... Stop being such a whiny little bitch all the time."

I raise an eyebrow. "What's gotten into you? You seem touchier than usual."

She takes another long suck on the straw and then places the drink beside her. "I'm just... I was thinking about how it was before, when we were taking the fight to the bad guys. We were on the move. We were invisible. We were ruthless. I guess I just envisioned it being much the same this time, and it's frustrating that we're just sitting here, hoping no one tries to kill us."

I'm surprised by how much sentiment she holds for me, in her own unique way. It reminds me just how much of her personality is part of the act. Part of the character she portrays when she's doing her job. I remember seeing her vulnerable, more human side and thinking there was no need for her to pretend she was anything other than who she was. But I suppose this life is easier to lead when you take yourself out of the job. A conscience will get you killed. She'll use *Ruby the Crazy Killer* to separate herself from what we do.

I know because I do the same thing.

I lean over and gently nudge her arm with mine. "I know how you feel, but this isn't a normal fight. We'd be foolish to approach it in the normal way. It's hard to rush headlong into something when you don't know which direction to go."

Her expression softens and she smiles. "Since when did you become smart and patient?"

I smile back. "About three weeks ago."

She holds my gaze. For the first time since I met her, she looks exposed and defenseless. It's strange to see her like that, but it's also nice to know she can be normal.

I frown questioningly. "What?"

She shakes her head. "Nothing. Just admiring."

"Ha! Don't tell Josh. I think he likes you."

She rolls her eyes. "Not like that, you idiot. I mean, after what we went through together and what you went through afterward... seeing you here now, dealing with this the way you are... I'm proud of you."

I fight to stop my cheeks from flushing. I never would have pegged her as the complimentary type.

I look away. "Thanks. Now quit being nice to me. It's weird."

She laughs. "You got it, asshole."

As we share a rare moment of escapism from the shit-storm that is our lives, I see Josh making his way across the bridge toward us. He's been at our hotel, waiting for his people to deliver the Holy Trinity rifle and some other goodies from his compound. He's carrying a paper bag in one hand.

We both get to our feet as he crosses the street and stops beside our table.

"How did it go?" I ask.

He nods a quick greeting to each of us. "All good. Every-thing arrived without any problems. I think we're good to go." He rests the bag down on our table. "Presents for you both."

Ruby looks inside, and a smile creeps across her face. "Hugh Grant, you sexy man!"

She reaches in and takes out a gun, which she quickly tucks at her back. I move over and take out another. I quickly look it over before doing the same. They're both Berettas—the latest M9A3 model.

I look at Josh. "Thanks, man. Did they not have any 92s? You know they're my favorite."

He shakes his head. "Sadly not. This latest version of the M9 was the easiest to track down since they're manufac-tured in Italy. A few months ago, the U.S. Army began the phasing out process. They're switching over to the Sig Sauer P320s—which I'm not happy about. GlobaTech bid for that contract, but they actually wanted something more low-tech. Would you believe that? Anyway, it meant they had a large stockpile right here, so it was straightforward enough to borrow from."

"So long as it fires, I'm happy."

"I figured. Oh, I called Schultz again and told him we were here."

"I take it he still won't help us directly?"

He shakes his head. "No, he won't budge. He also reiterated how unhappy he'll be if we make the news back home."

I smile wryly. "I'm pretty sure what we're about to do will make the news everywhere."

"Agreed. But it would be nice if our names and faces stayed out of the headlines, eh?"

Ruby sighs heavily, and we both turn to see her pouting. "This isn't going to be any fun."

Josh frowns. "Were you really expecting this to be *fun*?"

She raises an eyebrow as if that was a silly question. "Are you kidding me? I get to work side-by-side with the most famous assassin on the planet *again* to take down the *actual* Order of Sabbah? What's not to enjoy? It's a once-in-a-life-time job!"

He looks at each of us in turn. "Wow... talk about separated at birth."

We all share a moment of reprieve, laughing like old friends, but it's interrupted by the ringtone of Josh's cell phone. He reaches inside his jacket for it, muttering to himself about getting no peace. However, he falls silent and frowns when he stares at the number on-screen. He answers and places it to his ear.

"Hello?" His expression hardens. After a moment, he holds the phone out between us all and presses the speaker button with his thumb. "Yeah, we're all here."

"Good," says Horizon's voice. "Now, Adrian, I see you've been doing some recruiting of your own. An amusingly futile gesture. Tell me, Miss DeSouza, do you really want to align yourself with this man? You have so much... potential. It would be a shame to see you cut down before you could fully realize it."

Horizon? How the hell did he get Josh's number? And how does he know Ruby is with us? Instinctively, I look around, quickly surveying the light stream of pedestrians around us, but I see nothing suspicious.

Ruby looks at me, silently asking what she should say. I can't tell if she's nervous or starstruck. I just shrug. I'm as taken aback as she is. I wasn't expecting him to make contact again.

She clears her throat. "So, you're the guy who recruited Adrian?"

"I am, although that transpired to not be one of my better decisions. Perhaps I should've considered you. After all, hiding out in an insane asylum between contracts is a stroke of brilliance. With my help, you could have executed it perfectly."

Her eyes grow wide. I stop myself from doing the same thing, despite being so surprised to learn he's had his eyes on her too.

"You've scouted me?" she asks.

"Briefly, yes."

"So, why didn't you approach me?"

He pauses. "Ultimately, you were deemed too amateurish."

She scowls, her mouth open. "Well, fuck you! Me? Amateurish? Why don't you come here and say that, and I'll show you amateurish, you sonofa—"

I put a hand on her arm and shake my head. We can't let him see he's getting to us.

I look at Josh and then at his phone. "What do you want, you old bastard?"

"I just wanted to give you one last chance to quit before you're all laid to rest."

I roll my eyes. "You don't give up, do you? You've lost, asshole. You're so blinded by your own sense of accomplishment that you've lost, and you don't even know it."

He chuckles. "Adrian, please, remember who you're talking to. There isn't anything I don't know or haven't already prepared for. I will admit, I was surprised you made it out of Sterling's offices alive, but it makes no difference. He gave you nothing."

Josh and I exchange a glance. "What makes you think that?"

Horizon chuckles, which sounds a little distorted on the line. "Because I detonated his tracking chip before he could."

I raise an eyebrow. "Wait. That was you? I figured he took the coward's way out and did it himself."

"Grant Sterling was no coward, Adrian. He was a visionary, like everyone else on the Committee. But I had to do what was necessary to preserve The Order, and I couldn't risk you getting anything out of him."

"Hold on a second," says Josh. "Are you saying you decided to blow his head off on your own? You weren't following an order from someone else on the Committee?"

"Yes, I took it upon myself to ensure the safety of our organization. A bold move, I confess, but a prudent one, nevertheless. So, I know you have nothing, Adrian. You're wandering aimlessly through the darkness, waiting to die."

I physically bite my tongue, resisting the urge to prove to

him what we know. Pride can be a bigger killer than I am, sometimes.

"Uh-huh. Well, okay, if that's the case, why don't you tell me your next move? Why don't you tell me what The Order really wants? Let me at least go out knowing how I was beaten."

He laughs. "You're a true warrior, Adrian. I respect that. You know when you've lost, yet you still want to know how. The Order's reach covers the globe, and we seek to solidify our position by finally assuming control of the largest organization on Earth."

"GlobaTech?" asks Josh. "I knew it! Although I wouldn't say we were the largest..."

"No, Mr. Winters, not GlobaTech."

Josh frowns, as if he's unsure how he could've guessed wrong. Ruby's eyes have glazed over a little. She has no idea what she's gotten herself into. I stare blankly at the sidewalk, running through everything we know and everything we've guessed, trying to see the big picture that has so far eluded us. I slow my breathing and close my eyes. I know I have all the answers. I just can't make sense of them...

Ah! Come on, Adrian. *Think*, goddammit!

Horizon wanted me to kill Josh. Sterling told us it was a power play to put someone in Josh's position. He also said The Order was working for God, and we know the camerlengo of the Catholic Church is the leader of The Order. Horizon just said The Order seeks to take control of the largest organization on the planet, and it's not GlobaTech.

Nothing makes sense. I'm missing something. I *have* to be. I can't...

...

...

...

Sonofabitch.

I look at the phone in Josh's hand. "You're going to kill the pope."

He chuckles. "Well done, Adrian. Yes, we intend to remove His Holiness from office."

Josh shakes his head. "But why? I thought The Order was on some sort of mission from God. Surely—"

"We're spreading His word, yes. We're carrying out His will. But to get where we wish to go, we need new direction. Now I have things to attend to. It's a shame you won't be alive long enough to see how all this plays out. I simply called to say goodbye. You have been a most interesting adversary, Adrian Hell."

I clench my jaw tightly, glaring at the device. "Oh, you have no idea, asshole. I'm gonna stop you."

"No, you're not. Every asset across all fifty states has been activated, with the sole purpose of eliminating the three of you. The Committee has authorized the awakening of America. A contract such as this hasn't been issued throughout all our history. You should be honored that you get to die under such... monumental circumstances."

I take a moment to process what he just said. Then I smile. He just made a mistake. Horizon just proved he doesn't know where we are. That means we're a step ahead of him, and I can finally enjoy a conversation with him.

"Wow. Sterling was right. You really *are* out of favor, aren't you?"

There's a moment's silence on the line. "What do you mean?"

I take the phone from Josh and hold it close to my face. "Listen carefully, Number Seven..."

"What?"

The shock in his voice was evident.

"Oh, that's right. I didn't tell you—you killed your own boss for nothing. I don't know what you think you knew, but he told us everything. I have the name of every single asset in The Order. I also know who your illustrious leader is, and I know your Committee was pissed with you long before you blew Sterling's head off—which, by the way, I don't think they're gonna appreciate. See, I already know that I have nearly four thousand of your finest on my ass. Sterling told me they did that because they lost faith in your ability to get the job done. I know you're the Horizon who controls the Middle East. What happens in North America has nothing to do with you. I also know that you're too late. I'm not in America. I'm in Rome."

I pause a moment to let that sink in.

"I'll admit, I didn't know what you were planning, but now I do. Thanks for that. So, you go and attend to whatever you've got going on. I'm going to kill your boss."

I smile to myself. Man, that felt good. I hate not being the smartest player in the game, and that bastard has been three steps ahead of me since day one. Finally, I have the advantage, and this was the perfect time to antagonize him and really throw him off his game.

Josh and Ruby look at each other. For the first time since I dragged him into this mess, I see genuine hope in his eyes. He knows we have the upper hand now, just as I do.

Ruby will be happy. It's about to get fun.

"Adrian, I... I don't know what to say."

"I don't care. I'll be seeing you, asshole."

I go to hang up, but Horizon starts laughing on the line, and I stop myself. I raise an eyebrow. "Something funny?"

"Yes."

"Care to share?"

"I'm laughing at your little speech. Was that your trademark attempt at pissing me off, so I'll make a mistake? Please. I know you're in Rome. I know you've seen Sterling's spreadsheet. I know you know I'm not the only Horizon. Tell me, did you see how many there are?"

I close my eyes for a second. I don't like where this is going...

"Yeah."

"You're correct in saying I oversee the Middle East. My counterpart in the United States has already informed me that you flew out of Vancouver yesterday. Do you really think our assassins can't leave their territories?"

"Whatever. They won't get here in time to stop me."

"Adrian, they don't need to."

My eyes snap wide. My arm drops to my side, and the phone slips from my grasp. Everything is falling into place. Everything makes sense now. I turn a slow circle, scanning the streets and the buildings. We're all standing on a corner. The sidewalks aren't too busy, and there's only light traffic on the roads. Ahead of us is wide open. The bridge that crosses the river leads to large, tall buildings.

We're sitting ducks.

Then I hear it. It's barely audible, but the sound of a single gunshot is unmistakable.

Oh, no...

I turn back to face Josh and Ruby. They're both staring at me. I can see in their eyes that they haven't yet realized what I have.

That we've lost.

I look at each of them in turn. "I'm sorry. I never—"

The words catch in my throat as my world turns black.

27

13:37 CEST

I take a deep, desperate breath. My face is warm and wet. I wipe my eyes and open them, blinking fast to remove the last droplets of blood from my eyelashes. The first thing I see is Ruby, standing motionless in front of me. Her eyes are wide, and her face is a dark crimson mask.

No...

Time stops. I catch my breath.

No...

She reaches out to me and puts her hand on my arm. "Adrian..."

Her voice sounds a thousand miles away.

I turn to Josh. He, too, is standing still, staring at me through unblinking eyes. His features are hidden behind a thick layer of blood.

I don't feel anything. No pain. No emotion.

Is this what death feels like? Is this what death *is*? Stuck forever in your final moment, trapped in purgatory as you watch the people around you stare at your corpse, covered in your blood?

Except... I'm breathing. My brain's telling me my chest is moving in and out as my lungs fill with oxygen. I can sense the movement.

So, am I dead or not? I don't understand what's happening. I heard the gunshot. I have to be.

I try to turn my head, but it feels heavy, as if I'm trying to roll a concrete block back and forth on my neck. I settle for moving my eyes and rest my gaze on Ruby again. She's staggering backward, her arm still outstretched, her eyes still wide.

"Adrian..." she whispers.

"R-Ruby?"

She stands still. I shift my eyes left and look at Josh. He's exactly the same. His gaze is fixed on me, unblinking, glazed with shock.

"J-Josh?"

He doesn't react.

It's hard to frown. All the muscles I need to do it are refusing to work. I look him up and down.

"Josh?"

Then I see it. On his face, beneath the blood. A dark spot in the center of his forehead.

Is that a hole?

No.

No, it can't be...

No!

His body falls backward in slow motion and lands with a dull thud on the sidewalk. His head lolls to the side. Blood seeps from the bullet hole above his eyes, quickly staining the ground around him. His arm falls lifelessly over the curb, and I hear a faint crack as his knuckles smack against the road.

"Josh!"

I sink to my knees as I stare at the dead body sprawled before me. The empty vessel that once belonged to my closest friend. I clutch at my chest, which feels as if it's locked in a vise. I can't breathe. I feel drunk with anger. I feel myself fading in and out of consciousness. My eyes are heavy with anguish. My brain is fighting to shut down, to protect me from the agony. My jaw hurts from clenching so tight, I fear my teeth will shatter. Each breath out is an increasingly louder growl—a guttural, primal vent of emotion. Finally, I lean back on my haunches and allow my head to roll back. I stare up at the bright, cloudless blue sky and scream until my lungs burn.

I feel a hand on my shoulder and snap my head around to see Ruby standing over me. "Adrian, we have to go!"

I shake my head slowly. "No. No more running. I'm done. It's over. All that matters now is making sure each and every one of those bastards turns cold, and I don't care if I have to tear this fucking world to the ground to do it."

"I know, and I'm going to help you, but we need to leave. They're everywhere!"

Huh?

The hollow, distant noises suddenly rush to the forefront. I notice the people screaming around me first. Then I hear tires screeching. I quickly look along the street. The corner nearest to me is part of an intersection. Both directions leading away from me are blocked by cars parked at a hurried angle. The doors are open, and men are walking toward us. They fan out into a wide semi-circle, holding guns by their side, watching me. Instinctively, I count them, noting the positioning. Eight guys, all roughly six feet apart, slowly closing in on us, trapping us against the café.

How could I have been so stupid? So blind? I've underestimated The Order from the beginning, and now Josh has paid the ultimate price for my mistake.

I look at the men again. Eight of The Order's finest. Eight of the best assassins the world has to offer. I'm guessing the sniper's moved now. He would've needed to be across the bridge to make the shot. Maybe even on the roof of the Supreme Court building opposite. He couldn't have been too far away, because the exit wound on Josh's head was small, which means it was a low-caliber bullet. Therefore, the shot had to have been fired from no farther than a few hundred yards. With so many of them surrounding us now, there's no need for the sniper to hang around and risk being seen.

But I'll find him. I promise. I'll find the guy who killed Josh, and when I do, it'll make what I did to Pierce look like a fucking back massage.

I slowly get to my feet.

I glance to my left and see the last of the innocent locals fleeing out of sight, leaving the street free for me to turn it red.

I blink, pausing for a few moments in between. In that short time, I see not only the scene before me in my head but also how events are about to transpire. The wide arc of soon-to-be deceased killers is roughly fifteen feet away, curving across the middle of the street. Through the gap between the two guys on the far right, I have line of sight to one of their cars. More importantly, I have line of sight to the cap of the fuel tank.

I need five shots. Ruby will need four.

She's standing beside me. Her body is tense, with what I imagine is a cocktail of adrenaline and fear coursing through her veins. I lean my head slightly toward her; the movement is barely noticeable.

"Follow my lead," I whisper through still lips.

The world around me slows almost to a stop. I instinctively raise my cast like a shield as I move my good hand behind me, reaching for the M9. Everything feels like an out of body experience, as if I'm looking on from afar, watching myself move with a practiced, lethal grace. My movements don't feel like my own. I'm on autopilot, allowing my subconscious full, deadly freedom.

I've got you, man. I've got you.

When the world stops making sense, you have to find the one thing inside you that still does and hold onto it with everything you have. It's the only way to survive.

I breathe slowly, almost meditatively, as I feel my hand wrap around the butt of the gun at my back. I watch the men in front of me react. They're fast but not fast enough. Their mistake was having their weapons by their sides when they approached me. Instead of simply squeezing the trigger, they have to lift the guns and aim first, which will take way too long.

I whip my arm out straight and fire off the first round. It covers the distance between me and the car almost instantly, penetrates the thin bodywork, and buries itself into the gas tank.

The explosion is sudden and deafening. The heat instantly rushes toward me, scorching the air around me. The vehicle is engulfed in flames within seconds. The smell of burning fuel is strong and strangely pleasant. The blackened carcass is pushed into the air. It flips over, landing on the hood of the other car.

The men all react the same way—by ducking and

bringing a hand up in a natural but ultimately futile attempt to protect themselves from the heat of the blast.

I don't waste any time.

I move my arm slightly and fire three more rounds, starting at the right of the semi-circle and working my way back along it toward Ruby. Each bullet finds its mark, punching into the skulls of each man with violent accuracy, sending them sprawling to the ground.

The fourth guy is standing at more of an angle, so I adjust my aim slightly and put a bullet in his chest, directly into his heart. He joins his friends a split-second later.

Five shots.

The sound of deliberate and precise gunfire stops a moment after I finish shooting. I look next to me and see the last of the eight men—and the last of Ruby's four targets—landing awkwardly on the road.

I turn to her. "You okay?"

She nods hurriedly. "Yeah, I am. Now let's get out of here before more of those assholes show up."

She starts running toward the bridge, veering right to gives the flaming wreck of the vehicle a wide berth. I start to follow her but stop when I draw level with Josh's body. I look down at him for a moment, then tuck my gun away at my back and kneel beside him. His lifeless eyes are looking away from me.

This... this doesn't seem real. It's Josh. He can't be dead. I mean, look at the guy—he's like Peter Pan. He's older than me, yet he looks exactly the same as he did twenty years ago. I don't understand. My brain can't make sense of it.

He can't be dead.

I stare at him. "This wasn't how it was supposed to happen. You were the one who lived, Josh. You were the one who always survived. I was supposed to be the one who dies... the one who goes out in a blaze of glory and divine retribution. It's what I deserve after the life I've led. That was always how it was supposed to be."

I sniff back a sudden wave of emotion.

"What am I going to do now, huh? Look what happened when I was without you for six weeks. I caused *this* shit! And I ended up in therapy. Jesus, Josh, you have to wake up. I need you."

He doesn't move.

"Damn it, Josh, quit screwing around and wake up!"

I slam my fist down hard on his chest. Once, twice... desperately trying to force some life back into him.

"Wake up, you selfish bastard! You can't do this to me! You're too smart to get taken out by a fucking bullet. Figure something out, like you always do. Come on!"

I hit his chest again, then my shoulders involuntarily slump forward in defeat. I stare blankly at my best friend as he lies motionless before me.

I shake my head. "I'm sorry, man. I'm sorry."

I sense movement next to me. I look up to see Ruby standing there, keeping a respectful distance but presumably trying to decide when she should tell me how important it is that we're no longer here.

I nod to her. "I know. Just gimme a sec."

I quickly pat Josh down, taking his cell phone, his wallet, and his keys from his pockets.

"Jesus, Adrian," says Ruby. "You're *robbing* him?"

I smile, which loosens the single tear from the corner of my eye, allowing it to roll freely down my cheek. "I don't think he'd mind. I need the phone, so I can call the president. I need his wallet because it has the keycard for the hotel room inside it, and the keys are for the rental car he would've parked over the bridge."

She doesn't say anything. She just takes a step back, giving me more space.

I reach over him and use my finger and thumb to gently close his eyes. "I'll see you soon, brother."

I get to my feet and look Ruby in the eyes. I don't say anything. I don't need to.

After a moment, she simply nods. "I know."

We set off running toward the bridge. We quickly cross over the Tiber and stop on the other side, facing the Piazza dei Tribunali. I glance left and right, trying to spot which car would be ours, but I see nothing that was obviously chosen by Josh. I hold the keys up, press the button on the fob, and see lights flash on a gray sedan across the street.

"Let's go." I toss Ruby the keys. "You can drive."

Within a few moments, we're on the move, heading east along the banks of the river, toward our hotel. We need to put some distance between us and the massacre back there. We need to lie low, so I can figure out our next move.

And I need to call the president and tell him about Josh.

I don't know how—

"Shit!"

A car just plowed into the side of us, appearing at speed from our left as we drew level with another bridge.

Ruby wrestles with the wheel as we spin counterclockwise, sliding us to a stop, facing the opposite way. Directly in front of us is another car, jet-black with a chrome fender. The passenger door opens, and the torso of a man wearing sunglasses appears. He rests his arm in the crook of the door and takes aim with the gun in his hand.

I'm already reaching for mine. "Ruby, get us out of here!"

Bullets start pinging off the hood as she stamps hard on the gas. We surge forward and head past the car, down the road it came from. As we draw level, I fire a few rounds in quick succession. I don't know if I clipped the guy, but it at least gave him something to think about.

I look ahead as we pass through a small plaza with grass on either side. Ruby's concentrating as she navigates the traffic that's coming toward us.

I glance over at her. "This is a one-way street, Ruby."

"I know..."

"And we're going the wrong way."

"I know! Will you quit complaining and start shooting those assholes behind us?"

I look over my shoulder, out the rear window. I see the black car following us and gaining fast.

The car lurches left, then right, then left again as we weave at speed through the stream of oncoming vehicles.

The tires screech as Ruby slams the brakes on and drifts right, onto another road. I reach across and grab the handle above the window with my left hand. "Holy shit, Ruby! Where did you learn to drive?"

"You can have lessons? Since when?"

I look over at her. "Are you kidding me right now?"

She straightens us up and hits the gas again, continuing to move in and out of the traffic. "Yes, I'm kidding, but no, I don't have a license."

"Then how the hell do you know how to drive?"

"Honestly? I watched a lot of *Miami Vice* when I was young."

I close my eyes with disbelief. "*Miami Vice*... fuck me." I stare ahead again. "Ruby, this is *another* one-way street!"

"Well, I don't know where I'm going! Quit shouting at me and keep us alive!"

"*You* keep us alive! You're driving!"

She slams the brakes on again and fishtails between two cars.

I chance a look behind us and see the car is keeping pace. Sitting on the right, it's hard to shoot comfortably with my left hand. I shuffle in my seat and twist my body, so my left arm is resting on the back of it. I wait until the car is directly behind us and then open fire. The first bullet shatters our rear window. The next three punch into their hood and grill but do little to slow them down.

The hammer smacks down on an empty chamber.

"Shit. I'm out. Ruby, I need your gun."

Without a word, she leans forward, and I reach behind her to pull it from her back.

"Try to keep us steady."

I line up my shot again and fire two more rounds. Both go through their windshield, hitting the driver in the chest. The car lurches one way and then the other before smashing into another vehicle traveling the opposite way. The impact lifts it off the ground. It flips sideways, rolling over once... twice, before stopping on its roof.

I shift back around in my seat. "I think we're clear."

Ruby slows us down, and we turn left onto a road where we're traveling in the right direction. "Thank God for that. Nice shooting."

"Yeah, thanks."

I stare silently ahead, still trying to make sense of what's happening. We're coming up to a large traffic circle with a stone fountain in the middle, surrounded by patches of grass. As she heads right, Ruby's forced to slam the brakes on again. Three more cars slide to a halt—one in front of us, one to our left, and one from behind. They have all stopped side-on to us, trapping us in.

We look at each other. "Shit!"

28

The doors to the car in front fly open. Men pile out, raising their automatic rifles. I can only imagine the same thing is happening behind us.

"Look out!"

I reach over and put my hand on Ruby's arm, pushing her down as I lean forward, using the dash for protection. A split-second later, the firing starts. The staccato roar of a dozen rifles spitting hundreds of bullets fills the air, accompanied moments later by the rapid thudding as they riddle our car. Glass smashes all around us, showering us with thousands of tiny shards.

"What do we do?" shouts Ruby.

A good question. Frankly, it deserves a better answer than the one I'm about to give.

"Punch it!"

"What?"

"The gas—punch it, now!"

Staying low, she grips the wheel and steps hard on the pedal. She keeps us as straight as she can as we surge forward. A few seconds pass, which feel like days, before we collide head-on with the front of the car facing us. The sound of metal crushing against metal drowns out the gunfire. The impact sends us lurching forward, slamming me into the dash. My shoulder takes the brunt of it, but Ruby goes head-first into the wheel. Almost immediately, a thin trickle of blood appears down the side of her face.

I put my hand on her arm. "Are you okay?"

She nods silently.

Good enough.

I bolt upright and quickly aim Ruby's gun out of the shattered windshield. I fire two rounds at the first two men I see, who are both standing, startled, on the left side of their car. The bullets find their mark, and they both slump life-lessly to the ground.

"Let's go."

We climb hurriedly out of the sedan. Ruby ducks low as she retrieves the guns from the two guys I just shot. I drop to one knee and fire a couple more rounds off, hitting the two remaining men standing to the right.

Holding both rifles, Ruby jumps feet-first and slides awkwardly over the crumpled remains of both hoods, landing in a crouch beside me. I tuck her gun at my back as she hands me one of the newly acquired weapons. We have some cover on this side of the cars, but it won't last long.

I look at her. "On three?"

She nods back. "Three!"

We turn and pop up, quickly bringing the rifles up to rest on the roof of what remains of our rental car. Behind us,

I see the other two vehicles. The first is parked at an angle, blocking the way we came. Three men and a woman are surrounding it, intermittently shooting at us. I vaguely recognize one of the men, but I can't recall where from. I suppose, with so many assassins chasing us, it was inevitable that I might know at least one of them.

To the right of them, the second car is fully side-on to us and came from the opposite direction to where we are now. Again, it's surrounded by four people, all taking turns squeezing off controlled bursts of automatic gunfire at us.

Without needing to talk, we do what we do best. I aim at the car farthest to the left and spray the area with bullets. I'm not trying to be accurate. I don't have the time to pick them off. I just want them to quit firing at me for a minute, so I can get the hell out of here.

Ruby does the same to the other vehicle. They soon stop, ducking behind their cars for cover. We both keep firing until the hammers thump down on empty chambers.

"We're done here. Follow me."

I discard the rifle and set off running away from the fountain. I slide to a stop behind the small arc of cars parked around the circumference. I glance behind me and see Ruby stooping to pick up another rifle as she follows me.

The firing resumes as she reaches me. I glance over to the right, looking at the far side of the traffic circle. Cars have been left abandoned, and I'm suddenly aware of the screaming coming from all directions.

"Shit. We're sitting ducks, Ruby. We have to move. There are *way* too many friendlies running around out here."

Ruby checks over her shoulder. "This way."

Keeping low, she starts running away from the fountain, heading along the sidewalk, past a small group of pedestrians huddling together for protection against the wall. I take out the M9 and squeeze off a couple of rounds behind me before following. As I draw level with the small group of scared bystanders, I shout, "You need to move! Go, now!"

I carry on past them without stopping. I don't know if they even understood me, but at least I tried. I catch up with Ruby. "You're moving like you have a plan."

"Nope... just don't like being shot."

We reach the end of the sidewalk, which presents us with an intersection, and we stop to catch our breath.

"Which way?" asks Ruby.

I have no idea where I'm going, so I instinctively draw on the rules that got me this far.

"When in doubt, go right."

"I thought you told me once that if there was ever any doubt, you go left?"

I frown. I did?

I shrug. "Left doesn't feel right. Right does."

"So, what? You just change your rules depending on how you feel at any given moment?"

"I won't tell anyone if you don't."

She rolls her eyes. "Whatever. Come on."

As we head right, I hear gunfire pepper the ground behind me. We cross the street, passing a small restaurant, and head for a rusted gate on the left, between two buildings. It's padlocked shut. I shoot the chain, which falls noisily to the ground, and Ruby pushes it open. We rush down the alley, which is shaded by the buildings on either side. The breeze here is refreshingly cool as we navigate past a couple of large dumpsters and emerge into the open area in the center of the block.

The buildings on our left and ahead of us bar our way.

The fire exits are closed, with no visible handles on the outside, so there's no getting in. The area stretches away to the right, covered by trees. Behind us, I hear renewed screaming, which I'm guessing means our attackers have given chase.

I point right. "Down here."

We run forward, keeping close to the trees, both for shade and cover. Luckily, there's no one around back here. After a couple of hundred yards, the area turns left and leads back out to the street.

We stop, and I gesture to Ruby's rifle. "How many bullets you got there?"

She quickly checks. "Almost a full mag. You?"

I eject the mag of her M9, catch it in the natural cup my cast forms my right palm into, and slam it back in a moment later. "Four rounds."

"What are you thinking?"

"I'm thinking we can't run forever. We need to get back to our hotel. We need to stay focused on stopping The Order. We can't be wasting our time with these assholes."

"So, stand and fight?"

I nod. "Stand and fight."

Ruby moves to the corner that leads back to the street, crouches, and aims back the way we came. I stay on the opposite side, put my back to the building, and aim around the corner of the small alcove, between two trees. We both have a clear view of the wide alley, and we'll be able to see whoever's chasing us before they see us.

We exchange a nod and wait.

...

...

...

That didn't take long. Six guys round the corner, skidding to a stop at the far end. I have a clear shot at two of them. I hope Ruby can see the rest.

I take a deep breath, slowing my heart rate down. I line up my shots and quickly practice the movement between both intended targets.

One... two.

One... two.

Nice and easy.

I take another deep breath, and—

I turn away, closing my eyes and gritting my teeth as images of Josh's body flood my mind, flashing sporadically before me. I see the pool of blood around his head, like a sick halo on a plate-glass window. I see his head turning slowly to look at me and his wide, bloodshot eyes gazing up at me.

"You did this!" he shouts, causing blood to ooze from his mouth. "You killed me!"

No...

No...

I shake my head, trying to shift the images. I don't want to see this. I can't. Not now. I need to—

Bullets splinter the thick trunk of the tree, mere inches from my head.

Shit!

The images disappear instantly, and I snap back to the alley.

"Adrian!" shouts Ruby before leaning out and opening fire.

I take a moment to clear my head and re-aim my shots. I squeeze the trigger twice, finding the mark only with the second bullet.

Damn it.

My second target drops, joining two of the others on the

ground, which Ruby must have taken out.

That leaves my first target, plus two others.

I step out and crouch, leaning around the farther of the two trees and taking aim again. This time, I don't miss. I fire my last two rounds, which both find their way into the chests of our remaining adversaries. Another burst from Ruby, and the final guy drops.

I sigh, relaxing for a moment before getting to my feet. I sprint over to Ruby, who's already heading out of the alley and back onto the sidewalk. I stop beside her and look out across the street. Both sides are lined with trees, and the road is bathed in a strip of sunlight.

We step out side by side to cross, eager to put some distance between us and the increasing number of dead guys behind us. I turn to her. "Nice shooting back there. You all right?"

She nods. "Yeah. What happened to you?"

"I dunno. I just—"

I hear the car screeching to a halt as it hits us both. I roll up the hood, my body twisting so that my back slams into the windshield. I catch a glimpse of Ruby flying away in front of me, but I don't see her land on the road.

I roll back down, landing hard and awkward on my front. Each breath I take feels like a hot knife plunging into my chest. I try to move, but nothing wants to. I'm also aware that I'm no longer holding my gun.

Where the hell did that car come from?

I try to call out for Ruby, but all I manage to do is groan quietly.

Before I can think to do anything, I feel something cold touch the back of my head. It's pushing hard against me, forcing my face against the rough surface of the road.

It's a gun barrel.

"Game over, Adrian," says a female voice. The tone is calm, and the broken English accent has a hint of Italian mixed with it. "You're done."

Shit.

29

"Get up. Slowly."

Well, this is a shitty end to a shitty day, isn't it?

I didn't see the car coming from the left. The road is narrow and lined with parked scooters on both sides. I don't know where Ruby is, or if she's even alive. She was a few steps ahead of me as we were crossing the road, but she was on my left, so the car would've hit her first. I saw her catapulted across to the far side of the street, but I was down before I saw her land.

"Move it, now," urges the female voice, still calm, still in control.

Honestly, I don't know if I *can* move. My back is pulsing with agony. Fresh cuts are registering on my arms and legs, but there's a difference between my brain telling me I'm bleeding and me feeling the actual wound. Every inch of me is numb—presumably from shock.

Shock is a wonderful thing. I think the name is a little

misleading, though. Shock implies something bad... a terrible surprise. But shock in the medical sense of the word is your own brain's gift to your body. If you get hurt badly, your brain activates shock, like flipping a switch. It tells your body it's currently experiencing something so bad, it's better off not knowing about it, and it effectively kills your pain receptors. Hence why I feel numb.

I bring a leg up slowly and press my weight down on it gradually, testing my ability to stand upright. I use my good hand to help push my body up off the road.

...

...

...

I'm doing all right.

Ah!

Maybe not.

I just tried moving my other leg, and it wasn't happy about it. Must be my back. The impact from crashing into the windshield hurt like hell, and there might be some swelling that's restricting my movements.

I glance down at my leg, as if staring at it will help it work better.

Oh.

Shit!

Well, it's not my back that's stopping it.

There's a three-inch shard of glass sticking out of my hip.

That might be what the shock is for.

It looks painful, although I can't feel it. I just have a faint notion of my leg being cold, but that's it.

Ugh!

The woman just jabbed the back of my head with the butt of her gun.

"Get to your feet, pathetic man!"

Pathetic? Really?

I'm down on one knee in the middle of the street. I'm resting my cast on my right knee; my left is against the ground, unable to straighten properly because of the glass sticking out of it. Does it look like getting to my feet is happening any time soon?

I glance up and over my shoulder, seeing her for the first time. It's the woman from the second car, back at the fountain. "Listen, lady... in case you hadn't noticed, I just got hit by a fucking car. I might need a minute. If you're going to shoot me, will you just get it over with? Save me having to struggle trying to stand up."

She smirks. "I will not execute you in the street. You deserve more."

"Huh, thanks."

"You deserve *worse*."

"Oh."

"The Order will make an example of you, Adrian Hell. You will die so that the whole world will know who we are and what we're capable of. Now... get...to... your... fucking... feet."

She emphasized each word by jabbing the gun harder into the base of my skull as she said them.

I hate it when people do that. Especially to me.

I try again, putting my weight on my good leg. I attempt to slide my bad leg underneath me, so I'm kind of standing on it by default, as opposed to through any effort.

...

...

...

Ah!

Okay, I'm standing on both legs, albeit uneasily. I haven't

straightened my back yet, though. I'm leaning forward, resting on my knees. I shuffle each hand up my leg, a couple of inches at a time, gradually raising my torso as I do, like a decrepit drawbridge.

...

...

...

And...

I'm up.

I slowly turn around to face the woman. She didn't tell me to, but I don't care. If this is it, and my number's finally up, there's no way I'm going out with a bullet from behind. I'll leave this world standing tall, staring into the eyes of the person who was finally able to best me.

She doesn't say anything. She's holding her gun steady, aiming right between my eyes in a professional, unwavering grip. I keep eye contact with her but use what I can of my peripheral vision to look around for Ruby.

I can't see her.

That said, my vision's a little blurry, and the fuzziness inside my head suggests I might be a little concussed.

The woman smiles, and her grin is loaded with sick satisfaction. I bet it's a big thing, taking me down. I mean, Josh said it himself. Thanks to the dark web, my reputation knows no bounds. Taking The Order out of the equation, it'll still be a career-changing kill for any assassin to bag a target like me. I can see it in her eyes. The arrogance. The pride. The—

BANG!

Huh?

The woman was just pulled from my line of sight, dragged away to the right as if attached to a stampeding horse. A needle-like whisper of blood chases after her, evaporating in the air as suddenly as it appeared.

I look left and see a man standing there, holding his gun in his outstretched hand. Smoke is still twisting up from the barrel. It's the guy I recognized from the group who attacked us earlier. He's the last one left now too.

I stare at him, frowning, trying to kick-start my brain into figuring out what the hell just happened.

He lowers his gun and moves next to me. "You don't have much time, Adrian. You need to get your ass outta here, now."

I move my head slowly from side to side. "But... you're..."

"The only friend you have right now. Go."

"Ruby?"

He steps aside, revealing Ruby, who's standing on the opposite sidewalk, holding her neck. She smiles weakly.

I look at him. "I know you, but I can't..."

He nods once. "The name's Monroe. We met once, years ago, when we both bid on the same contract. We did it together and grabbed a beer afterward. My handler is friends with yours." He pauses. "I'm sorry about Josh. I had no idea we'd put a man across the street back there."

I'm not even going to try pretending to understand what's going on here.

"So, you're in The Order?"

He shrugs. "They recruited me about five years ago. I haven't done much work for them, but the payouts are good. Kinda feel like I'm making up the numbers, y'know? They assigned me to Spain initially and then moved me to Italy about six months ago. When we got the call from Horizon to say we'd be going after you, I wondered why. Then the details came down the wire. Everyone I know got excited, man. The chance to take *you* down. But I wasn't buying it.

No way you'd go through the shit you have done if it weren't worth it."

"I... ah... I appreciate that. Thanks." I take a deep, painful breath. "Meeting you is the first bit of luck I've had in a long time, Monroe."

"Well, it won't count for shit if you don't get out of here." He puts his car keys in my hand. "Take my ride. Get you and Ruby out of here."

"You gonna be okay?"

He grins. "I'll be fine. Telling Horizon I was overpowered by you isn't exactly a tough sell."

I smile politely. "Appreciate it. Listen, you know your Horizon isn't the only one, right?"

He nods.

"Watch your back, man. I saw The Order's personnel files when I killed Sterling. My Horizon was number seven. Be careful with him. This coordinated effort to take me out has everyone on edge. People like him are keen to make a good impression in front of what's left of the Committee."

He pats my shoulder. "I'm guessing you're trying to make sure there's no one left to impress?"

"That's the plan."

"Good. When all this is over, the beers are on me."

"Count on it." I look over at Ruby. "You okay to drive?"

She nods slowly, so I toss her the keys. I turn back to Monroe. "Thanks again."

"Don't mention it, Adrian."

We get in the car and quickly put some distance between us and the latest dead body. That's eleven more people The Order have lost today, so they won't be happy. With a little more luck, no one else will track us down before we reach our hotel.

I turn to Ruby. "You okay?"

"I'm fine. I managed to jump out of the way, so the car only clipped my back leg. It'll bruise like a bitch, but I'll live. What about you? Are you—" She glances at my leg. "Holy shit, Adrian!"

"Yeah, I know. I'll be all right. It's high enough up my leg that it shouldn't have caught any major arteries. It's closer to my hip. A bandage and some aspirin will do me just fine."

We navigate the narrow streets until we reach an intersection. Ruby slows us to an anonymous speed as we merge with the rest of the traffic heading right.

She reaches over and squeezes my hand. We smile at each other, then I lean back in my seat and close my eyes.

This has turned into the worst kind of nightmare, and all I want to do right now is wake up.

30

The world is a blur as I slowly open my eyes. A mist of confusion allows only the most basic of light through. Everything else is unidentifiable.

Where am I?

I feel something cool and moist on my forehead, which stimulates my mind enough to begin registering more things. Like the dull ache resonating around every inch of my body.

I hear a distant, faint groaning, which I assume is my attempt at speaking.

"...okay now. Just relax," says a female voice, which sounds hollow, yet smooth.

I squeeze my eyes closed, then snap them wide open, blinking fast to clear them.

I'm lying on my back, staring up at a ceiling. I'm... yeah, I'm on a bed.

Is this my hotel room? When did I get here?

The cooling sensation leaves my head. I turn slightly, trying to see where it went.

Sitting next to me, holding a sponge and looking concerned, is Ruby. She smiles at me. "Hey."

"Uh..."

"Don't try talking. Just take it easy."

She gets up, moves over to the desk in the far corner, and sets a bowl of water down on it. She ambles back to my side and kneels on the bed.

"Wha... what happened?"

"You passed out in the car. I managed to slap you awake long enough to help me get you to the room, but you blacked out again as soon as you lay down."

"How long—"

"About five hours. We're safe here. Don't worry. We weren't followed."

I try to push myself up the bed.

"Ah! Shit..."

She puts a hand on my chest. "Yeah, don't move either. I had to do a little improvising with your leg wound. It'll hurt for a while."

I frown and glance down at my left hip. The large shard of glass is gone, and a thin piece of material is tied around the top of my thigh.

I've also just noticed I have no clothes on. Besides my boxers, I'm lying here naked.

I look up at her and raise an eyebrow. She looks confused for a moment and then smiles sheepishly. "Yeah, I had to undress you to wrap your leg wound."

"Then why is my top off?"

"You were running a temperature, so I've been trying to cool you down."

"Right. Sorry. Thanks."

I allow myself a moment to relax. I close my eyes and take slow, deep breaths to calm my mind and focus on one thing at a time.

...

...

...

Right, where does it hurt?

Most places, apparently. My left leg, my right shoulder, my right hand, most of my back, my head...

Shoot me now.

I keep breathing, pushing past the physical issues. Pain is temporary. It's defeat that stays with you. If you get yourself to a point mentally where you can ignore any physical discomfort, you can concentrate on the important things.

What's next?

I need to figure out how to take out the camerlengo, which will effectively kill The Order of Sabbah. I can shoot him from almost anywhere, using the Holy Trinity rifle, but that's not going to happen while he's inside Vatican City. Plus, the pope is their next target, and his public appearance tomorrow is the obvious time to take him out, so time's a-wasting.

I feel Ruby's hand on my chest. "Adrian, while you were sleeping, you... you were talking a lot."

I open my eyes and look at her. "Sorry."

"No, no, it's fine. It's just... the things you were saying..." She pauses. "How are you doing?"

I swallow back a rush of emotion. "How do you think I'm doing, Ruby? I just need to focus on what I'm doing, okay?"

She doesn't say anything for a couple of minutes.

Eventually, she moves her hand. "It's not your fault, y'know?"

"Yeah, it is."

"No, it's not. It's The Order's fault. They're the ones responsible, and you're going to get even by taking out their leader. Focus on that, not on your own misplaced guilt."

"Misplaced? He wouldn't even have been here if it weren't for me. Up until three days ago, he thought I was dead. He was miserable, sure, but he was living his life in blissful ignorance, and I should've left it that way. I brought him back into this world. I got him involved with The Order. His death is on me."

"Adrian..."

"No, Ruby." I try to shake my head, which is harder to do than I would like. I can feel the raw emotion erupting inside me, spilling out with no control. "You don't understand. You don't get it. Josh is *dead*. He wasn't just my friend... he was my brother. He was family. He was all I had, goddammit! When I lost my wife and daughter, he was there to get me through it. When I lost my way and my days were perpetual darkness, he was there to guide me. You don't even know half the shit I've been through. Since day one, it's been me and him. Even when we weren't together, we were together. He knew the real me. He was the better half of my conscience, and now he's dead. I left him lying on the street in his own blood. All those times he was there for me, and the one time... the *one time* he needed me, I let him down. Today, I lost the final piece of my soul. I don't know who or what I am anymore. All I know for certain is that I'm alone. All the loss I experienced in my life, yet he made sure I was never by myself. But now... what? What have I got left? What have I got to live for?"

She doesn't say anything. She just stares into my eyes as a tear rolls down her cheek.

"No, Adrian. You're wrong," she says after a few moments of silence. "The Order might have hired you to kill him, but regardless of Horizon's sick little power play to have you do it, it wasn't you who pulled the trigger. And you didn't make him a target either. The Order would've gone after him whether you were around or not. With him being in their crosshairs, it was inevitable. The fact he stayed alive as long as he did... *that* was because of you. He wouldn't be angry with you... he'd be proud of you."

Her voice starts to crack as more tears roll down her face. She sniffs back her emotion.

"And as for being alone? Adrian, you're not alone. Not now and not ever again. We're in this together, and when it's all said and done, whatever comes next, we'll do that together too. I've got your back, and I promise you, you won't lose me."

I let her words sink in. There's a part of me that knows she's probably right about Josh, but I don't think I deserve to feel anything but guilt and blame for his death. Not yet.

I know that everything else she said couldn't have been easy for her. She's like me. She knows emotions will get you killed. She knows the more you care for something, the more you have to lose. Yet she said it all anyway.

I rest my hand on Ruby's knee. "Thank you. For everything."

She wipes her face dry and smiles. "Thank me when the job's done."

I try to push myself up again, grimacing at the effort.

She puts her hand on my shoulder. "For God's sake, Adrian, will you stay still?"

I shake my head. "No. I... I need to make a call. Help me up, would you?"

Ruby rolls her eyes but moves to stand beside me. I swing my legs over the side, then pause to catch my breath and refocus on ignoring the pain I'm in. She hooks her arm underneath mine and helps me to my feet.

I stay still for a minute, ensuring I have enough balance to avoid falling over and that I can actually walk.

...

...

...

Yeah, I'm good.

I pad carefully over to my jacket and reach inside it for Josh's cell. I scroll through his contacts list and select the number I want, which starts dialing automatically.

"Who are you calling?" asks Ruby.

I don't reply because the phone has already been answered.

"Josh? Goddammit, son, what did I tell you? I'm watching your boy Adrian's handiwork on CNN. It's a goddamn disaster over there! What are you playing at?"

I sigh. "Mr. President, it's not Josh. It's Adrian."

"Well then, what are *you* playing at? I told you to be discreet. Nineteen dead bodies, an explosion, a car crash... Jesus H. Christ, son! How can you—"

"Twenty."

"What? What does that mean?"

"You said nineteen dead bodies, Ryan, but that's not right. There were twenty."

"Why does that matter? Anyway, why are you calling me from Josh's phone?"

I sigh again. This conversation is going to suck.

22:09 CEST

. . .

I'm sitting on the bed, leaning against the headboard, with my legs stretched out in front of me. Ruby is beside me, eating pizza. We've not spoken much since my phone call with President Schultz. In fact, for the last hour, we've sat here in silence watching CNN. It's the only news channel we can access that doesn't broadcast in Italian.

He was right. Most of what's happened today has already made headlines around the world. Thankfully, most people are jumping to the same conclusions—that it was an act of terrorism. It seems to be the go-to reason for anything nowadays. Luckily, there haven't been any witness statements or security footage to prove otherwise.

Unfortunately, the Italian press also started reporting that one of the dead bodies littering the streets of Rome was Josh Winters, CEO of GlobaTech Industries. The news reporter said that America is rocked by his death and that the nation will mourn him as a hero for all the work he's done to help the world as a whole in the aftermath of 4/17.

The sad truth is that no one will ever actually know *half* the shit he's done to help this world.

Schultz was genuinely upset when I told him about Josh and passed on his sincere condolences, which I appreciated. He promised me Josh would be given a full state funeral, shown every courtesy, and treated like the patriot he was.

I told him everything we knew, including what Horizon gave us. I knew his hands would still be tied regardless, although he made sure to reiterate how much he couldn't help me.

His final words to me were a promise. He told me to, and I quote, *get each and every one of those sorry son'bitches* and unofficially gave me his blessing to do it however I wanted. *Politics be damned,* he said.

I'll have to remind him of that when this is over.

But before he hung up, he also told me if I were successful in saving the pope's life, stopping The Order once and for all, and made it back to the U.S. in one piece, he would publicly exonerate me of all the crimes I was sentenced to death for committing. He didn't give me the specifics but said he would explain everything to the American people in a way they would accept and understand, which would allow me my life back.

More incentive, I guess.

Ruby offers me a slice of pizza, but I wave it away. I'm not hungry. I'm too busy thinking.

"How do you think The Order is going to kill the pope?" I ask her.

"Mmm-hmm," she replies, with a mouthful of pizza. "I don't know, but we need to figure it out soon if we're going to stop them."

"I've never had to reverse-engineer a hit before. It doesn't feel right."

She doesn't respond.

I frown. "You okay?"

She reaches over without looking and fumbles her hand over my face, then finds my mouth and holds her fingers over it.

I silently hold my hands up in the universal *what the hell* gesture. She points to the TV, then picks up the remote and turns up the volume. On the screen, a woman is standing on the street, talking into a microphone. Over her shoulder, St. Peter's Basilica is illuminated from beneath, making it glow against the backdrop of the night sky.

"...where tomorrow, commencing at ten a.m., His Holiness will hold a special Papal Mass in front of an expected audience of eighty thousand people, despite the events that have rocked this city throughout the day. A spokesperson for the Vatican said earlier that tomorrow's Mass is being held to show the world, not just Catholics, that we can be united in the face of adversity. The tragic events of today, which claimed the life of GlobaTech Industries CEO Josh Winters, among others, only serve to highlight the need for such a strong message.

"Tomorrow will also mark the first time His Holiness is joined by all six cardinal bishops—the highest-ranking members of the College of Cardinals—while delivering Mass. While this is both unorthodox and unprecedented, His Holiness himself issued a statement explaining why he felt it was important to show the extent of the church's support in these dire times."

The screen changes to show a file photo of the pope, along with all six cardinals who will be accompanying him tomorrow.

"They will all assist the pope during Mass and Communion by offering prayers and blessings. In other news, the forecast for tomorrow isn't favorable, with low cloud, high winds, and even a storm front moving in from the Mediterranean, though it's unlikely to deter the thousands of people who have traveled from all over the world to be here. The pope, along with his cardinals, will no doubt conduct the service from beneath the canopy at the top of the steps leading inside the famous basilica, should the conditions deteriorate. This is Diane Webber for CNN, reporting live from Vatican City."

Ruby clicks off the TV. "Holy shit."

I stare blankly ahead. "I know."

"Did you see—"

"I did."

"What are you thinking?"

I turn to her and reach for a slice of pizza. I've suddenly acquired an appetite. "I'm thinking I've figured out how The Order intends to kill the pope. And I've also got my shot. Which means tomorrow, all this shit ends, one way or the other."

31

The thing about luck, in my experience, is that you typically get more bad than good. Also, more often than not, regardless of which kind you get, the timing is rarely useful. That's why, last night, in our hotel room, eating pizza and watching TV, Ruby and I were so shocked we caught a massive break just when we needed it the most.

We're standing side by side at the foot of one of the beds, which has every weapon and gadget Josh brought with him for the trip laid out on top of it. Nearest to us are the handguns—more M9s, along with several spare magazines. Just above them is a row of tech, including comms units and a custom range-finding device with a built-in anemometer for tracking wind speed and direction. I can't remember what he said it's called, but he was proud of it. Next, there are three assault rifles, which are upgraded, tactical versions of GlobaTech's AX-19, which I've had the pleasure of using more than once in the past. Finally, at the top end, raised slightly because it's resting on the pillows, is the case containing the third Holy Trinity sniper rifle.

That CNN report we saw last night presented us with the opportunity we needed to bring down The Order *and* save the pope at the same time. See, in less than two hours, His Holiness is going to walk out in front of tens of thousands of people to deliver Mass, and he'll have all the cardinal bishops with him. These guys are the six highest-ranking members of the College of Cardinals. One of them is Antonio Herrera Martinez—the camerlengo and leader of The Order of Sabbah.

Now, ignoring previous advice to stop showing these bastards too much respect, I'm assuming they will be thinking as I would when planning how to take out the pope. My first instinct is a long-distance, high velocity sniper round. BANG... one and done. But the problem, as I've found out myself, is that there aren't all that many buildings in Rome that offer a good vantage point for a shot like that. Plus, knowing The Order as I do, if they're going to assume control of the Catholic Church, they'll want to make a statement. This will be their long-awaited opportunity to step out of the shadows and present themselves to the world as a group that can be relied on to guide us... blah, blah, blah. Plus, with Josh dead...

...

...

...

Bastards.

Sorry.

With him gone, GlobaTech will be in turmoil for a while, which means their ability to keep doing what they have been for this world might be compromised. It's the perfect time to announce their replacements, right?

That's how I'm thinking, anyway, and I reckon that's how The Order will be thinking too. So, they won't just shoot the guy, and they won't have just anyone take him out. That reporter said it herself—today will be Mass and Holy Communion. If I were Martinez, I'd want to do it myself, to set an example to everyone who works for me. And I'd do it by poisoning the cup that one of the cardinals will pass to the pope during Communion. No one will understand how it's happened. They'll just see the pope die on the steps of St. Peter's Square and then BAM! Camerlengo to the rescue.

That's what I'd do.

I told Ruby my theory last night, and she instantly agreed.

Every now and then, it's beneficial to have a mind as dark and twisted as mine.

But then she raised a good point. It's great that we know how The Order intends to do it, but we need to figure out how to stop them. This is where a little reverse psychology and some poker skills come into play. Let's not forget, they know I'm here too. I'm also sure that, by now, they know what we know, which means they'll be expecting me to try to stop them. I'm going to assume they will be thinking along the same lines as I do, which means they'll be expecting me to intervene in a less obvious way. Just as they're going to poison the pope up close, they'll be figuring I'll look for a way inside the Vatican to take out the camerlengo before any of this can happen.

But if they're thinking like that, they would be wrong.

I look at the case containing the Holy Trinity rifle and smile to myself.

I'm going to shoot the bastard.

. . .

09:38 CEST

The change in the weather from yesterday is mindboggling. I know the reporter mentioned something about it last night, but I didn't expect it to be this bad. It's not raining yet, although I think it's inevitable at some point, given how dark and gray the sky is. The wind is howling in all directions. I'm wearing a hooded sweater, with the hood tied up tight around my head. It's thick, but I'm still getting shivers up and down my spine.

I don't know... maybe that's not the weather?

I've taken more painkillers than I probably should have, but I'm walking almost normally, despite the leg wound, the sore back, the sore shoulder, and the pounding headache...

Just another day at the office, right?

I'm carrying the Holy Trinity rifle beside me, as if it's a normal briefcase. I don't have any other weapons on me. Ruby, however, looks like Rambo. She's walking beside me with a backpack worn over both shoulders containing one of the AX-19s. At her back are two M9s. Strapped to her thighs are two more, holstered on the outside of her legs. She's wearing a sleeveless duster coat that runs down to below her knees, concealing them. Beneath it, she's also wearing a thick, hooded sweater, with the hood up over her head.

We're walking with purpose but calmly enough that we don't stand out among the other pedestrians. As expected, the streets are busy today, which we're trying to use to our advantage. Right now, we simply look like two tourists braving the poor conditions, making the most of our trip.

The main issue with my plan to shoot Martinez is the same one anybody would have had: where do I take the shot from? As I said, not many buildings in Rome are tall enough to see over the Vatican City walls, and the ones that are tall enough are too far away, even for me and using this rifle.

There was a tablet included with Josh's stuff, so we sat up until the early hours of this morning, using GlobaTech's satellite network to find somewhere suitable. Eventually, we did, but while the location is perfect for the shot, it presents new problems for us to work around.

Namely, it's very public.

But I can't let a little thing like that stop us. Not now. There's too much at stake.

I glance over at Ruby. "You ready for this?"

She keeps looking ahead. I see her eyes darting in all directions, constantly checking for threats in the crowds. She nods curtly. "Yeah. We've got this."

We cross the street and turn right onto a bridge, navigating the growing throng as we make our way across. I look down over the side at the river. The water is moving violently in the strong wind. I feel myself slowing down, and my vision blurs as I focus on the turbulent surface.

I feel Ruby's hand on my arm, distracting me. "Hey, you with me, big guy?"

"Hmm?" I snap my head around to look at her. "What?"

"Are you all right?"

My gaze rests behind her momentarily. Over her shoulder, I see the bridge farther along the Tiber, where Josh had walked yesterday. Just to the right of that, I see the police cordon, blocking off the intersection where he was killed.

I blink slowly, tearing my focus away from it and back onto Ruby's emerald eyes. "I'm fine."

We approach the end of the bridge. "Good, because if you want to change your mind, now's the time."

I shake my head. "No, this is the only way."

We stop as the bridge merges with the clean, cobbled sidewalk on the other side, which stretches away from us in both directions.

"Are you sure? I mean, what happens if this doesn't work?"

I shrug. "If this doesn't work, then Schultz's promise of exoneration won't mean shit. We'll probably be dead."

"But if it does?"

"Then we have to hope Schultz can include the crimes we're about to commit in his presidential pardon. Although, right now, I honestly don't care. I just want to get the job done."

I feel her hand grab hold of my cast. We both stare up at the large, bronze statue of the Archangel Michael, sitting atop the spire of the Castel Sant'Angelo—the Castle of the Holy Angel.

Ironic, really. There's nothing holy or angelic about what I'm going to do.

32

This is going to be either the most brilliant thing I've ever done or the most stupid.

The castle opens at nine a.m., which means, by now, it's already going to be busy inside. There's also extra security because of the mass. However, because of what's happening in Vatican City in just under ten minutes, only the first floor of the castle is open to visitors today. This means A... there are fewer people in there than normal, and B... no one's on the roof, so I won't be disturbed.

The only thing left to do now is empty the place, which is where Ruby comes in. This is the trickiest part, which is why we've intentionally left it so close to showtime. We want everyone out, so I can work, but if we do it too soon, we allow more time for word to reach the Vatican and risk the mass being postponed. It also opens things up to the possibility of The Order learning where we are and trapping us inside.

We walk toward the entrance, which consists of two thick, wooden doors adorned with large, metal rivets. They're standing open, with a security guard stationed on either side. We pass through anonymously, part of the larger crowd shuffling through the outer wall of the castle and into the courtyard, which is nothing more than a narrow alley running around the outside of the castle itself.

There's another door ahead, with a ticket booth just inside, on the right. There's a handful of people in front of and behind us in the line. I check my watch again. Not long to go. I look at Ruby, who's staring straight ahead, her game face on.

We inch closer to the booth. Once we're inside, we just need to—

Uh-oh.

I close my eyes and whisper, "Shit..."

"What is it?" asks Ruby.

I turn to her. "Security are checking bags."

She sighs. "Shit."

I think about it for a moment and then shrug. "Well, at least this means we don't have to pay the entrance fee now."

She rolls her eyes and smiles. "Every cloud, right?"

I nod. "Be ready, and remember—we want noise, not casualties."

"Yeah, yeah, I know."

We're next in line. I have a clear view inside now. There's a small walkway formed by two rope lines heading away from the booth, which opens out into the main reception area of the castle. Straight ahead leads farther into the castle itself, while each side features a curving staircase leading up to the galleries and, presumably, the roof.

It's busy down here, but it's not crammed. There's still room to move.

We step forward and draw level with the booth. The woman inside it speaks to Ruby, initially in Italian but then again in English, asking her how many tickets she wants. One of the two security guards standing on the left steps in front of me points to my extra-large briefcase. "We need to check inside your bags, *signore*."

The other moves in front of Ruby. "You too, *signora*."

We exchange a glance and nod.

Here we go.

Ruby unfastens her coat, brushing it around both legs, revealing her thigh holsters. The guard's eyes grow wide, and his mouth falls open. Before he can react, she steps forward, lashing her leg out and kicking him firmly in the gut. She draws both M9s as he keels over. She aims one at the other security guard and one at the woman in the booth.

Behind us, people start screaming and running back to the street. Inside, everyone is standing still, exchanging looks of confusion and disbelief. I step away to the side, trying not to look affiliated with her.

She nods to the woman in the booth. "You. Out here, now." The woman complies, stepping out and around, moving in front of her. "I want you to stand by this door. Make sure no one else comes in and that the people trying to get out do so quickly and safely. Do you understand? Ah... *comprendere*?"

The woman nods hurriedly.

"Good." Ruby steps forward and slams the butt of her pistol in the second guard's face, putting him on his ass. She raises the gun in the air and fires twice in quick succession. Screams quickly ring out around the castle. "Everybody out of here! Now!"

The sound of stampeding footsteps grows loud as the people inside merge together to form a herd, which then rushes for the doors. Ruby moves to the side, standing next to the booth, ushering everyone out.

That was easier than I thought.

I slip away, staying close to the left wall, and head for the steps. As I reach them, I quickly set the case down beside me and reach inside my pocket for the comms unit. I put it in my ear and activate it, then continue my ascent. I stop halfway up and glance back over my shoulder at Ruby. We catch each other's eye, and I gesture to my ear, signaling for her to put her comms unit in too. She nods once. I continue up the steps, two at a time, trying to ignore the increasing discomfort in my leg as a result.

They wind up to the next floor, which leads to a balcony looking out across the main area below. I look down and see the back of the group clamoring for the exit.

That's good. They're nearly all out already. Ruby's done well.

I turn and head along the small corridor, which brings me to a circular space with a display case in the middle. Branching off to the right is a café. Straight ahead is the gift shop. I head left and through the door marked ACCESSO AL TETTO.

Roof access.

I climb the damp, stone staircase and burst through the door at the top.

Oh, Jesus!

Lightning forks across the sky, followed a moment later by a loud rumble of thunder. The rain is still light, although the strong wind is making it look worse than it is.

There's a crackling in my ear. I hear Ruby's muffled voice, but I can't make out what she's saying. I clasp my hand over it. "...you hear me? Adrian?"

"I hear you, Ruby. How's everything your end?"

"The place is empty. I've locked the doors shut, and I'm positioned at the bottom of the stairs. I have a clear view of the first floor, and I'm covered with no blind spots. No one's getting in here without me being able to shoot them if I need to."

"That's great!" I'm shouting over the storm. "Listen, we have a problem."

"The weather?"

"Yeah, the storm's bad out here and only seems to be getting worse. The way it's going, it won't be long before they give the damn thing a name."

"Shit. What are you gonna do?"

"I don't have a choice, Ruby. I have to take this shot."

"Do what you gotta do, Adrian. I've got you."

I stride across the roof and head back inside the main tower. I quickly climb the narrow, winding metal staircase. There's no door at the end this time. The steps simply go up and lead me back out into the storm, on top of the castle.

Dead ahead, the gray skyline of Rome stretches out before me. More lightning flashes behind the clouds, illuminating the heavens. Directly behind me, the tower shoots up, and the statue of Michael looms ominously over me, like a gothic beacon against the storm-ridden sky.

I move to the right edge and look out across the city. In the mid-distance, maybe eight hundred yards away, I can see the dome of St. Peter's Basilica.

But that's all I see.

"Oh, fuck off…"

"What now?" crackles Ruby's voice.

"That goddamn satellite feed we used wasn't helpful. I don't have a shot."

"What do you mean?"

"I mean, from here, I can't see the canopy at the end of

the square. It's blocked by the buildings on the right side of the street approaching the Vatican City walls."

I let out a low growl through teeth gritted with frustration.

I don't have a shot.

33

I turn my back on the view and pace away, frustrated and angry.

"Shit!" I wipe rain from my face and let out a muted cry. "Shit, shit, fuck, shit!"

So much for catching a break. Now what do I do? This was it. This was the one shot, the one chance we had at stopping this. I check my watch. Any moment now, Martinez is going to fulfill his Order's goal and take out the pope in front of the world. No one's going to know he did it, and they're going to win. He's going to control everything, and Josh will have died for nothing.

I switch direction, pacing side to side, instead of back and forth.

Come on, Adrian. Think!

There's too much noise...

I stop in the middle of the roof, facing the statue, and

drop to one knee. I set the case down in front of me, close my eyes, and take a deep breath. And another.

...

...

...

I can't feel the world slowing around me.

Shit!

Come on, damn it!

Clear your mind.

I take more deep breaths, each one slower than the last.

...

...

...

Hey, Adrian. You miss me? Yeah, that's right. It's your Inner Satan here. Forgot all about me, didn't you? Listen, I'm gonna let you off because of all the shit you got going on, but you need to pay attention now, okay? I know he's dead, and that sucks, but now isn't the time to mourn or sink into the darkness. Losing your angel doesn't mean your devil stops working.

Now someone's about to wage war on God. Are you really gonna pass up a chance to cash in on the irony here? The biggest evil the world has never known is about to kill the pope... and the King of Assassins and his pet Satan are gonna stop them. Now... get your ass up, Adrian. Open your eyes, open your mind, and do what you were born to do. Get up!

I open my eyes and slowly get to my feet, grabbing the case once more. I look to my left, staring out at Vatican City again. This time, though, it looks different. This time, I don't see a problem. I see a challenge.

I walk toward the edge behind me, away from the statue. I'll lean out as much as I can to see if I can get line of sight on the canopy. If I can see the shot, I'll find a way to make it. But time's running out, and I need to—

Well, fuck me sideways.

I smile to myself as I look over the side. I thought I would see the street, the bridge, and the river below... but instead, I see another roof, about eight feet down, jutting out maybe fifteen feet.

Sonofabitch.

I don't think or hesitate. The end is in sight, clear in my mind. I know what needs to be done, and my instincts are taking over, guiding me and focusing me on getting the job done.

I place a foot up on the ledge and step up onto it.

Jesus... that eight feet just became fourteen!

I swing the case around and let go, dropping it onto the roof below me. It slams down, loud and heavy. It'll be fine—it's titanium, so it'll protect the rifle. Plus, it's down there now, which means regardless of how much I don't like the idea of jumping, I don't have a choice.

Talk about incentive.

Trying to keep any pressure away from my injured leg, I carefully crouch. I turn my body, preparing to hold onto the wall with my one good hand as I lower myself over the edge. If I hang down, that fourteen feet becomes two, which is much more manageable.

I kick against the side of the tower, searching for any grip with my feet as I place more of my body weight on my left arm.

Oh, man, this is going to suck.

I'm using my cast as much as I can, but the lower I go, the less use it is. I take it as slow as I dare, gradually shuffling my feet down the wall, flattening my body out against it. My left hand is throbbing. Just a little more...

A loud rumble of thunder crashes overhead and brings with it a renewed wave of rain.

This is not—

"Whoa!"

...

...

...

Ugh!

"Ah, shit!"

I lost my grip and fell backward. I must have dropped six feet easily, and I landed hard, flat on my back, on the roof below. I'm gasping for breath, having just had the wind knocked out of me. Thankfully, I lifted my head a little before impact, but my lower back took the full brunt of the fall.

"Adrian? Adrian, is everything all right?" crackles Ruby's voice.

I grimace. "Yeah... kinda."

"What's going on?"

"Nothing. I just... ah... I just fell off the roof."

"You did *what*?"

"It's not as bad as it sounds. There's a lower level above the entrance. It's only about eight feet down. I'll be fine."

"Jesus, Adrian... be careful."

"Yeah."

I roll over on my side and use my good arm and leg to push myself upright. I stretch as much as I can, hearing and feeling the crack as my back protests. I stagger toward the edge and peer over. The bridge leading back across the river is central, directly below me.

I look over toward the basilica.

Please tell me I can see—

Yes!

I have a full view of the canopy and the sea of multi-colored umbrellas filling the square.

I rush over to the case, ignoring the discomfort in my... well... pretty much everywhere. I drag it back over to the far edge and click it open. Everything's still intact. I take out the rifle and fold down the bi-pod stand attached to the barrel. I rest it on the ground and then take out the scope, which I attach in place on top of the upper receiver. Finally, I slam the five-round magazine into the breach and move to the upper-left corner of the roof, which is the closest point to the target.

More lightning flashes behind the dark clouds, momentarily igniting the sky. The rain is heavy but holding, and the visibility is poor but manageable. I reach over to the case and take out Josh's fancy anemometer, which I stand to the side of the rifle. I turn it on and glance at the display.

Holy shit!

I've got a seventeen mile per hour wind coming in from the south, which is now on my left side. That's going to make a tough shot even harder.

I shuffle on my front until I find a position that's borderline comfortable. The ground is soaked, and the rainwater is seeping inside my hoodie, making me shiver. I tuck the stock firmly into my left shoulder and place my eye in front of the scope.

Straight away, St. Peter's Square rushes toward me with frightening clarity. I can see the pope standing central beneath the canopy, wearing his white robes and gesturing with his hands, clearly mid-speech. He has three cardinals on either side, standing a small distance behind him, wearing their red outfits.

I can see Martinez. He's the one standing immediately to the right of the pope as I look on.

I adjust the focus on the scope, squeezing as much clarity as I can out of it. My display says nine hundred and eighty-eight yards to the target. The distance itself isn't much of an issue for me. The problem I have is the cross-wind. I'll need to shoot way left of the camerlengo, so the wind can carry it back toward him, but doing that means the bullet is going to drift in front of the pope. If there's a sudden drop in the wind speed, even by half a mile per hour, it might not make it far enough right, which means I could end up shooting His Holiness, instead of his piece of shit secretary.

I take a long, deep, tired breath.

No pressure, then.

I take as much time as I dare watching the scene. It'll take a fraction over a second from me pressing the trigger to the bullet finding its mark, but that's a long time to hope for zero movement from the target and zero changes in the weather.

The rain is still beating down, wetting my face and hands. I blink away drips that threaten to impede my vision as I focus solely on the next shot. I'm lying prone, with my right arm bent beneath me and my chest resting on my cast for support. I'm trapping the stock between my chin and shoulder, and my left hand has a firm grip of the handle. My index finger is straight, resting against the trigger guard.

Never put your finger on the trigger until you're sure you want to squeeze it.

I use the slightest of movements to adjust my view, looking along the line of cardinals. The pope still looks in full flow of his sermon. Each of the cardinal bishops is standing stock-still behind him, respectful and disciplined.

Wait. Is that...

Yeah, it is.

Shit. I hate being right all the time.

I'm focusing on the camerlengo. I can see a chalice in his

hands, held low in front of him. He's preparing to give it his boss as part of Communion. That's how he'll do it—I knew it!

Right, I need to do this now.

I flash a glance at the anemometer again. The wind speed is still the same. I refocus my gaze through the scope and adjust positioning for the shot.

The display is helping, but honestly, shots like this are made on instinct. You just *feel* when it's right. Your heart rate increases naturally with excitement when your brain sees the shot that will find home. I inch the view left, so I'm looking almost at the cardinal on the other side of the pope.

I hope for his sake that the wind doesn't drop.

I move the rifle along the line again, lining the crosshairs up with Martinez's head. I turn the first knob on the scope to adjust for the wind. Four clicks should do it. Next, I turn the second knob, to factor in the natural dip in trajectory as the bullet loses its velocity over the distance. I keep the crosshairs resting on Martinez's head, right between his eyes.

Got you now, you bastard.

I can't tell if it's rain or sweat that's running down my face right now.

Breathe, Adrian, nice and slow.

I move my finger through the guard, so it's resting gently against the trigger. I throw a final glance to the anemometer. No change. One last look at my target. He hasn't moved.

No, wait!

Fuck!

He's just stepped to the pope's side and placed the chalice on the pulpit in front of him.

Damn it! I'm out of time. I need to—

"Shit!"

I catch my breath and frown. "Ruby?"

"Adrian, we've got a problem."

As her words register in my ear, so does the noise of cars screeching to a halt below me, carried up on the wind, subtle compared to the rush of the storm around me.

The Order!

"How many?"

"I count four cars."

"You have to hold them off. I'm about to take the shot."

"I'll do what I can, but you need to hurry, or we're not making it out of here. There's only so much I can—"

"Ruby, relax. You've got this. Just buy me as much time as you can."

The line goes quiet.

"Ah!"

No, it doesn't! The high-pitched squealing of gunfire rings out in my ear. I quickly yank the device out and throw it over to the case.

She'll be fine, and I need to concentrate.

I look back through the scope. The pope hasn't reached for the chalice yet, and Martinez is back in line. He seems to be smiling...

I line the shot back up, same as before. I feel my heart begin to race. This is it. Time slows to a familiar, comforting crawl. Everything I've been through, everything I've done, everything I've lost... it's all led me here, to this moment, to this shot. My finger tightens on the trigger. I fight to control my breathing as adrenaline and excitement try to take over.

I've got this.

I've... got... this...

...

...

...

"Drop your weapon!"

Oh, fuck off!

I don't move. I stay focused on my target.

"Back away from the rifle, right now!"

That was a different voice. I heard it clearly enough, despite the ambient noise surrounding me. So, there's at least two of them. Great.

I also noticed that voice was American, so I'm assuming some of The Order's men have finally followed me across the pond.

There's more movement. If I were to guess, I would say they were shouting down from the top of the tower at first, and now they're trying to jump down to the level I'm on to physically grab me.

Weird that they haven't just shot me, but I'm not complaining.

If they're climbing down here, I only have a few seconds.

I can see Martinez as clear as if he were ten feet away. The reticle is lined up, and the shot is calculated. My body is tensed, my breathing regulated...

"Put down that weapon!"

I hear the impact as at least two people land on the roof. They can't be more than a few feet away from me.

I breathe in...

And out...

In...

"Drop it, now!"

And out...

I squeeze the trigger.

A split-second later, I feel a hand on my arm, pulling me. The rifle is knocked over as I roll over on my back to see two faces glaring down at me. I stare at the barrels of their guns, both pointing at me.

The scene freezes. I hold my breath, waiting for their bullets to riddle my body.

"Shot fired! Shot fired!" yells one of them into a mic attached to his cuff. He looks at me, holding my gaze for several moments. "Say again... Is the primary hit?"

More silence. I continue to look up at him. I'm trying to ignore the guns, trying not to think about if Ruby's still alive...

"Copy that." His eyes refocus on me. "You lose, asshole. You missed."

I frown. "I did?"

"Yeah, the pope's still alive."

Wait, what?

"But I... was anyone hit?"

"One of the bishops standing beside him."

"Which one?"

"Why do you care, asshole? It doesn't matter. You're done. After this, you better believe your life is over."

"If that's the case, there's no reason not to tell me. Who was hit?"

The man exchanges a quizzical look with his colleague and then looks back at me. "It was Cardinal Martinez."

My whole body relaxes, and my right arm hangs loosely over the side of the roof. I stare up at the sky, feeling the rapid patter of the rain on my face, and smile. Then I start chuckling to myself, lightly at first, but it quickly degenerates into an uncontrollable fit of laughter.

I got him, Josh.

It's over. Whatever happens now, I don't care. It's all over.

We did it, man.

We did it.

34

I loosen my tie and shift awkwardly on the spot. I hate wearing suits. The sun is high and bright, and while it isn't scorching, the warm breeze is making me hot and uncomfortable.

A respectful silence rests over the crowd. The gentle flow of the Potomac is faintly audible behind me.

It's been a long few days.

I did what I set out to do. The Order is dead. I took out Martinez, cutting off the head of the snake. Those guys on the roof and all those cars that surrounded me and Ruby in the castle... that was the FBI, dispatched from the U.S. Embassy in Rome on the president's authority. They didn't know what the hell was going on. They just knew where I would be and had their orders to escort me back to American soil.

When we arrived at the embassy, we were immediately detained until official orders came through from Washington to expedite us back to the U.S. Everything from our hotel room was brought over and handed to the Feds as evidence. All our weapons were confiscated.

We were questioned for a few hours, and I was open and honest about what I was doing in Rome. They confirmed they had their analysts working on Josh's laptop, so I knew they had the evidence to back up my claims about The Order.

I confirmed my identity, which caused some initial outrage. Once everyone had calmed down, I simply detailed my involvement in the events that took place the day before and reiterated why I was there.

I kept Schultz's name out of it. I figured there was no sense in trying to drag him into all this if he had suddenly decided to deny all knowledge of me, which was a genuine concern.

But I was wrong. President Schultz came through for me, just as he promised he would. He ordered the FBI director to personally release both me and Ruby, then made a public address to the nation to explain everything.

Or, at least, the version of things he promised me he would tell them.

He told everyone the truth about Cunningham's involvement in 4/17 and how me killing him was self-defense after I discovered evidence of the conspiracy. Upon learning of the much larger threat from The Order, it was agreed that the U.S. Government would fake my death, using Cunningham's murder as justification, and send me to infiltrate the ranks of the shadowy organization to uncover what they were planning and bring them down from within.

He said it was my decision to take that risk because I believed the American people had suffered enough, and I wanted to protect the ideals of a government they could trust.

A slightly exaggerated twist on what really happened, obviously, but still plausible.

He also went on to explain that I've been a life-long member of the Special Forces, not a hitman, as was previously documented. The operation in Rome had to be conducted in secret to avoid being compromised, although he was clear about having told the Vatican what was happening beforehand.

Again, not *quite* how it happened, but under the circumstances, I doubt anyone from the Vatican is going to come forward and say he's lying.

The FBI has all the information Josh and I took from Sterling's office, so they know the true extent of The Order's reach, which I imagine they will keep to themselves. Last I heard, they were heading up a massive, coordinated, global effort to track down every name on that spreadsheet.

Better them than me.

That was a big list, which would result in a lot of dead bodies if it were left to me.

Finally, he confirmed the operation resulted in the tragic and untimely death of Josh Winters, CEO of GlobaTech Industries. He explained how Josh had served this country alongside me for many years, and he would be granted a military funeral in recognition of everything he had done for the United States and the world.

His statement made headlines everywhere, as you would expect, but people seemed to buy it. He officially exonerated me the next day and wiped my slate clean. So, here I stand, a free man for the first time in my life, beside a fresh plot in Arlington National Cemetery. I'm surrounded by a whole bunch of people I've never seen before. I'm staring blankly at a large coffin with the American flag draped over it, which contains the body of my best friend.

I smile to myself. I hope he appreciates the fact that I wore a suit. If this were the other way around, he'd be standing here in jeans and a T-shirt!

Next to me, Ruby snakes her arm underneath mine, linking me, and moves closer. I glance sideways at her. She's wearing a black dress and heels and looks amazing. Schultz's act of generosity wasn't limited to helping me. Ruby had her slate wiped clean too, for which we're both grateful.

A few bodies farther along the row, President Schultz stands, solemn and tall, surrounded by Secret Service agents. He really stuck his neck out for me with this. I owe it to him not to waste this second chance.

I owe it to myself.

I owe it to Josh.

I can't speak for Ruby, but when the dust has settled, I'm leaving. I don't know where I'm heading yet, but it'll be far away from here. Far away from any memory of Adrian Hell. This will be my second attempt at burying him, and this time, I'll do it right.

The father has just finished his service, and the seven Marines are moving into position for their three-shot salute.

They lift their rifles.

I take a breath and close my eyes as I place my cast over my heart.

The first shot rings out.

I flinch involuntarily as I feel Josh's blood spray across my face.

Second shot.

I fight to stop myself lunging forward as I watch his body fall slowly to the ground.

Third shot.

I feel Ruby's hand tighten around my arm as I open my eyes again. My breathing is fast, and my vision is cloudy from tears I can't escape.

Until now, I hadn't really taken the time to process anything that's happened. After I saw him die, I didn't allow myself to stop and mourn him. I had to focus on the shot, on taking out Martinez, and stopping The Order for good. Then, in the days that followed, it was a whirlwind of inter-rogation, de-briefing, and reacclimatizing to life in the United States as a free man.

But now, as I watch the soldiers expertly folding the flag that covered Josh's coffin, the enormity of what's happened is hitting me like a wrecking ball, over and again on my chest. I feel as if I'm standing still, and the whole world is rotating around me, turning itself on its head. If it weren't for Ruby holding my arm, I would probably fall over right now.

I focus long enough on what's going on to notice one of the Marines standing before me, holding the triangle of the flag out to me. Josh and I weren't just friends... we were the only family each other had in this world.

"I... er..."

Ruby reaches for the flag on my behalf and takes it from the Marine, who immediately salutes me and marches away.

I shake my head. "Thanks."

Ruby smiles kindly. "Don't mention it."

I lift my head and stare out at the sea of headstones as the father finishes his prayer. "...as we commit his body to the ground, earth to earth, ashes to ashes, dust to dust..."

I watch as the Marines begin lowering the casket into the grave.

This was never meant to be you, Josh.

This was always supposed to be me.

The crowd slowly disperses. People pay their respects as they pass by the coffin and the president. Few people acknowledge me.

Ruby grabs my arm and turns me to face her. She steps in close and reaches up, kissing me on the cheek. "You okay?"

I nod but don't say anything.

"Listen, I'll give you a few minutes alone." She gestures to the flag. "I'll keep hold of this until you're ready to leave. Take your time."

She walks away without waiting for me to respond, heading toward the car that brought us here.

Someone clears their throat behind me. I spin around to see President Schultz standing there. His protection detail keep a minimal but respectful distance.

Without thinking, I extend my hand, which he shakes without hesitation. "Thank you, Ryan. For all this. For everything."

He nods. "For Josh, this was the least I could do. For you... hell, son, it's the least you deserve. Did you know, it's been two months to the day since Matthews sent the world into chaos? Two months. In that time, you've assassinated a sitting president, faked your death, joined and subsequently waged war against a secret organization of killers, and taken out the man behind it all as he stood three feet from the pope. You've done all that with most of the world on your ass, and not once have you blamed anybody. Not once have you complained about it. You just picked up a gun and kept shooting, right to the end, no matter the risk."

I smile briefly. When you put it like that...

"I once said to you that I would never like you because of who and what you are, regardless of the good you've done along the way. But some things change. The world owes you a debt it'll never know."

"I appreciate you saying that, Ryan... Mr. President. Thank you."

He steps closer. "Just... don't waste this second chance, son. You won't get another one."

I glance over my shoulder and look back at the casket as it disappears into the ground. "I won't. Don't worry. Adrian Hell is down there with Josh. I'm done."

"Huh. I seem to remember you saying that once before..."

"I did. But this time, Josh isn't around to bring some crazy terrorist shit to my front door, so things will be different."

I try to smile to show him I'm joking, but any attempt I just made was weak at best.

"If you want my advice, Adrian, be who you are. Just learn not to answer your door when shit comes knockin'. You'll find the life that awaits you after today will be a lot easier to live that way. Oh, and that girlfriend of yours... Ruby, is it? She seems good for you. Maybe try keeping her out of trouble too."

He pats me on my shoulder and walks away, quickly followed by the secret service. I turn back to face the grave. The crowd has gone now. I take a moment to look around and soak up the scenery. It's an incredible sight, seeing all these graves belonging to fallen soldiers. It's peaceful but not in an eerie way, like you would expect from a cemetery. The sound of the river behind me, the birds tweeting in the trees lining the borders... it's serene. It's humbling. It reminds you that nothing worth having in this life comes free or easy.

I crouch beside the hole and gather up a fistful of dirt in

my left hand. I stare down at the lid of the coffin. I let out a long breath.

"The last time I stood in a place like this, I was visiting my wife and daughter for the first time. That was one of the hardest things I've ever had to do, but I got through it because I knew you were waiting in the car. You had my back. From the day I found them murdered, all the way through the ten years I spent running, up until the moment I looked down at their graves and said sorry, you kept me going. You protected me from myself. You kept the barrel out of my mouth. And now I'm here, and I can't help but wonder who's going to get me through *this* if you're not around. I guess that makes me a selfish asshole, but hey, who's left for me to piss off, right?"

I smile and blink away the tear I feel forming in the corner of my eye.

"You know I've been trying to get a handle on all this emotional shit, but now that the dust has settled, there's just so much of it I haven't had chance to deal with. I'm not sure I know how to cope. I've been so caught up in everything that's been going on, I suddenly realize how alone I am. Tori's gone. Cunningham basically blew up Texas, which destroyed any remnants of the life I had there. Lily was a kindred spirit, and she was taken from me by the same enemy who took you. And without you, I have nothing tying me to this world. Is it wrong that I'm angry with you for dying? You were the last one to go, so it's your fault. I'm blaming you. You're the selfish one for leaving me. You're the stupid one for not seeing the bullet coming. You're the..."

I trail off and take another long breath.

"Sorry." I rap my knuckles on my cast, directly above my WWJD tattoo. "If you were here now, you'd shout at me for wallowing, or feeling guilty, or just plain talking shit." I smile. "Yeah, I know. You were always smarter than me. I still blame myself for your death, even though I had no way of knowing it was coming—or preventing it, even if I did. Don't be mad at me about it. It just feels like something I need to do for a while. But I'll be all right. I promise."

I glance over my shoulder and see Ruby leaning against the car, absently staring out across the Potomac, at the Washington skyline beyond.

"Yeah, now that I think about it, I reckon I'll be fine. Eventually. I'm gonna miss you, man. You were my brother, and I owe you my life. So, I'm going to honor you by living it for once."

I stand and throw the dirt onto the lid below me.

"Say hi to my girls for me. I'll see you soon."

I walk away without looking back, wiping the tear from my eye as I approach the car. Ruby walks to meet me. "Hey. You say everything you need to?"

I nod. "I think so, yeah."

We get in the car. She's driving. She starts the engine and turns to me. "What now?"

I think for a moment. "There's one last thing I need to take care of."

She frowns for a moment, then smiles and drives away, leaving Josh in our rearview, resting in peace.

35

Each step I take along the dusty road kicks up a small cloud at my feet. The streets of Baghdad are gridlocked as an endless stream of fifty-year-old cars inch ever closer to their destination, sounding their horns at every opportunity.

When the 4/17 attacks happened, it was southern Iraq that took the brunt of it. Basra was decimated. Survivors and refugees fled north, and Baghdad was the natural destination. Consequently, this place is busier than ever.

I'm wearing a loose-fitting white shirt and combat pants, with heavy boots and a scarf wrapped around my head, covering my nose and mouth. The black sunglasses shield me from the relentless glare of the sun and from the perpetual whirlwind of sand. They also offer anonymity.

I keep a relaxed pace as I navigate the market stalls lining the streets, absently pausing every now and then to look over the wares. No one looks twice at me. I'm invisible.

So, why Baghdad? It's a fair question. Iraq isn't exactly renowned for its retirement community. But I'm not retired. Not yet. There are still a couple of things I feel I need to do... some loose ends that I need to tie up.

I tried not to push my luck with Schultz, in terms of asking for more favors. Not after everything he's done for me. So, I asked for only one—access to the FBI's ongoing investigation and their efforts to track down every last piece of shit who was affiliated with The Order of Sabbah.

He did, on the condition that he never finds out why.

That's fair enough.

Ruby wanted to come along, but I told her this was something I needed to do alone.

I have a rough idea where I'm going. I don't have anyone telling me where to turn anymore, which will take some getting used to. Even when I was with The Order, separated from Josh, I still had them feeding me intel—albeit minimal and mostly bullshit. But I recognize the street I'm walking down from the GPS feeds I studied, so I must be close by now.

...

...

...

Yeah, here it is. There are two stalls selling fruit and vegetables near the curb, in front of a café. I slide between them and head down a narrow alley that runs between the café and the building next to it. It's dark, and there's a pungent smell of urine all around me.

I step out at the opposite end, into a square formed by the buildings lining the circumference of the block. Stone steps lead to broken doors in all directions. There is a handful of people around, sitting on old chairs or on the steps, smoking and drinking. A couple of them throw cautious glances in my direction, but most ignore me.

I look all around, studying the buildings, the upstairs windows, the ways in and out of the square... familiarizing myself with every aspect of my surroundings.

Plan your exit long before you make your entrance.

Finally, my gaze settles on the doorway in the bottom corner, just to the right of the alley. I head over to it and try the handle for luck.

It's locked.

Figures.

I risk another glance around, checking that no one's paying me any attention. They don't appear to be. I turn my back to the square, shielding the view of the door as best I can. I discreetly move my hand beneath my shirt and slide the knife out of the sheath attached to my belt. It's a ramshackle door, and its weak wood is scorched colorless from years of harsh sunlight. My blade is five inches long and made from thick, serrated steel. I jam it between the edge of the door and the splintered frame and press down on the latch. I grip the handle as best I can with my cast and turn it, applying more pressure with the knife.

The door opens easily, leaving almost no visible damage.

I step inside, welcoming the shade. There's a single door on the right wall, which I'm guessing leads into the back of the café. Straight ahead of me is a staircase, which I know leads to the apartment above.

I close the door behind me and climb the stairs, taking two at a time, as quietly as I can. The pain in my hip is almost gone now. The wound is healing nicely, and any ache tends to subside so long as I keep it moving.

There's another door at the top, on the right, and I

repeat the process from before to open it. Inside is a dirty, barely furnished living space consisting of three rooms. The bathroom is on the left, just inside the entrance. The door's open, and I glance inside as I pass. The mirror above the sink is cracked, the john hasn't been cleaned in years, and there's a towel on the floor with a damp stain around it.

Someone's used it recently if it's still wet.

I walk into the main living room, which is no more than a ten-by-ten cube of dirty tiles and cracked plaster. On the left, there's an archway leading into a kitchen area. On the right, a single, unmade bed sits in the corner, facing the open window opposite. In the left corner, next to the archway, is a chair. It looks uncomfortable. I can see the springs protruding through the cushion. Still, I'm not standing around for God-knows how long, and there's no way I'm sitting on that bed...

I lower myself carefully into the chair, sit back, and relax.

Now we wait.

11:16 AST

I hear the door to the apartment open and close. I hear keys jangle and grip the arms of the chair, ready to push myself up quickly, should I need to.

I hold my breath.

A man steps into the main room, facing right. He's wearing a long, white robe with a thin, sleeveless black jacket over it. He unravels the scarf from his head, revealing his white, disheveled hair.

Slowly, quietly, I get to my feet and lean casually against the wall, watching the man as he empties his pockets onto the bed.

I smile. "Considering how smart you're supposed to be, you didn't do a good job of hiding, did you?"

Horizon spins around. His gaunt face is frozen with shock. "Adrian? How did... how did you find me?"

I walk over to him. "Friends in high places."

He backs away, stumbles against the edge of the bed, and sits heavily. "What are you doing here?"

I roll my eyes. "Oh, you know, taking in the sights, enjoying the local beer... what do *you* think, you fucking idiot?"

"Now wait a second. Let's... let's talk about this, okay? I have nothing you want. Nothing you need. You won. You were right. I... I underestimated you. You beat me. You took down The Order. You have nothing to gain from—"

"Horizon? Number Seven? Colonel Sanders? Shush." I step back but make sure I put myself between him and the door, just in case he gets any ideas. "See, you've got it all wrong. Well, a bit of it wrong. You were right about most things. I'll give you that. But you *do* have something I want. And you're going to give it to me."

He holds his hands up and nods hurriedly. "Of course. Anything. Whatever it is, you've got it."

This is actually quite sad. He was the man who recruited me. The man who orchestrated my fake execution. From the moment I met him, like him or not, he's always exuded confidence. He was always intelligent, tall, and calm. And now look at him. He's a scared, frail old man. It's almost hard to enjoy this without feeling cruel.

Almost.

"I want to know who did it."

He frowns, appearing genuinely confused. "Did what?"

I stare at him and raise an eyebrow. I don't say anything.

He gazes around the room, looking at anything except me. "I... ah... I don't know."

"Sure, you do."

"No, I... I can't—"

"Sure, you can."

"But I don't have—"

"Yes, you do." I move in front of him and grab a handful of his beard, yanking down hard on it, pulling him with it. "Listen to me carefully, you sanctimonious prick. Even if you didn't give the order yourself, you would've spoken to the version of you who did. That means, at the very least, you know the name of the asset who put a bullet in my best friend. Tell me."

I let go, and he sits upright, rubbing his face. "Even if I did know, what use is it to you? Assuming he's not already been apprehended, you'll never find him. The Order employed ghosts, remember?"

I smile. "He's not, and I will. Just give me the name."

"And if I don't?"

I shrug. "Then your last minutes on this earth will be more painful than you can imagine."

"But if I do?"

"Then they won't be."

He thinks about it for a moment and then slowly gets to his feet. He moves over to the small table beside the window and takes a pen and a piece of paper out of the drawer. He writes something down and hands it to me. I look at the name, memorize it, and then tear the paper into multiple pieces.

"Thanks, Horizon. That small gesture has helped you atone for almost all the shitty things you've done to me."

I see a small spark in his eyes. Hope.

I lunge forward and wrap my hand tightly around his throat, like a snake clamping down on its prey. He grabs my wrist with both of his weak, bony hands, but it's futile. His eyes bulge with fear as they stare into mine.

"Unfortunately for you, you did a *lot* of shitty things to me, and some of them I just can't forgive." I reach inside one of my pockets, using the finger and thumb of my injured hand, and take out a small, tubular pill. "Now open wide, asshole."

I squeeze tighter and shove the pill into his mouth. I release his throat and grab his hair, yank his head back, and push his jaw closed. "Swallow... swallow... There's a good boy."

He does, albeit grudgingly.

"Show me."

The fear in his eyes has been replaced with anger, but I don't care. He opens his mouth, and I look inside, making sure he's not hiding it beneath his tongue or something. Happy he's not, I let go of him and shove him down on the bed. I move to the short hallway that leads to the front door.

Horizon coughs and splutters. "Is that it? You're going to poison me? You goddamn coward!"

I laugh. "Please..." I take out a small device that looks like a tube of lipstick with a button on the top. "That wasn't a poisoned pill. That was GlobaTech's version of the tracking device you implanted in me."

"Wh-what?"

"It has a lot of the same features. For example, I can now track your location to within a couple of feet, anywhere in the world."

He looks around the room, as if plotting his escape,

despite the fact that I just told him I can now find him anywhere.

Dick.

"It also has a small explosive charge in it, although GlobaTech's versions offers a little more bang for your buck than yours did."

He's sweating, and his hands are restless with nerves. "So, what, you're going to keep tabs on me? Is that it? Torture me by forcing me to look over my shoulder for the rest of my life, constantly afraid that you might one day press that button? You sick bastard! I'd rather you just killed me."

I stare at him silently, keeping my expression neutral.

It's fun watching him squirm.

"Come on!" he yells. "Do it!"

I smile. "See you around, asshole."

I turn and head for the door. Behind me, I hear him screaming through gritted teeth and hitting the thin mattress with his fists out of frustration and fear. That's his life now. I did that. And it's no less than he deserves, right?

Right?

I head back along the hallway and poke my head around the corner. He looks up at me, confused. I smile at him. "I'm just fucking with you."

I duck away and press the button.

The muted sound of a wet, sticky explosion fills the apartment, followed almost immediately by the squelch of thick blood spraying against the walls.

I wait for a moment and then turn around.

I laugh. "Holy shit!"

The room is painted a dark red. Sprawled across the bed is the remains of his torso. His head's hanging off, and there's a large cavity in his chest. His legs are resting in the middle of the room, separately.

I toss the detonator onto the bed. "Bet you didn't see that coming, did you?"

I take one last look at the remains of the man who helped ruin my life and then I walk out of the apartment, closing the door gently behind me.

EPILOGUE

June 23, 2017 — 18:34 HAST

The sound of the waves lapping on the white, sandy beach nearby is one of the most relaxing noises I can think of. It's hotter than hell, but the shade from the palm trees lining the beach makes it tolerable.

I'm sitting on a high stool at a table, sipping an ice-cold bottle of beer. My shirt is open, allowing air to brush against my scarred body. Opposite me, sipping something through a straw from a coconut, is Ruby. She's wearing a bikini top and a short, white skirt, with large sunglasses covering her eyes.

"I've gotta hand it to you, Adrian," she says, tipping her drink toward me. "You sure know how to celebrate freedom."

I smile. "I promised Josh I would live my life. Drinking beer with a beautiful woman in a bar that's a few feet from the beach in Hawaii... sounds like living to me."

She takes her sunglasses off and smiles coyly. "Beautiful? Are you flirting with me?"

I roll my eyes. "Just calling it how I see it. Don't get excited."

We share a laugh.

She shrugs. "Well, it's not like you're Hugh Grant or anything..."

My smile fades, and I take another sip of my beer.

She sighs. "Shit, I'm sorry. I didn't mean—"

I wave away her apology. "I know. Forget about it. Truth be told, I think he and you would've been happy together. God knows he needed someone like you to take that stick out of his ass."

"Ooo, kinky!" She slurps her drink loudly. "I reckon he did all right with the ladies. He was a handsome man. And British. Women love a British accent."

I nod. "Very true. Hell, *I* used to love it. When he got angry and started cussing, it sounded so funny and so aggressive at the same time. I think he just got so caught up in his job, he stopped having fun. I mean, all the shit he did for GlobaTech, the stuff with the Security Council... the belief that I was dead... I guess you can't blame him. But you would've given him some much-needed perspective."

Her cheeks flush a little, and she holds her drink up. I touch it with the neck of my bottle.

"To hear you say you thought I was good enough for your friend, knowing what you two meant to each other... that means a lot to me, Adrian. Thank you."

"No problem."

"Y'know what I still don't get? How you seem immune to me."

I frown. "Immune? You're not a disease..."

"I mean, I've spent a lot of years in this business, perfecting my persona, making the job easier. I look after myself. I know a lot of guys who would love to get their hands on the merchandise. Y'know what I mean?" She pauses to gesture to her body. "But you don't seem to be attracted to me. Why is that?"

I smile. Most people would find her arrogant, but I don't. I know what she means.

"It's not that I don't find you attractive, Ruby. It's just that I see through the act. Because that's what it is—an act. All the flirting, the extroversion, the constant nudity... that's not you. At least, not completely. It's who you make yourself out to be to help you cope with the job. If you're anything like me, your persona is simply a version of who you really are but with the volume turned way up. I'm the same. Josh made me into Adrian Hell, and I made that person... that *character* work for me. I am who I am, but when I'm him, I'm just a little more violent." I pause as we smile at each other. "When I look at you, honestly, I see beyond all that. I see the kind-hearted, loyal, passionate, sensitive woman who, as things stand, is the only friend I have left. Does that make sense?"

She doesn't say anything. She looks at me for a moment, her lips slowly curling into a smile. She pushes herself off her stool and walks around the table, stopping in front of me. She puts a hand on the back of my head, leans forward, and kisses me softly.

...

...

...

She pulls away, looking deep into my eyes. "I've got your back, Adrian. You have my word. We're a team now, whether you like it or not. And I'm not looking to replace anybody—not Josh, not your girlfriend... nobody. I'm not here in any specific capacity. I'm simply like you. I have a second chance at life and few people I can share it with.

Now what say we get another drink and start enjoying ourselves?"

Holy crap.

I nod. "Sounds good to me."

She moves back to her seat, and I head over to the bar. The counter is made from thick bamboo wood and is lined with stools. The roof is thatched with grass, and the two barmaids serving are wearing coconuts and hula skirts, with white flowers in their hair. It's pretty quiet in here. There are a few tables that are occupied with couples or small groups, and there's one guy sitting at the bar, but that's it.

The guy at the bar disappears to the bathroom as I'm ordering the drinks. I signal to the barmaid that I won't be a minute and head back there myself. I push the door open, noting the two empty cubicles as I walk along the row of urinals. I stop in front of the one that's two along from the guy from the bar.

I glance over to him. He has a tanned complexion, which looks natural, not a product of the Hawaiian sun. His hair is thick and dark.

I nod. "Hey, man."

He returns the gesture but says nothing.

"Beautiful, isn't it? This bar, the beach..."

He shrugs. "I guess."

He has an Italian accent.

"I'm on sabbatical from work. The wife and I are taking some time to see the world. You're Italian, right?"

He finishes up and begins fastening his shorts. He nods.

I smile, excitedly. "No way! We've just come from Italy!"

"Small world," he replies politely.

"Yeah. We were in Rome about a week ago."

He ignores me, turning his back to wash his hands.

I move beside him. "It was a bit crazy over there. Did you hear about it in the news?"

He shrugs, remaining silent.

"Yeah, all that shit with the pope. Man, that was messed up. I was with a friend over there, actually. It was the strangest thing. We were just hanging out at a café, when all of a sudden, this no-name piece of shit called Alfonso Moretti put a bullet through his fucking head..."

He stares ahead, looking at me in the mirror.

"Y'know what? Come to think of it, you look a lot like him. Say, did you used to work in The Order of Sabbah?"

He spins to face me, a wave of aggression washing over his face. He raises his hands, but he's too slow. My left hand is already on the side of his head. I whip my body around, twisting at the hip for added momentum, and drive his head forward and down, smashing it into the ceramic basin. I let go, and he bounces back, falling to the floor with blood gushing from his broken nose.

I don't allow him a second to recover. I step over to him and drag him to his feet by his collar. I grab the back of his head and ram it into the wall opposite. Once... twice... three times—each one harder than the last.

I let him go, and he sinks to his knees. I raise my right hand and swing the solid cast toward him like a dead weight. The dull smack as it connects with his temple echoes around the bathroom. He lurches sideways, banging his head on the side of the urinal on his way down.

I crouch beside him, lifting his head again. He appears to be out cold, but I'm not interested. I rest his face on the edge of the urinal and force his jaw open, so his mouth is clamped around the yellow-stained rim.

I get to my feet and move behind him. I pause for a moment, staring down at the prone body of the man who killed Josh. I feel as if I should say something—a final few words on behalf of the man he shot, or something derogatory and cruel, so I can think back to this moment in years to come and smile fondly, knowing I defeated him mentally as well as physically.

But I've got nothing.

Huh.

Never thought I'd see the day.

I bring my leg up and slam my foot down on the back of his head, snapping his jaw around the urinal, killing him instantly.

I'm breathing heavily from both the exertion and the adrenaline. I look down at his body, slumped face-first in a bowl of piss.

"Well, Josh... *now* I'm done."

I walk over to the sink and wash my hands. I splash some water on my face and head back outside, where I'm greeted with a warm, welcoming sea breeze. I walk over to the bar, where my drinks are waiting for me. I pay my tab and head back over to Ruby. She smiles at me as I approach.

"You took your time."

"Yeah, I went to the restroom."

She glances over at the door and then at the bar. She smiles at me. "You feeling refreshed now?"

I nod. "Like you wouldn't believe."

I place the two shots of bourbon on the table and push one toward her. She picks it up and looks at it, frowning. "What the hell is this?"

I raise mine to her. "If you're gonna be hanging out with me, you need to start drinking real drinks. None of that fruity, rainbow-colored shit. And definitely no cold coffee."

She rolls her eyes. "Whatever, old man."

We smile, and she raises her glass to mine. I take a breath. "To those we've lost..."

"Gone but not forgotten."

"And to new beginnings."

We tap our shots together and throw them back. Ruby winces and breathes loudly through gritted teeth. "Oh my God, that was awful!"

I move beside her and hold out my arm for her to link. "Come on. Let's take a walk along the beach and watch the sun go down."

She wraps her arm around mine. "Sounds good to me."

We step out of the bar area, straight onto the sand, and start walking toward the sea.

"Can I get a cocktail from somewhere?"

I shake my head. "No. You can get a beer."

"I don't want a beer..."

"Then you'll be thirsty, won't you?"

She punches my arm. "Asshole."

We laugh, and she rests her head on my shoulder. We walk side by side, listening to the waves lapping on the beach, wondering what tomorrow will bring.

THE END

A MESSAGE

Dear Reader,

Thank you for purchasing my book. If you enjoyed reading it, it would mean a lot to me if you could spare thirty seconds to leave an honest review. For independent authors like me, one review makes a world of difference!

If you want to get in touch, please visit my website, where you can contact me directly, either via e-mail or social media.

Until next time...

James P. Sumner

JOIN THE MAILING LIST

Why not sign up for James P. Sumner's spam-free news-letter, and stay up-to-date with the latest news, promotions, and new releases?

In exchange for your support, you will receive a **FREE** copy of the prequel novella, *A Hero of War*, which tells the story of a young Adrian, newly recruited to the U.S. Army at the beginning of the Gulf War.

Previously available on Amazon, this title is now exclusive to the author's website. But you have the opportunity to read it for free!

Interested? Simply visit the below link to sign up and claim your free gift!

smarturl.it/jpssignup

CPSIA information can be obtained
at www.ICGtesting.com
Printed in the USA
BVHW051404111122
651671BV00022B/1566